Not Pink

Margaret D. Kasimatis

ISBN: 1548167592
ISBN 13: 9781548167592
Library of Congress Control Number: 2017909854
CreateSpace Independent Publishing Platform
North Charleston, South Carolina

*For my parents, my sibs, my husband, and my kids,
who loaned me their faith when I couldn't find my own.*

Chapter One

A Little Time

1963

"Hang on, sweetheart," Mama whispered, a kind hiss easing between the bobby pins clenched in her teeth. "That's my brave girl."

Mae Panos stood as tall and stiff as she could, holding her breath, not voicing "ow-ow-ow" as her mother jabbed another bobby pin close to the roots of her wavy chestnut hair and into the crown of her white straw hat. A band of silk daisies, all pink and yellow, hid the half dozen bobby pins fighting the fluttering, sharp bursts of a dusty Chicago breeze. Mae had danced when Aunt Sophie bought the hat for Mae's first train trip by herself. She'd spun in front of the long mirrors at Marshall Field's department store, admiring the spirals of pastel ribbons, momentarily forgetting the impending separation from her mother. Now she wished she'd never seen the hat, never given a hint that she felt elegant in it, never lost sight that this was all about going away, far away from her mother and her brother, and she didn't want to go. As if that mattered.

Mae blinked hard, trying to ignore the ripped roots of her hair and the penetrating August early-morning sun. Mama's smile was too bright as well, matching the forced cheerfulness in her voice, at odds with the worried shadows in her eyes. "There! Now keep that hat on, Maisie—you've my fair Irish complexion, too many freckles! And put your white gloves back on. How grown up you look, every bit of ten years old." Mama gave her a genuine, sad little smile, then startled and turned. "Where's Michael?" She scanned the platform, the luggage carts, and locked in on Michael whipping pebbles up against the weathered Chicago–South Shore sign at the end of the platform. "Michael!" she whispered fiercely, waving him back to her side between anxious glances in Uncle Nick's direction. But Uncle Nick's back was to them as he leaned into the ticket counter, head stooped low to confer with the agent. Aunt Sophie, by his side, nodded with the tiniest wave of her lace-gloved hand.

Michael threw his hands high in the air, as if cornered by the police, his eleven-and-a-half-year-old voice shrill: "Don't shoot! I confess! I threw a stone, more than one. The coppers'll send me to the slammer for sure!" He shuffled in imaginary wrist and ankle cuffs toward his mother and his sister, with tragic eyebrows but a wobbly grin.

Mama gestured to him to put his arms down. "Michael, no clowning, and pick up your feet! Your shoes are scuffed enough!"

Michael glanced down, licked his thumb, and rubbed off a dark streak on his dingy saddle shoes. He slapped at the dust on the cuffs of his trousers, then pulled himself up straight, almost a full head taller than Mae. Shrugging, he pushed his crooked bangs to one side.

Sighing, Mama smoothed the frown from her brow, putting on her calm and proper face, adjusting the veil on her velveteen pillbox. She drew Michael close to her side. "Now, Mae, Michael, company manners. The train will be here any time, so please? For me?"

"Ma, I wasn't doin' nothin'!"

"That's 'anything,' and I know, Michael, but this is a big day for your sister."

"But, Mama," Mae whispered, very low, hoping that Michael would not hear her, "Mama, I don't wanna go. Please can I stay?" Her voice grew too quivery to say any more, but tears welled up and over her dark eyelashes, spilling past the faint freckles on her cheekbones, curving along her jaw.

Mama insisted in her chipper tone, "Sweetie, it'll be fine!" And as Mae's tears hit the concrete platform, Mama stooped down and gently lifted Mae's chin, dabbing at the tears with her cotton hankie, whispering in her real voice. "Oh, Maisie, baby, I know this is hard, and I'll miss you too, but it's the best we can do right now. Don't cry."

"But, Mama, Michael and I could babysit ourselves after school. Cross my heart, I'd start dinner for you, and we'll pick up, do our homework..." Mae scanned Mama's face for any sign of indecision, any cue to keep pressing her case, but even through the veil, Mama's gaze was dull, lost in hazy resignation.

Michael scowled. "Mae, cut it out! You're no baby; you're almost ten now. Uncle Nick's decided, picked the best schools around. You're goin' to Indiana; I'm goin' to Wisconsin. Boarding school's not so tough. We'll be back for Thanksgiving, so don't fuss at Ma and make her feel bad."

Mae's eyes darted back and forth between their faces, one flat with pain, and the other flashing with a black irritation that was almost never directed toward her. She held her breath, trying to fade from her brother's glare. Then Mama patted Michael's arm.

"Michael, no, you've been away before, but Mae hasn't." Mama peered keenly into Mae's eyes. "You know if I could keep us all together, I would, don't you, Mae? I simply can't right now, but maybe by next year, there'll be enough money to have everyone together. But, sweetheart, till then you'll be at a lovely school, getting a first-rate education, one I wish I had now, so I could support us all. South Bend's not so far away, just an hour or so. And just a little stretch until Thanksgiving." Mama pinched the air between her thumb and finger, less than an inch. But the light was back in her eyes, and Mae knew she should reassure her mother.

"I'm all right, Mama," Mae forced out.

Mama brushed her hand down Mae's cheek, pursing her lips in an apologetic kiss, just as Aunt Sophie appeared at her elbow. Instantly the air was thick with perfume.

"Here we are. Sorry that took so long. Heavens, the South Shore will arrive any time now. And, Mae," Sophie added, her tone conspiratorial, "Uncle Nick and I have a treat for you." Aunt Sophie held out a small, shiny white cardboard box wrapped in gold cord with a tightly rolled one-dollar bill tucked into the center of the bow. "Spice drops from Field's. And, Michael," she said, winking, "you'll have the same next week for your trip!"

"Thanks, Aunt Sophie," came Michael's dutiful response.

"Yes, thank you, Aunt Sophie, Uncle Nick," added Mae as Uncle Nick loomed above the ladies.

Uncle Nick nodded, resting his hand on Mae's shoulder. "The best thanks is to be a good student, make your mother and father proud of you. And I say your father, too, because he looks down on you from Heaven." His square, sober face was deeply shaded by the brim of his fedora. *Does he ever smile? Maybe Uncle Nick is trying to be kind, but his voice is so distant, as if he's the one far away, not Papa.* Mae frowned, trying to see Papa in his brother's face, maybe the same broad Greek nose, the black eyebrows, but no grin like Papa, no sparkle, just—

A train whistle shrilled, and the tracks buzzed with a low rumble. Mae clenched her mother's hand as Mama swept up her veil, stooping to face Mae. "Take care, sweetie. Remember the train stop on the note in your pocket. Sister Mary Anthony assured Nick she'll be at the station to meet you, and I'm saving for a train ticket for parents' weekend. Remember, just for a little time." Mama again pinched an inch of air as the brakes screeched and let out a long, low whine.

Michael tugged Mae to the side, tweaking a lock of her hair. "Don't worry, Maisie, you'll be okay. Just don't turn into a nun or nothin'. And listen, Maisie," he added, abruptly serious, "I promise I'll always write back. I'll answer. May take me a while, but I will. Cross my heart."

"Thanks," Mae choked out. She grabbed both of his hands.

He squeezed back but then let go with a little push, tipping his head toward the train. "Go on."

"Don't I get a hug?" pleaded Aunt Sophie, already wrapping her arms full circle around Mae. Sophie kissed the crown of the straw hat with an audible smack and gave Mae one more squeeze. "Love you, sweetheart." Her brown eyes shiny with tears, Sophie turned Mae toward Uncle Nick.

He bent low to brush a kiss on Mae's cheek, murmuring, "Safe journey."

The conductor held a hand out to Mae. Her gloved hand in his, she hopped onto the first step, hesitating. *Call for me, Mama, call me back.*

Mae bit her bottom lip. *Mama, please?* Mae glanced back at Mama, who sadly signaled “Just a little” one last time. Mae did the same, took a very deep breath, and disappeared into the coach car.

Chapter Two

The Mixer

1970

"Earth to Mae, earth to Mae...hey!"

What the hell? Nora?

Mae squinted, eyes just half open in the wash of colors swirling about the room. The chapel was drenched in every shade of turquoise, teal, and navy-blue glass, dancing abstract mosaics tightly contained in perfect oak-framed arches on each side of the chapel. Softer and deeper greens flecked the stained glass, with only a very occasional trace of gold or white. Offertory candles flickered within pale-blue votives. The marble of the altar railing swirled white and dove gray, a gentle barrier to the altar itself, covered in a simple white cloth edged with a few gold threads. Only the golden tabernacle was ornate, a blur of gold and silver tones in a deeply engraved image of the Lamb of God. Mae sighed, inhaling the sweet, stale air, laced with the smoke of the candles and the residue of incense from morning Mass. And a trace of smoke lingering from her joint.

"Knew I'd find you here." Nora sounded amused. "Old chapel, fifth row, maybe sixth, on St. Joseph's side...jeez, Mae, you're predictable."

Mae stretched, rolling away from the bright aqua light shooting off the stained glass. She licked her thumb and index finger, good and wet, pinching out the burning tip of the joint. "I know what I like."

"Yeah, but then I gotta walk back to Trinity Hall to get you. Why don't you use the high school chapel like the other seniors?"

Mae propped up on her elbows, bracing herself against a floating feeling. She shuddered as she eased upright. "Dunno, like this chapel better.

Hardly anyone comes in between Masses, and they stay in the back pews when they do. Don't be so uptight." She brushed off her blouse: no seeds, no traces. Slipped the last of the joint under her bra strap.

"You're gonna get busted...anyway, coming with or not?"

Mae wrinkled her nose dismissively. "Like ten- and twelve-year-olds would know what's incense, what isn't. Wait, coming where?"

"The fall mixer tonight, dope. Bus leaves at seven-thirty, so we've only got an hour to get ready before dinner. And you definitely need a shower." Nora sniffed Mae's hair. "Like an ashtray."

They slipped out of the chapel and the side door of Trinity Hall. The September sky was brilliant. Mae squeezed her eyes closed and grabbed Nora's elbow. "Whoa, hold on."

"Jeez, how stoned are you? If you don't wanna go, fine, but I need to fix my hair before dinner."

Mae frowned, rubbing her forehead, and then opening her eyes a sliver. "Mixer, right. No, yeah, I wanna go." She blinked her eyes wider, feeling the tickle of the tips of her long bangs. "Okay, shower now, straighten my hair fast after dinner."

Nora looked skeptical. "You gotta move."

"Watch me." Mae let go of her elbow and strode ahead, double time.

Nora scurried to catch up. "Faster if we cut through the meditation garden. Shh, I'll check." Easing halfway into the bank of lilac bushes, Nora paused and then waved to approach. She continued through as Mae followed her path, shrinking back against the scratching branches.

Mae emerged into the shadowy garden of blues and violets: hastas, columbine, some kind of faintly blue ground cover, all shades honoring the Blessed Virgin Mary, whose marble statue rested serenely on a solid, low pedestal in the center of the crescent-shaped nook. Nora reached to pull a stray lilac out of Mae's hair and then gasped and jerked back.

"Jesus! What did you do?"

"What?" Mae raised her hands to feel and then grinned as she gingerly traced the outline of the large safety pins hanging from her ears. "Oh, these? Fun, huh?"

"No, not fun. Gross!" Nora pulled Mae behind the statue and held out her hand. "Take them out now, before one of the sisters sees you and you get another write-up."

"Come on," Mae whined, even as she complied. "The one last week wasn't fair. I was only out of the building ten steps, to put my letter to Michael in the mail."

"After hours and braless."

"In my red halter. It was hot!"

"Well, don't even think about wearing it to the dance—you'll never get past Sister Mary Ruth." Nora handed back the safety pins. "And normal earrings."

"Why do they inspect us anyway? Like cattle call, all of us shuffling past to get onto the bus. The herd in search of a bull. Mooo..."

Nora snickered. "Pathetic, yeah, but we seniors must be proper, right?"

Mae tossed the safety pins inside the crown on Mary's head.

"Mae! That's sacrilegious!"

"Lighten up."

"You know how close you are to being on probation?" Nora demanded. "One more write-up this month."

Mae snorted. "Jeez, like I'd risk getting sent home to my mother. Anyway, thought we were in a hurry."

Nora nodded, and they scurried into Regina Hall, taking the stairs two at a time. Mae ran her fingers through some of her tangles while Nora unlocked their door.

Mae plopped on her bed and lifted her feet to examine them. "Guess my clogs are out, huh? But pumps will look too dressy."

"Borrow my silver sandals again, but move! We finally get to go to college mixers, meet Notre Dame guys, and I need time to get fixed up."

Mae stared at her Rolling Stones poster as Nora opened the closet door. "How 'bout music? Moody Blues?"

Nora flipped rapidly through the hangars. "How 'bout a shower?"

♦ ♦ ♦

The bus was packed: every senior at St. Mary's was going to the mixer. Mae pressed closer to the window, staring out, ignoring the excited chatter and the sickly blend of colognes and bus exhaust, vaguely aware of Nora's arm brushing against hers with every bump in the road. Sunset came earlier now: the trees pressed dark against the streaky light lingering below the cloud line. Felt trapped behind the glass. Again.

Stepping into the aisle of the South Shore coach, Mae slipped into the first bench, tight against the seat back, careful not to get her face near the window. Hanging back in a shadow, she peered out at the platform. Mama was still, as she and Aunt Sophie scanned the length of the train car. Only Uncle Nick's back showed as he towered over Michael, Michael's hands shoved deep into his pockets. Mae watched, sitting still as a stone, until a twingy, prickly sensation at the nape of her neck made her turn. A girl with a perfect heart-shaped face, framed by perfect copper-colored braids, standing in the aisle, forced a smile.

"Hi, I'm Nora."

Mae just stared.

The girl glanced back toward her mother, who gestured to keep going. She locked her green eyes on Mae. "Um, my mom wants me to ask if you'd like to sit with us. You know, not by yourself."

Mae hesitated.

Nora made a face. "C'mon, I'm supposed to invite you. Going to St. Mary's, right? My mom says come sit with us." Nora gestured back toward her parents with her head and then rolled her eyes.

"Sure," Mae mumbled, gathering up her Marshall Field's box and tagging after Nora to the far end of the coach. Nora scooted between her parents' knees and plopped down close to her mother. Her dad stood to let Mae move to the window seat facing Nora. Mae nodded her thanks and slipped past, gingerly settling in.

"Nora, this is...?" her mom prompted.

"I'm Mary Therese. Panos. Hi."

Nora's mother nodded. "Nice to meet you, Mary Therese! We're the O'Tooles. You're headed to St. Mary's, like our Nora?"

Mae nodded.

"Shall we ride together? You two can make friends before we even arrive!"

Mae shrugged and then corrected herself with a smile. "That sounds very nice."

Mrs. O'Toole smiled sweetly, her coral-colored lips framed by deep dimples. Her soft blond curls were almost like a halo. "Wonderful! Nora, get to know Mary Therese!"

"Well...what's the matter?" demanded Nora in a low, matter-of-fact tone. "Why don't you want them to see you?" She pointed out the window.

Flushing, Mae stared, speechless, as Mrs. O'Toole chided, "Nora, don't be silly. She'll wave good-bye." The train whistle trilled, making Mae squirm in her seat. "But now, Mary Therese!" clucked Mrs. O'Toole. "We're pulling away!"

With a defiant glare toward Nora, Mae leaned into the window, one gloved hand and the tip of her nose resting against the cool glass. The train lurched into motion, and she pressed one cheekbone against the window, wiggling her fingers as Aunt Sophie looked her way. Aunt Sophie beamed and grabbed Mama's arm, pointing to Mae, waving with great energy. Mama's face brightened, too, as she waved and then rested her hand on her lips. Uncle Nick looked up, as did Michael, but neither moved, much less raised their hands. Mae sank back into her seat, watching her family shrink into the yellow morning haze. She could still feel Nora's gaze on her, but she didn't care now.

And for a moment, the only sound was the clack-clack-clack of the train wheels, but then came a kindly, "How 'bout a stick of gum, Mary?" Mr. O'Toole held the pack toward her, with an encouraging nod.

"Oh no, thanks anyway," Mae whispered.

"You sure? Thought everyone liked Juicy Fruit." He pushed the pack closer to her face.

"All right, thanks," Mae acquiesced. Tugging off her gloves, she unwrapped the stick of gum and folded it three times on her tongue. Her

eyes darted like a hummingbird around the ceiling of the coach until Mrs. O'Toole's voice broke in.

"So did your mother attend the academy as well?"

"Oh no, ma'am..."

"Well, then how is it that you're going there?"

"Uncle Nick. Uncle Nick's sending both Michael and me to boarding schools, to help my mother out."

Mrs. O'Toole cocked her head. "Help your mother out?"

"Yes, ma'am, it's been hard since Papa died."

Mrs. O'Toole gasped, "Oh dear, your mother's widowed?"

"Mm-hmm, almost six years now. Papa died in a car crash on Lake Shore Drive, near Navy Pier, the day before Michael's birthday. Mama says he was probably lookin' out at the waves on Lake Michigan, never knew what hit him."

Mrs. O'Toole shook her head gravely. "I'm sorry."

Mae leaned closer to Mrs. O'Toole, drawn to the softness in her voice. The way Mama's voice used to be. Before.

"See, when Mama got a job as a seamstress, Michael was s'posed to babysit me after school, but he didn't always come straight home, so then last year, Uncle Nick sent Michael to St. Scholastica boarding school, you know, on Sheridan Road, and he came home weekends, so I stayed with Aunt Sophie after school. But then—" Mae tipped in even closer. "Then Michael got kicked outta school, and Uncle Nick put his foot down that both of us were too much for Aunt Sophie. So Uncle Nick said Michael goes to military school, 'n' I'm old enough to go away to school too, and so"—Mae bit her lower lip—"that's why."

Mrs. O'Toole's mouth hung open as Mae raised her eyebrows for emphasis. "See, we're Greek, but Mama's not. Plus she had us baptized Catholic!"

"Oh my," faltered Mrs. O'Toole. "Well, I..." She looked expectantly at Mr. O'Toole. "Isn't it too bad, Bill?"

"Yeah." He nodded, scratching his forehead. "Too bad."

Nora's "Whoa!" under her breath confirmed Mae's too-late sense that she had said too much. Determined to salvage the moment, Mae swallowed her gum, adding, "So, anyways, it's not that important 'cause it's only for a year. But look, Aunt Sophie sent candy with me, from Field's." Her hands trembled as she tugged at the gold cord. "Anybody like some?"

"Sure," jumped in Nora. "What kind?"

"Spice drops." Mae pried the lid back. "Try 'em: they're really good."

Mrs. O'Toole chose one, and then Nora took a small fistful. Her father cleared his throat with a meaningful frown that froze Nora, until Mae grabbed a few and added in her cheeriest tone, "Good to mix flavors. I do it all the time." Mr. O'Toole sat back, and Nora nodded, grateful. "Try mixing the orange and yellow, but the green doesn't go with anything. It's mint, not lime."

♦ ♦ ♦

"Breath mint?" Nora was rummaging through her patent-leather purse as they shuffled inside.

Notre Dame's gym *was* pretty. They'd put up one of those new disco balls, the kind with hundreds of tiny mirror squares, and specks of light were flickering like lightning bugs, silently, randomly, with just a hint of a clockwise spin. With the bleachers folded back, an enormous banner, letters all glitter gold, spelled "Welcome St. Mary's" across the whole length of the wall. Even the DJ was all right, playing new stuff from Pink Floyd and not talking too much. Mae had danced a couple of times, but now she was hanging back near the sign, huddled with Madonna and Lisa.

"Shouldn't it be time for a break?" Mae started to grind her heel back and forth and then, abruptly realizing the sandals were Nora's, planted her foot back flat on the floor.

"I guess," Lisa frowned. "Bathroom, fix our faces?"

"Nah, too dim for anyone to see anyway."

Tears of a Clown ended, the feedback whined over the intercom system, and then the DJ's voice boomed. "Just one more song in this set, and then we'll bring up the lights for a break. But since this is a mixer, I need everyone to step onto the dance floor."

"Oh brother," muttered Mae. "Queer." Still, the girls peeled themselves off the wall.

"C'mon, everyone," the DJ cajoled. "Find a spot: literally, step onto one of the colored dots on the dance floor. One person per dot."

Mae scanned the gym floor. There were fifty-some dots the size of paper plates, lots of different colors, splashed all across the room. She'd assumed they were part of the decorations.

"Okay, everyone finding a dot of their own? Pick one, plenty to go around."

Any cheerier and you could be a kindergarten teacher! Good God. With an annoyed sigh, Mae slid onto a rose-colored spot, folded her arms, and tapped her left foot.

"Okay then!" the DJ crooned. "Now, girls, stay put. Guys, take note of what color dot you're on and then locate a young lady near you on the same color dot. Go up, introduce yourself, and ask her for the next dance."

Mae watched the shiver of embarrassed excitement wash through the crowd. Nervous glances darted left and right. Some girls blushed; others tossed back their hair and tried to smile confidently; yet others seemed to be holding their breath as they stared down at their purple or aqua island. Mae shook her head, closed her eyes, and tilted her chin up. *Beam me up, Scotty! Quick!*

"Hi there." A low but assertive voice, coming from just behind her left shoulder. Mae opened her eyes and fixed a polite but not overly enthusiastic smile on her face as she turned.

Tallish, dishwater blond hair, long sideburns; kind of a heavy brow, but nice enough hazel eyes; straight nose, crooked smile. *Wise guy, or did he think this was queer too?*

"Hi." Mae stuck with her perfunctory smile.

"I'm Ron." He held out his hand, and Mae shook it.

"Hi, Ron." Mae kept shaking his hand. He smiled wider: *okay, he was cool.*

"This is the part where you say, 'Oh hi, Ron, I'm...'"

"Mary." Mae dropped his hand, edging back a little.

"Mary, nice to meet you, Mary."

More firefly lights started to flit, and the opening notes of *Color My World* cued Ron. "Dance, Mary?"

"Sure." She let him wrap her arms around her back, hesitated, and then rested her head on his right shoulder. *Lord, a slow dance?* He pulled her in a little too tightly. She tilted her hips back enough that they wouldn't brush against him but decided to let him nestle his face in her hair. Kinda weird, him smelling her hair, but at least she didn't have to make small talk.

Left, right, left, right, a comfortable blur. Ron's breath warmed the back of her head, washed down the nape of her neck, and faded away just as it slipped under her blouse.

Mae opened her eyes to slits, just enough to take in the dance floor through the screen of her eyelashes. Slow motion, the wordless, shuffling spins, the sparkle lights, like one of those silent movies, where the click-click-click of the projector seemed to push the figures across the dim screen. Only instead of a tinny piano, the deep, smooth horns of the band Chicago pulled everyone in a swirling stream, rocking, turning, fading into the shadows. Mae let her eyes slip closed again.

Michael and Nicky under the dining room table, giggling, flicking red poker chips at each other. "C'mon, Maisie," Michael beckons. "Over here!" But Mae is snuggled under the crook of Papa's arm, happy just to watch, happy to feel him wrapped all around her. Mama and Papa and Uncle Nick and Aunt Sophie chat over their cocktails, and they don't notice her any more than baby Alex sleeping in the bassinet. And when Papa chuckles, it echoes on Mae's cheekbone, almost like Mae's laughing too. And when he's quiet, Mae can feel his heartbeat on her cheek.

With the last few notes, the lights brightened immediately, and Mae stiffened.

"So..." Ron let his hands run the length of Mae's arms as he took a too-small step back. "Thanks for the dance, Mary."

"Sure." Mae corrected the space between them with a visible lean away.

"Which dorm you in?"

"Regina," Mae muttered, her eyes traveling around the room. "Most seniors are, you know." Her trademark irritated-but-mannered tone.

Ron winced. "Right." He twisted a bit to the left to catch her eye. "Can I bring you some punch?"

"Sure, that'd be great." Mae offered a scripted smile. "Shall I come with you?" *Don't sound too snotty.*

"No, wait here while I brave the crowd," he answered, taking off before he finished his reply. Mae felt her cheeks glow with embarrassment. *Must've wanted to get away. Bitchy, Mae, being bitchy: be nicer when he gets back.*

She checked out the couples on the floor: Nora looked like she was joking around with her partner, some boxy blond guy. Monica was making small talk, too, but her arms were folded tightly, and her guy looked resigned, hands in his pockets. Loretta returned Mae's glimpse with a shrug—*guess she's waiting for some punch too*—but she was flushed and was standing with her boobs thrust out. Just then Loretta flashed her toothy, Miss America smile as her dance partner emerged from the crowd, a flowered Dixie cup in each hand. She barely came up to his shoulders. *Football player? Pretty cute, though, how he leaned low to hear whatever she was saying. Was she talking quietly so he would have to bring his face close to her, wait, cleavage? Jeez, Lori! Kleenex?*

"Here ya go." Ron offered Mae a cup, and she offered a friendlier smile in return, before she took a sip.

"Thanks, I was thirsty." *Cherry cola.*

"Sip, sip, sip!" Papa chuckles, holding Mae's glass steady for her.

"Johnnie, don't fill it to the very brim," Mama points out for the umpteenth time. "At least use a plastic cup for the children."

"Nah, then they can't see the prize at the bottom, right, Miss Maisie-Daisy?"

"Papa, I got cherries too?"

"Of course, Michael, one more than your sister, since you're older."

"Neat-o!"

"But your mother's right: careful not to spill. Here, baby, let Papa hold the glass for you. Go play with Nicky and Michael—scoot!"

"Hello? Mary?"

"Oh, sorry. What?"

"I asked if you're hungry: cookies?"

"No, thanks anyway." *Focus, Mae!* She smiled enough to show her dimple. "So!"

"So Regina Hall, right?"

Mae nodded.

"Then you know Margie Hill, Vicki McAllister?"

Blah but why not. "Yeah, both on third floor: third north."

"Right. Margie's the twin of one of my buddies."

"Really? Huh. Didn't realize Margie had a twin. How 'bout that."

"You're not on third?"

"Nope, second. That's enough exercise for me." She shrugged.

"Oh, gotcha. We're on fifth and the elevator's slow, so we're taking stairs all the time."

"Oh, drag." Mae wrinkled her nose sympathetically.

"Yeah." Ron hesitated and then brightened as someone behind her caught his eye. He grinned, gesturing them closer. Actually a pretty nice smile, Mae had to allow, as she turned to see who was joining them.

Two guys, two girls, four Dixie cups all in a row: Cathy and Marianne from four north. And a kind of short but sweet-faced blond boy, and... Mae audibly gasped. The other guy: the lightest maple-colored hair and fiercely blue eyes, such a wintry blue that they should've been scary, but no, somehow framed by bristling lashes, crinkles in the corners as he smiled, somehow seemed like the eyes of a sweet old man. *Santa eyes.*

He nodded hello to her and turned to Ron. "Join you guys?"

"Sure, man." *Good friends?*

"Thanks." The cute guy gestured toward the girls. "Cathy, Marianne, this is my roommate, Ron. Ron: Cathy, Marianne, and this is...?" He focused on Mae and paused, his smile fading a touch.

"Mae." Mae thrust her hand out. As he wrapped his hand firmly around hers, Mae's heart tripped, and her scalp tingled. Again, a bit of a gasp as she inhaled—sounded like she was preparing to say something. "Mae Panos."

"Mae?" Ron frowned. "Thought your name was Mary."

Mae flushed again as she pulled her hand back, turning toward Ron. "Mae's my nickname. It's really Mary Therese."

"Oh." Ron still looked perturbed. "Anyway, this is my roomie Jack, and this guy's Otto; he's on our floor too."

"Hi." Mae forced herself to acknowledge Otto but was drawn back to Jack's face. Even his ears were so graceful that she couldn't resist studying the curves in them. Jack, apparently taken aback by her scrutiny, turned toward Cathy. *Was he blushing? Oh cute!*

"Mae." Ron's voice startled her. "You know Cathy and Marianne?"

"Sure," Cathy answered for her. "It's a small class, so you pretty much know everybody after this many years." All the girls nodded their heads.

Marianne chimed in, "Right; in fact, Mae and I are both from Chicago. I'm south side, and Mae, you're a north sider, right?"

Irritated, Mae sensed she was losing the small-talk competition. "Aw, Marianne, I'm amazed you remember that about me! That's right, St. Ignatius. And Wrigley Field!" she added, looking to the boys for approval.

Marianne modestly dipped her head, glancing up at Jack. "Guess I'm just a people person."

Mae's eyes narrowed. *So obvious! Marianne, you're not keeping him.*

Jack added, "Otto here, he's from Gary, practically next door to you guys, right?"

"True, I hail from the armpit of America," Otto boasted. "Otto's my name from German class, but it stuck, anyway kinda like it. But Jack's our really exotic one, all the way from Kansas."

"Right," Jack protested, fending off a punch in the arm from Otto. "Munroe, Kansas: so exotic! Ouch!" Otto nailed him on the second shot. Jack ducked his head for a second as he rubbed his shoulder, but Mae met his sidelong glance without blinking.

"Why are you here?" Mae blurted out.

Jack hesitated. "Here where? At the dance?"

"No." *Crap, sounded flustered.* "I mean, why school in Indiana?"

"Oh. My granddad, my dad both went here."

"Then how'd you end up in Kansas?" Mae stepped closer.

"Well, Dad went to medical school there and then the Clinic—you know, Menninger—that kept his practice there, I guess." Jack was only addressing her now.

Marianne slipped in front of Jack, catching Mae's eye and then focusing on Ron. "So, Ron, what color spot were you and Mae standing on? Jack and I were on green." She reached back to put her hand on the crook of Jack's elbow.

Scram, Marianne, he's mine.

"Pink, right?" Ron asked Mae, his tone tinged with defeat.

Mae turned toward him, smiling apologetically. "Yes, pink." She gulped, trying to think of something to add, even though he clearly held little expectation now. *Sorry.*

"So pink's your favorite color?" Jack asked, right over the top of Marianne's head.

Mae turned only her head, but she felt off-balance as she met his eyes. "No, not really. Blue."

Chapter Three

Biding Time

1963

Sister Louisa paused in front of a room near the end of the stark third-floor hallway, sorting through her keys. Mae heard voices in the stairwell and stepped back to make space but bumped someone, turning as she offered, "Oh, sorry," only to face a life-size statue of the Blessed Virgin Mary, reaching with open arms toward her. Mae stumbled backward, stepping on Nora's foot.

"Ow!" Nora complained.

"Sorry," Mae whispered.

Sister Louisa exclaimed, "Here we go: Mary Therese's key!" She pressed a key attached to an oversize safety pin into Mae's palm, saying, "Careful! There's a two-dollar replacement charge." Her tone suggested grave responsibility, yet she winked when she caught Mae's eye. Sister drew them all into Mae's room, pointing out its features: a single bed with two wide drawers built underneath, a corner desk and built-in bookshelf, a sink in the corner, and a closet so narrow that it could hold only four, maybe five dresses and perhaps three pairs of shoes below. Mae's two suitcases, lined up neatly in the center of the room, seemed to fill all the floor space.

"Oh my," frowned Mrs. O'Toole. "I'd forgotten how small these rooms are."

"Well, yes," Sister Louisa allowed, "they were originally for our novices, so rather modest, all set up the same."

Mr. O'Toole considered aloud, "We may have to take Nora's trunk back with us."

"Or," Sister offered, "we can put it in storage, as you wish."

"Hmm..." Mrs. O'Toole pondered as she patted Mae's back gently. "Mary, are you all right to start unpacking by yourself? We'll just be down the hallway if you need us."

Mae nodded.

"Well then, Sister, if you can show us Nora's room," continued Mrs. O'Toole. "There's work to do!" The adults brushed out the door; Nora shrugged and followed.

Mae stood silent, nothing moving but her eyes. Beige walls, blond wood, white ceramic...a clean, grim little room. She was glad, at least, that it wasn't any bigger: the emptiness would be too much. Even so, the walls seemed to echo the voices of other girls with their parents. The chatter buzzed around Mae's head like a pesky fly. She climbed over her suitcases to crank open the dusty window, hoping for other sounds to fill the space. But no, just an empty tennis court below, and beside it an old, mossy cemetery. Mae stared out, and a sob started to well up. She clapped her hands over her mouth and then swatted at a stray ribbon from her hat. Tears spilled down her cheeks as she wrestled to pull off the stupid hat. As bobby pins gave and hair roots tore, Mae flung the hat on the floor, grinding her heel into it for good measure.

♦ ♦ ♦

"What color should her face be?" Some of Sister Eva's salt-and-pepper bangs peeked out as she cocked her head to the right, studying Mae's canvas. *Art class: the worst.*

"Color?" Mae wrinkled her nose.

"Mm-hmm. Notice you'll need different values for each side of her face—the light from the window hits this cheek sharply plus, there's that shadow from her nose and her lower lip. See it?" Sister's eyes flicked back and forth.

Mae frowned at the model. Thought it was a good drawing of Madonna's face: the wave in her bangs, one ear a little lower than the other. Looked like her. But Sister Eva didn't seem to appreciate Mae's careful lines.

"I guess, this side whitish, and the shadowy side more, um, tannish?"

"Remember, a portrait conveys the subject's mood as well. What does she feel? And how can you convey that?"

"I don't...I guess she looks tired."

"What else?"

Mae wished Sister Eva would move on to the next student. "What do you mean?"

"Feelings, Mary Therese, how might she be feeling?" Mae glanced over at Judy's easel, hoping to find a clue. Sister offered, "Would you say her expression is happy? Thoughtful? Sad?"

"Sad? Maybe?"

"Okay, good, sad: so how will you convey that?"

"Like, the corners of her mouth?"

"Fine, and what about through color?"

"Well..." Mae hesitated. "I, um, the background could be dark, maybe dark blue?"

"Ah, feeling blue, we use that expression, don't we? How would you feel about putting the color in her face?"

"Well, her face can't be blue."

"Why not?"

Mae shook her head. "Her face?" *Was she making fun? Oh, please move on to Judy.* Mae bit the inside of her cheek.

"Really," Sister Eva persisted. "Why can't her face be blue?"

Mae's tone was polite but flat. "Because it isn't?"

Sister Eva sighed as she studied Madonna. "Ah well, if you don't see blue...but if sadness is what you see in her, that's one way to communicate it. Just play with the idea." Finally, Sister turned toward Judy's easel.

Mae shook her head, glancing up at the clock. Seventeen more minutes.

♦ ♦ ♦

"Much homework tonight?" Nora flicked one fuzzy orange slipper across the room as she stretched out on Mae's bed. She pulled out her ponytail holder, shaking out her glinting auburn waves.

"Nope, only chapter three vocab for French tomorrow. Just writing home first."

"Already got your mail today?"

"Yep, a letter from my aunt."

Nora's eyebrows shot up. "Again? More money too?"

"Another two dollars."

"Gosh, you get more mail! I've only had two letters from my mom since we got here."

"That's a lot," Mae reassured her. "It's just I've got Michael and Aunt Sophie too."

"I guess." Nora's eyes narrowed. "You write back to your aunt more, huh?"

Mae flipped her daisy note card closed. "Maybe, but I write my mom too." She tugged on the corner of her pillow with her toes.

Nora raised a hand in protest. "Hey, I would too, for those two-dollar bills."

"It's not just for the money, though: I've been asking her..."

"What? For clothes?"

"No, never mind." Mae slid the card into the corner. "Anyway..." Mae smoothed her starchy pillowcase with one foot, casting around for another subject.

"Whattaya think she'll get you for Christmas?"

"Dunno, that's still pretty far away. She said to bring home my summer clothes at Thanksgiving, and she'll take me shopping at Field's for a winter jacket."

"Neat."

"Yeah." Mae tried again. "Anyway, your folks picking you up for Thanksgiving?"

"Driving here, sounds like. At least that's what they're doing for next weekend. You?"

"Think my mom's sending me a train ticket. She doesn't drive, or else she'd be coming for parents' weekend. I gotta wait for Thanksgiving, but she promised, she's gonna have me come home a day early. I'm excused to go home Tuesday afternoon. Michael too."

"Wow, lucky duck. My folks aren't coming till that Wednesday, pretty sure."

"Too bad."

"So," Nora mulled, "your aunt and uncle are pretty rich?" She twirled a lock of hair with her index finger.

"Guess so." Mae shrugged.

"How'd they get that way?"

"Dunno exactly. He owns a lot of stuff, buildings I think."

"Oh." Nora looked thoughtful. "But no kids? That why your aunt buys you so much?"

"I guess, but they did have two boys. But my cousins died."

"No kidding. Died when they were little?" Nora sounded just like her mom.

"Pretty much." Mae tried to summon up the faces of her cousins. They kept turning away in her mind's eye: just a glimpse of a nose, a blur of shiny coal-black curls, and yet she could hear Nicky laughing, perfectly clear. But Alex, like a silent movie. Mae sighed. "I guess Nicky and Alex got the whooping cough. I remember playing with them under the dining room table, but can't really remember when they got sick. But Mama says Aunt Sophie used all her strength to get through the funerals, and then she took to her bed for, like, two months."

"Gee. And your uncle? Is that why he's so scary?"

Mae bristled. "He's not scary, just, just serious. But he takes care of Aunt Sophie, Michael, me. Mama says he's 'old school,' so he only takes care of blood relatives..." Mae wasn't sure how to finish. *She and Nicky used to be eye-to-eye, and the grown-ups would measure them with their backs together. This time, Mae was a quarter inch taller, but just wait, said Papa, Nicky was gonna be tall like his dad.*

"Has he always been like that?"

"Like what? Who? Nicky?"

"Your uncle, Mr. Boss, who else?"

"It's just his way. He's in charge of our family, knows what's best for us. Mama says we're blessed that he feels responsible for Michael and me." Mae heard how unconvincing she sounded. Kicking her pillow, she wriggled up straight in her chair. "I gotta finish this note before lights-out."

"I'll see if the hall phone is free—should call my mom about parents' weekend."

Mae fell silent for a moment. "You're lucky your mom's coming."

"You know you can come with us."

Mae shook her head. "Nah, that's okay." *Maybe Mrs. O'Toole would insist that she join them.* "But like I said, gotta finish my note." Still she guarded it with her hand until she heard Nora dialing in the hallway. She reread from the beginning, slowing for the important part.

Dear Aunt Sophie,

Thank you for your last card and for the two dollars. I will buy treats with it this weekend. I hope you and Uncle Nick are well. You are right, Thanksgiving is almost here. But, Aunt Sophie, did you read in my last letter about Christmas? About how if Michael and me stay home and start public school in January, it would save Uncle Nick a whole lot? You didn't say anything about that in this letter. Mama's working plenty now, so it's a good idea, right? Please show my letter to Uncle Nick and decide by Thanksgiving. That would make it an extra good Christmas. Please ask Uncle Nick, OK?

Love, Mae XOXO

Chapter Four

Best Thanksgiving Ever

1970

"Aha!" Nora cheered. "Letters!" With a well-practiced right-left-right, she tugged the brass mailbox door open. "Let's see: Grandma, Dad. Check time!" She held one envelope up to the ceiling light. "Yes, Daddy, thank you." Ripping one end open, Nora tipped and shook the envelope until a check and a handwritten note glided out. "Twenty-five bucks!" she beamed.

"Cool!" Mae agreed. "My aunt still only sends fives." Only one letter, but it was from Michael. Mae frowned, trying to decipher the smudged postmark. *Nope, could never figure out where he was stationed.*

Nora scanned down her father's note. "Yeah, but your aunt writes every week, so you end up with almost as much at the end of the month. My dad writes once a month, if that. *He* sends me to boarding school, so Mom won't spoil me..." She looked up with a toothy grin. "Now he sends me spending money. Joke's on him, huh?"

Mae didn't respond, absorbed in Michael's letter.

Nora grew serious. "Your brother?"

Mae nodded. "Yeah, but this is dated almost a month ago. Sounds like he's still pretty far south in 'Nam but never says exactly, and who knows from week to week?" She tapped the paper, sighing.

"Mae, know it's hard, but don't psych yourself out: he said they don't move medics much, so he's probably still there. Better than on some front line, right?"

"Right." She reread the letter: maybe she missed some cryptic reference.

Nora waited.

Mae looked up with a deep, perplexed frown. "Dunno...guess he's okay, but sometimes when he says less, I get the feeling things are worse. Man, ten months to go on his tour. Just wish he'd get home sooner than August. He hated last summer."

"I know, but maybe he'll miss rainy season."

"I guess." Mae stared at Michael's disciplined script. No loops. She sniffed the inside of the envelope. *Pot?*

"What?"

"Oh, sometimes I think it smells like pot." Mae poked around the inner corners of the envelope. "Nothing, just my imagination. Heard they have great pot there."

Nora wrinkled her nose. "Well, not like he could send a joint to you. You have your own stash anyway."

"So what?" Mae bristled.

"So nothing, cool it. Anyway, you don't go through it as fast as you used to."

"True. Dunno, lately I just don't want to smell like an ashtray."

"Or taste like one?"

Mae shook her head, trying to look disdainful. "Maybe."

"Ooh, blushing? C'mon, let's go figure out what we're wearing tonight." Nora turned toward the stairs.

"You got a date, too? Who with?"

"Tony, you know, Kathy's boyfriend's teammate. A linebacker. We're doubling, I think a concert downtown. Hope he drives: sick to death of that bus. You're so lucky to have a steady boyfriend with a car."

My boyfriend. Mae bounced up the flight of stairs.

"Somebody's got it bad!" Nora teased. "Slow down, kid; you've only been going out a couple of months."

"I know that," Mae countered.

"Just remember, gotta kiss a few frogs!"

Mae fumbled for her room key. "Maybe not everybody has to do that. Some people must get it right on the first try. Sandra's engaged already. So's Barb."

"Oh brother! Stuck on an Irish guy, no less: your Uncle Nick's gonna freak out. Do they even know about Jack?"

Mae pushed the door open with her hip while she tucked her key back into her purse. "Not Nick's business."

Nora flopped onto her bed. "Not what I asked. And college?"

Mae plopped onto her bed, hugging her pillow. "College can come later. Jack's got Peace Corps first. He's graduating in December, so he can start early. We'll get married in June, then I'll join him, and then we'll take turns putting each other through school when he comes back."

Nora shook her head. "Lotta plans, Mae. Really think your mom'll go along with this?"

Mae shrugged. "She'll have to."

"What about Michael? Don't you want to wait till he's back?"

Mae studied her pedicure. "I know, not ideal, but Michael will understand. If I wait, Uncle Nick will have me shipped off to college, and Jack could be super far away, and it'll all get complicated."

"This is the *simple* plan? Shit!"

"God, yes. The only trick's getting Jack back from wherever in June, but we'll work it out. Or I'll go where he is."

"I know, just, look, don't take this the wrong way, but are you sure, well, this is what Jack's planning? I mean, is Jack saying this too?"

Mae fluffed her pillow. "It's okay. Don't worry; he's hinting. He knows he leaves in a few months. I think he's proposing by Thanksgiving—I really do."

Nora opened her mouth and closed it. She cleared her throat. "Mae, Thanksgiving's, like, two weeks away."

Mae lit up again. "I know. Gonna be the best Thanksgiving ever! What?" she added, not liking Nora's expression.

"Nothing," Nora responded, collecting her terry cloth robe and slippers. "I gotta shower."

"Best Thanksgiving ever!" Mae called after her. *This time, this time a good Thanksgiving.*

♦ ♦ ♦

1963

"Nick, look how handsome Michael is in his uniform!" Sophie turned Michael by the shoulders so that he faced Uncle Nick. Her hands rested on his navy-blue epaulets while Michael tugged the dove-gray jacket straight. "Oh my," Sophie murmured. "Almost as tall as I am. When did that happen?" As Nick stepped closer to inspect him, Sophie ran her hands down Michael's arms. "Look, Nick, our cadet!"

Uncle Nick nodded as he scrutinized Michael head to toe. "Polished shoes too!"

"Yes, sir," Michael snapped.

"Very good." Nick patted Michael's back and repeated, more vigorously, "Very good." He moved past Michael to Mae, gave her a perfunctory kiss on the forehead, and turned toward Sophie and Ellen. "Ladies, wine? Sherry?"

"Yes, let's have a glass of wine," Sophie suggested, motioning toward the couch. "Ellen, you and Mae sit down because I want to hear all about the academy, and Michael, sweetheart, help Uncle Nick serve the drinks? Nick, dear, make Coke-tails for the children. Maraschino cherries are on the bar."

Mae sank into the cushion next to Mama, her right hand imperceptibly stroking the velvet beside her. Everything felt warm: the golden cast of the lamps, Mama's arm brushing against hers, the heavy scents of turkey and gravy and rolls. As Michael shuttled back and forth, wineglasses and cocktail napkins in hand, Sophie and Mama momentarily forgot about Mae, and Mae was thankful.

"I'll have to get back the gravy in a moment," Aunt Sophie warned.

"Sophie," Uncle Nick boomed from across the room, "you should have had Dorothy stay to serve dinner!"

"Oh, don't be silly!" Sophie scolded right back at Nick. "I'm capable of putting Thanksgiving dinner on the table. Plus, she has her family, Nick! As it is," she continued, turning toward Mama, "Dorothy came in early this morning to do the rolls and pies while I prepared the bean casserole and turkey. The table was set last night before she left. Honestly, I don't know why people think I cannot host a holiday meal!" Sophie arched her eyebrow at Nick.

"Of course you're capable," Nick conceded, "but I don't want this to be work for you. That's why we pay for good help."

"And Dorothy's wonderful help," Sophie agreed. "But certainly Ellie and Mae and I can take it from here, can't we, ladies? In fact," she gasped, "the gravy! Mae, sweetie, will you go stir the gravy, and your mother and I will join you in a moment? You gentlemen relax and visit while we finish up. Ten more minutes."

Mae stood as Michael approached her with her drink. He handed it to her wordlessly, grimacing at the prospect of being abandoned to Uncle Nick. Mae mouthed, "Sorry," as she turned toward the kitchen. Taking one good sip so she wouldn't spill, Mae slipped through the dining room and pushed the kitchen door open with her back, into more light and more heat. Inspecting the pots on the stove, Mae found the gravy in front, with a dry skin forming on top. She poked at it with the ladle, trying to push the torn pieces down deep, and then stirred energetically until it looked all smooth and glossy again. Resting the icy glass on the Formica counter, Mae crouched down to take a good look inside the crystal tumbler. The cola had a reddish tinge from the cherry juice, and three maraschino cherries were bumping around on the bottom. She smiled at Uncle Nick's extravagance. *Just like Papa that way.* The door swung in as Mama and Sophie entered. Mae resumed stirring.

Aunt Sophie peeked in the pot and then gave Mae a perfumed squeeze. "A good cook like your mother."

Mama demurred. "Well, I'm no fancy cook, but Maisie's a big help."

"So tell me, Mae, how's the food at St. Mary's?"

Mae stuck out her tongue. "Not so great." Her mother shot her a disapproving look. "I mean, pretty good but nothing like this."

"Oh." Sophie chuckled as she patted a stray lock of hair into her chignon. "I guess that's to be expected. But on the whole, good?"

Mama was watching Mae closely. Mae understood. "Oh yes, Aunt Sophie. There's dessert every night with dinner!"

"Ah!" Sophie beamed at Mama. "Heaven!"

"And," Mae added for good measure, "my friends and I can buy M&M's or Good-n-Plenty on Saturdays, from Sister Louisa."

"Fun! I'd be doing that too. And speaking of buying..." Sophie turned back toward Mama. "Can we still plan to go downtown this weekend, while Mae and Michael are here? The Christmas windows will be up at Field's."

Mae closed her eyes. *Christmas! Maybe Uncle Nick decided! Maybe, maybe he will say something at grace.*

"Now, Sophie," Mama began, "you and Nick have already given us so much, I don't want Nick thinking that we want, well—"

"Oh pooh!" Sophie interrupted. "This is my pleasure to take you shopping. My goodness, Nick barely glances at our accounts anymore, and besides, I've already said I want to buy the children good warm coats."

"Well, maybe just coats then." Mama looked embarrassed.

"You, too, Ellie."

"No, no, that's too much. I can get another winter out of my coat, really."

"Now, Ellie," Sophie dropped her voice, and she motioned Mae closer, "you just listen to me, and, Mae, you're old enough to keep a secret, so you listen too."

Mae gasped. *Secret? Is she about to tell Mama?*

Aunt Sophie continued, "I have a one-hundred-dollar bill just sitting in my purse to spend, and I'm going to spend it on a few extras for all of you, and no arguments about it."

Oh. Well, maybe at dinner. Uncle Nick, he'd be the one to say so.

Mama looked stunned. "A hundred dollars?"

Sophie gave a dismissive flick of her hand. "Oh, I know that sounds like a lot, Ellie, but really, what good is it if I can't have fun spending it on the children? Nick gave it to me three weeks ago to buy something special for the table for the holidays. Well, honestly, we don't need a thing! I have my china, his mother's serving pieces; it's just silly to buy things just to buy them!"

"But Nick..." Mama cautioned.

"Oh, I'm not about to hurt his feelings. I'll let him think I did as he asked, and then I have a little money of my own. Don't worry, Ellie, I do this from time to time. He's a dear, so generous, but I'm always feeling it's his money I'm spending, and what do I contribute? Why, sometimes I even send Dorothy home when I know Nick will be gone all day, and I get down on my hands and knees and scrub the floor myself. And believe me, it feels good! I can't spend my whole life on solitaire and knitting!"

Mae was astounded. *Defying Uncle Nick?*

"Mae, sweetie, as you get older, you'll see we ladies have ways of managing the men in our lives. We love them, let them feel that they're in charge, but..." Sophie stage-whispered, "Honestly, in most homes the ladies rule the roost. But that's just between us girls now, right?"

But wait, so Aunt Sophie decides about staying home after Christmas?

"Still..." Mama muttered.

"Ellie!" Sophie insisted, "who else do I have to spend it—not Nicky, or my little Alex—oh dear!" Her voice quivered as her hands flew up to press hard against her lips, holding back a choking sob. She turned her face away from Mae, but Mae could still see her back shudder in little spasms as she fought crying.

Mama grabbed Sophie's shoulders and pulled her closer. Catching Mae's eye, Mama tipped her head toward the door with a no-nonsense expression even as she said in the most casual of tones, "Mae, Sophie and I will finish the gravy and set up dinner. You go join your brother." Mama silently mouthed, "Go!"

"Actually," Aunt Sophie hiccupped, still not facing Mae, "Mae, sweetheart, will you go get the box of lemon slices sitting on Nick's desk? I want you to take them home, and I just know I'll forget after dinner, so go put them by your mother's purse, please."

"Yes, Aunt Sophie." *Not now. Maybe at dinner.*

"Thanks, sweetie." Aunt Sophie's voice had that tremble again, and Mama squeezed her shoulders. Again Mama mouthed, "Go!" and Mae scurried out, letting the door close on the murmur of her mother's voice.

♦ ♦ ♦

The study was always dim. Mae had never seen the thick wooden blinds opened, and the slats only allowed light to filter in around their edges. Still, the shadows were not what gave the room its air of heaviness: rather, Uncle Nick's presence lay on the oversize furniture like early-August humidity, painful to inhale. The oak desk was tidy enough; the pine-green leather chair tucked behind it was graceful enough; the cream-colored carpet and walls, although plain, offered up as much light as they could muster, but still, there was a palpable uneasiness saturating the room. The white Marshall Field's box glowed, asserting it didn't belong there; yet as Mae picked it up, she was surprised that even sugar would weigh so much. Absently, she nudged the framed picture over a few inches to fill the space left by the box. She paused to inspect the picture of her cousins, slipping into the leather chair to study them from her uncle's vantage point.

It wasn't the greatest photo: not like the professional one on the mantle but, instead, a snapshot from their yard. Nicky and Alex filled up the rectangle, a tumble of arms and legs, sprawled on the grass like goofy puppies. Alex's face was a little blurry, just starting to turn away from the camera as he fell over his big brother's back. Strange that Uncle Nick would not have a more proper portrait on his desk. But Mae smiled at her cousins, patted the frame gently, gathered up the lemon slices, and tucked Uncle Nick's chair back into place.

♦ ♦ ♦

Everyone sat tall and silent as Uncle Nick stood at the head of the table. Mae bowed her head, taking care to cross herself in the Greek way, right shoulder before left. "Let us give thanks for God's bounty, on this day and every other day. And we offer special thanks for the time we had with those we love, John and, and..." Uncle Nick blinked several times. "And our Nicholas, our Alex, who now sit at Your table. Amen." Again, that awkward sign of the cross. He hesitated and turned to Sophie, whose head was still lowered. "Would you like to add anything?"

Mae held her breath, staring at Sophie. *Please, Aunt Sophie, please?*

"No," she whispered, pulling up her head with a wan smile. "That was perfect, dear." He studied her expression, obviously concerned, and she brightened her smile and raised her wineglass. "Happy Thanksgiving, everyone!" She raised her eyebrows encouragingly. Uncle Nick glanced at Mama, who gave him a meaningful nod.

"Yes, happy Thanksgiving," followed Mama, urging Nick to lift his glass.

"Happy Thanksgiving," echoed Mae and Michael, lightly clinking their Cokes together.

All heads turned toward Uncle Nick, who joined in the toast and then rather ceremoniously paused, lowering his glass and lifting the carving knife. "Please begin."

Mae clutched her hands in her lap, pressing against her nervous stomach. *Maybe later? Or when we go shopping? Eat a roll. Be polite.* Michael dove right into his salad, while Mama accepted the butter patties from Sophie, noting, "The table looks lovely, Sophie. So elegant."

Sophie's smile was more relaxed as she ran her hands along the edge of the table, responding, "Thank you, Ellie. You know, it's fun for me to pull out the sterling and china every now and again. In fact"—Sophie turned toward Nick—"like the new pieces, Nick?"

Mae stopped chewing. *Sophie was that bold?*

Nick frowned as he surveyed the table. "Fine, just fine."

Sophie pursed her lips in a pretend pout. "You can't even tell what's new, can you, Nicholas?"

Now Mama was as still as Mae. Mae shook her head in disbelief.

Nick looked irritated. "Does it matter?"

Sophie stroked his arm with a conciliatory smile. "You're right, Nick; it doesn't matter. I just was hoping you'd notice the new silver platters."

Nick hesitated. "They're different?"

Sophie chuckled, turning toward Mama. "Well, Ellie, I guess we ladies shouldn't expect our men to recognize silver patterns, should we? They have more important matters on their minds."

"Yes, Sophie."

Sophie turned back toward Nick. "I'm sorry, Nick, I shouldn't have put you on the spot. The pattern's similar, that's why I bought them: they blend in beautifully, hmm?"

Uncle Nick nodded, cupping Aunt Sophie's cheek with his hand. "Just so they please you."

Sophie slipped her hand into Nick's and kissed his knuckles. "Oh, I'm very pleased with them, Nick. Thank you, dear." Nick and Sophie squeezed hands for a long moment, and then Nick picked up his wineglass, offered Sophie a little salutation, and returned to his dinner. Mae slumped in her seat. *Not now.* Sophie put on her hostess face and picked up her salad fork.

Chapter Five

Or Maybe Christmas

1963

"Mae, are you sure you don't want to sit with your mother and me? We can squeeze in."

"No, thanks, Aunt Sophie." Mae gripped the L train's handrail and planted her feet.

"They're fine, Sophie," Mama insisted. "Only a few more stops."

"When I gave Leon the holiday off, I didn't think about needing him today. I suppose the children can help with the bags."

The bags! Soon there'd be so many bags bumping against her legs, against Michael's bags! Only two, three times a year, Aunt Sophie brought them to Field's, maybe for an Easter dress, maybe for back-to-school shoes, but the mystery was in the extras. There were always a bunch of bags by the time they left, plus the white paper one from the candy counter, waxy white boxes filled with sugared fruit slices or Frango mints. Sometimes they bought so much that Aunt Sophie had things sent out to their home. Or sometimes her driver, Leon, would meet them at the revolving doors on State Street, filling the trunk with all the parcels, and take everyone home in Uncle Nick's long, black Cadillac. Then Michael would sit in front with Leon, and they'd go on about engines and makes and models the whole way home.

The brakes screeched brightly, drowning out the driver's voice as he announced the next stop. Mae squinted to read the platform signs, still blurred by the train's speed, but Michael knew. "Diversey. Twenty-eight hundred North. A couple more stops 'n' then we go down."

Anticipation pricked up her spine. "That part's cool," she whispered. "Kinda scary."

"It's dark all right. Everything feels bumpier 'n' noisier till your eyes get used to it."

"Yeah." Not that it had really occurred to Mae until he said it just now.

"No hands?" One of his favorite challenges.

"Um, not today, too crowded. We might bump someone."

"Have you ever fallen? Keep your hands just an inch off, during the down part."

"But..."

"Jeez, Maisie, don't be such a sissy about it."

Mae bristled. "I didn't say no."

Michael stooped to be eyeball to eyeball. "Then you will?" His eyes, glinting golden brown, were the exact same color as his eyebrows. Even the few freckles on his nose were the same milk chocolate shade. Mae loved his face this way, didn't want his eyes to darken, the way they did when he was bugged, so she nodded, sticking out her tongue to show it was no big deal.

"Okay, then let's try for ten. We haven't made that in a while."

"Fine." Mae had never made ten, but she let Michael think so.

"Hold on, here comes Fullerton." Mae pressed into the steel pole, slippery with the oil and sweat of many palms, while the brakes whined and strained. They stopped, and the doors popped open. Two silver-haired ladies got off. A man stepped on, holding the hand of his daughter: three years old, Mae guessed. Seeing no empty seats, the man scooped up the little girl into the nook of his left arm, grabbing a pole with his right hand. The little girl buried her face in his shoulder: her shiny wheat-colored pigtails were a corsage on his lapel. They blended together.

The doors snapped closed, and the train lurched forward. "What's Aunt Sophie buying you?"

Michael shrugged. "Dunno, whatever Ma thinks. I gotta wear the uniform jacket, but she said I'll need gloves and a muffler to go with it. Maybe earmuffs."

"Hmm. I get a snow jacket with a hood. Don't know if I get anything with it."

"C'mon, it's Aunt Sophie."

"Yeah, I guess." They stared out the grimy windows.

"Hold on," Michael warned. Sure enough, the tug of the brakes. They braced together. The doors popped open; the man carried his little girl off.

Mae looked away, back to Michael. "What's Wisconsin like?"

Michael squirmed. "Okay." The doors sealed close with another lurch forward. "Lots of trees, kinda pretty that way, but more mosquitoes too, and these stupid things called deerflies, they bite a chunk outta you." He pushed his sleeve up to point out the scabs.

"Ouch."

Michael shrugged. "No big deal. I'm waiting to see the snow, though. Hope it's a lot. But it's only four hours north o' here, so how much more snow could it be?"

Now Mae shrugged. "Beats me. Wasn't really thinking about winter yet."

"Too busy with your rosaries, huh?" Michael flashed his wonderful wicked grin.

"Right, I'm preparing for the novitiate," Mae countered.

"My sister the Sister." Michael puffed up a little, obviously proud of that one.

"Ha-ha," she panned.

"Get it? Sister Mary Therese of the Perpetual Novenas?"

"Funny." Mae tried not to respond to Michael's smirk by looking past him and thinking about her real complaints. "You know, they make you go to Mass, every single morning. You're only excused from Mass if you're in the infirmary."

Michael grew somber. "Guess I'll take calisthenics over that. Sorry you don't like it."

Mae flushed. "No, it's just—it's all right, I guess. We can watch TV in the lounge on weekends. It's just, I dunno, far."

"I know. But look, Maisie, we're home now. We'll be back for Christmas and then Easter and then for the whole summer. You just gotta take a few weeks at a time." The brakes squealed and grabbed.

"Mama said we might be able to stay home then, that it's just for one year, maybe."

Michael looked away. "Yeah, maybe." The doors snapped open: no one came or left, but Michael stared at the door anyway. *Oh no, his eyes: milk chocolate turned to dark chocolate, just like that.* The doors closed. Michael's mouth pulled tight too. *No, Michael, what?*

"So..." Mae moved to catch his eye. "It's not so bad, Wisconsin?"

"Nah, it's okay...well..." He dropped his voice and looked Mae straight in the eye. Dark cocoa, no light. "Only thing I hate, really hate, is the marching. Marching even in the rain. Soon we'll be marching in the snow. What's the point? It's absolutely useless, and they make us do it anyway, every day, in formation, every single day. March, march, march. Stupid... anyway, here comes the drop. To ten, right?"

"Ten, yep." Mae stepped back slightly, showing Michael her hands hovering close but not touching the pole. "Ten."

"Cross yer heart, no hands!" The train pitched downward, clacking and rattling, diving under street level. The black swallowed them: no sight at all, just the groans and clicks of the wheels, echoing against the tight tunnel walls, and the wobble and lurch of the car and then Michael's steady whisper, " One...two...three...four...five...six..."

Mae kept her hands off the pole, but she pressed her thigh into it. *Was that cheating?*

"Seven...eight...nine," he whispered as the tunnel lights started to whiz past them. She pulled her leg back.

"Ten!" Mae grabbed the pole, grinning triumphantly. The train slowed as tunnel lights flooded the car.

"You made it?" Michael sounded skeptical.

"To ten," she insisted.

"Cool." An approving smile and milk-chocolate eyes again. *Yeah, better.*

The doors popped open again. A number of people exited as Mama called to them, "Mae, Michael, not yet. Watch for Randolph Street."

"Wanna ditch them at the next stop?" Michael whispered. Now his eyes were flecked with amber sparks, and his wicked grin was back too. Mae loved that wicked grin.

"Shut up." She giggled, feeling a little wicked herself.

♦ ♦ ♦

Michael tugged the massive door open and held it staunchly. Ladies brushed past him, some offering an appreciative nod, others a soft, "Thank you." Mae slipped through, into the basement level of Marshall Field's. She marveled that the department store had its own L stop. But then, why not? It had everything else. Aunt Sophie said that they could take care of you, cradle to grave. Well, maybe that was true for Aunt Sophie: she shopped here lots. For Mae, hardly ever, and that made these real occasions.

Ladies continued to stream by, pulling off their gloves and unbuttoning their coats. Fabric swooshed and high heels clattered as they fanned out toward housewares, toward luggage, toward the escalator. Aunt Sophie and Mama paused. Mae tugged at her buttons as Michael caught up to them.

"This way." Aunt Sophie shooed everyone toward the humming escalator. "Let's make a plan as we head upstairs." Her eyes were fixed on the tiny face of her gold bracelet watch as she took a measured step onto the moving platform. "Now," Aunt Sophie calculated, "let's aim for being up at the Walnut Room by eleven thirty; there certainly will be a line today for tables. But I don't want us to feel rushed, so let's see...we can divide and conquer, can't we, Ellie?"

Mae and Michael exchanged knowing grins: big lunch, hot chocolate with whipped cream, dessert too, way up on the third floor. *Lots of escalators today!*

Sophie snapped open her wallet and slipped out four or five folded bills. "Here, Ellen, take these, with Michael, and let Michael pick out some warm pajamas, and socks and underwear, the things a young man doesn't need his auntie seeing." She winked at Michael. "Then we meet up at small leather goods in, say, forty-five minutes, and find those gloves for him before lunch. Oh!" She frowned. "Unless, well, is it all right if I help Mae pick out her jacket? Or did you want to? Watch your step, children." She glided onto the gleaming tile of the first floor.

The others followed suit. Mae slowly turned in a circle as she stepped away from the escalator. She faintly heard her mother answer, "That's just fine, Sophie," as she took in the glass counters, the stylish ladies behind them, the ping of the elevator, the crackle of the dark green paper shopping bags, and oh, the Christmas decorations! From the ceiling spilled a thousand glittering snowflakes, spinning on fine clear threads, dancing to the Christmas carols playing over the speakers. *If just the ceiling's this magical, imagine the windows on State Street! Imagine what the tree must look like in the Walnut Room! This might be the best Christmas ever.*

♦ ♦ ♦

The saleslady stooped low, took one measured tug at the base of the zipper, and eased it all the way up to Mae's chin. The cold metal of the zipper pull didn't matter, because the white fake fur of the hood was tickling Mae's cheeks.

"Isn't that darling! But is it too big on her?" Sophie stepped back.

"Oh no, ma'am." The saleslady smoothed the jacket across Mae's shoulders and down her back. "You want a little room to grow, about a half size, to take her through the winter. And if she doesn't grow too quickly, you may get a second winter out of it. But, see, it's not too long at the cuff, so I don't think you'd want to go any smaller. Turn around, dear," she abruptly addressed Mae, pushing Mae's shoulders to spin her slowly. "Let your mother see how it fits."

Sophie chuckled. "No, I'm her aunt," she demurred, but she sounded pleased by the mistake. "Well, what do you think, Mae? Do you like this jacket?"

Mae studied her reflection. The navy blue was very deep, but the trim along the zipper and cuffs was white with Kelly-green stitching, and then snowy white fur edged the hood. Better than the red and pink ones. This looked more grown up.

"Yes, Aunt Sophie, this one."

"Better than the pink? That was sweet on you, and pink flatters a lady's complexion!"

"Well..." Mae knew she shouldn't argue. If Mama were here, Mae would have to reconsider the pink. "Well..."

Sophie took Mae's hand and patted it. "Sweetheart, if you like this better, it's fine. It's a beautiful jacket." Sophie caught Mae's eye. "We like the blue, right?"

Mae nodded almost imperceptibly.

Sophie was more emphatic: "Yes, we'll go with this one." She turned back to the saleslady. "Now, to go with it: some warm white gloves, and a pretty hat, but warm, for when she doesn't want the hood. What do you think, Mae—white or perhaps green?"

"White?"

"Yes, good." Aunt Sophie squeezed Mae's hand, didn't let go even as she turned toward the saleslady. "White hat and gloves?"

"Oh, I have several that would be just darling with this jacket, madam. I'll be right back." She bustled off.

Aunt Sophie took Mae's other hand. "Now you're sure this is what you'd like, Mae? I don't want there to be any disappointments, not today."

"Yes, please, Aunt Sophie." Mae threw her arms around Sophie's neck, surprising even herself with the ferocity of her hug.

"Oh!" Sophie exclaimed, holding Mae just as tightly. "Well, I'm pleased if you're pleased, sweetheart." Her voice quivered.

Mae held on, pushing her face deep into Sophie's fox collar. *Now, just ask now, Mae!* But the clack-clack of the saleslady's heels grew louder. Mae pulled back, while Aunt Sophie focused on two white fur caps, one more of a pillbox shape, the other with ties that had pompons on the ends. *Fur pompons!*

Mae looked back and forth between the two. The pillbox was more sophisticated, looked like something Nora would choose. But those pompons!

"Why not try both on?" Aunt Sophie suggested. "Try the pillbox first. Yes, that's nice," she noted. "Now the other. Oh my!" Her approval was clear. "Well, your choice, Mae. Whichever you like."

Mae turned back and forth, studying herself in the mirror. The pompons danced with each twist. "I think maybe…this one?"

"Good, then it's settled! We'll take the jacket, this hat, your heaviest white knit gloves, and let's see…the jumper's on hold at the desk. Tell you what, let's get both blouses that matched. Something pretty for when you're not in your uniform, right? And then I think we'd best find your mother and Michael. Are we forgetting anything, Mae?"

My letter! Please? "Aunt Sophie?" Mae caught her eye. "Remember?"

"What, dear?"

Mae pulled up right to Sophie's ear. "Remember my letters?" Mae whispered, barely getting the words out. "About Christmas, staying home after Christmas?" Mae felt Aunt Sophie stiffen slightly, and then after a long pause, Sophie slowly pulled back to meet Mae's eyes. *No. She looks sad. It's no.*

"Mae, sweetheart," Aunt Sophie whispered back, "let's not worry about Christmas just yet. The grown-ups will take care of everything. Let's just have a nice time today. For your mom. Okay?"

So maybe? Maybe for Christmas? But she looks sad. Don't make her sad, Mae. "Yes, Aunt Sophie, okay. And, and thank you."

"Oh, Mae, believe me, it's my pleasure." Sophie sighed and stood up, squeezing Mae's hand. "Come along, sweetheart."

Chapter Six

Jack

Dear Michael, *11-14-70*

Your letter came yesterday. Sure hope you're hanging in there. Can't wait for you to meet Jack—know you guys'll really hit it off. He's sweet, really fun. This is the happiest I remember being... It's just perfect, except for you not being here. In January Jack starts with Peace Corps, but once we know where he's gonna be and when you're gonna ship home, we'll figure out how to get everybody together, promise.

I kinda feel bad telling you how great everything is for me. What's happening with you? Guessing you're all tied up at that hospital. In a real hospital, a building, I hope? Not back in the field in one of those evac hospitals, right?

Don't know how hush-hush you gotta be as a medic, just hoping you're safe. Please don't get yourself transferred back out again near the fighting: you're doing plenty of good right where you are, helping those guys get back on their feet. Come home in one piece.

You're the only one I'm telling about Jack for now. I'll sound Mama out at Thanksgiving, I know she'll think I'm rushing into things, but I can make her understand. MISS YOU! PLEASE get home SOON!

Peace-love—Mae

Tonight was *Butch Cassidy and the Sundance Kid.* Last week, they'd seen *Paint Your Wagon.* Well, most of it anyway. Across the last month, with each movie date, they'd move a couple of rows further back, further from adults in the theater, and more and more twisted over the metal arm between their chairs. What had started as brushing fingers as they passed popcorn progressed toward holding hands, stroking arms and shoulders, and nuzzling ears. Mae's mouth was the more insistent of the two, searching for a throbbing vein in Jack's neck or the tingle of his tongue tracing the edges of her teeth. Fridays and Saturdays were all they were allowed, and it wasn't enough. Sundays through Thursdays they spent hours on the phone. Nora understood and would head over to the library.

And in the front of Jack's Camaro, after the movie, sitting in the parking lot outside the dorm, more quiet talk and, even better, more necking. Still, he was more restrained when there was no armrest between them. He wouldn't slide away from the steering wheel, wouldn't slip down, even unbutton Mae's jacket. Granted, it was colder than normal for mid-November, but so what? Mae felt such an urgent need to feel his cheek against hers, to warm her fingers in his hair. Tonight she opened her jacket, straddled his legs despite the steering wheel pressing into the small of her back, and whispered, commanding, "Come on, Jack, don't hold back." She nibbled on his earlobe, watching the steam from her breath wrap around the nape of his neck.

Jack buried his face in the curve of her shoulder and wrapped his hands around her ribcage, pulling her in tighter. One, two, three kisses along her collarbone, more straight on her mouth as his hands ventured, trembling, to her bra clasp. Mae held her breath, mentally willing him, "*Yes, yes.*" Jack paused and then abruptly drew his hands back and tugged her pea jacket closed. Grimacing, he tucked his head under her chin, murmuring, "No, Mae, not like this."

Mae tipped her face up, away. *Why not*, she demanded mentally, her lips pinched tight. A flash of anger, the first anger she'd ever felt toward him, stabbed in her throat. She blinked back tears.

Jack looked up and clasped her arms, but she kept her chin tipped away, wouldn't meet his eyes. "Mae, please." He gently pulled her face back. His eyes were grave, and Mae's heart sank: she'd made him sad. "Mae, I couldn't stand it if you were angry with me."

She kissed him between the eyes. "No, not mad. Just..."

"Mae"—Jack sounded firmer now—"where's that gazebo you told me about? Near the river?"

"What?"

"Really, is it far from here?"

"On the edge of campus, past Trinity and Augusta and the convent, that way." She pointed. "Why?"

"Let's go there now."

"But it's open, being a gazebo and all—it'll be really cold."

"We'll be okay."

Mae sighed. "I guess." She rebuttoned her coat, flipping the collar up. *Shoulda worn a hat.*

They wiggled out the driver's door, snickering at the tangle of legs trying to reach the icy pavement. Jack slammed the door closed and gripped Mae across both shoulders as they set out. It was so cold that the patches of snow squeaked under their shoes. Mae pressed her face into the velvety suede of Jack's coat. In the dim light of the frosted-over windows of Trinity Hall, they could mostly pick a path between low piles of snow, but once they were past the convent, they had only the starlight as they stumbled through a few drifts and over obscured brush.

The marble gazebo glowed, just barely, under the night sky: not exactly white but less black than the space around them. Round, with perfectly spaced pillars and three small crescent marble benches. In the summer the leafy trees surrounded and obscured the view, so Mae could sit there undisturbed in a soft green cocoon. Now the bare branches glittered with hoarfrost, creating a sparkling mesh that faded down the ravine toward the St. Joe River. It felt less private now but also felt right that Jack was here, the first time she'd ever shared this space with anyone.

Jack gestured to sit down, and again he wrapped his arm protectively across her shoulders. Mae was vaguely aware of the chilly marble bench as the cold penetrated even through the back pockets of her jeans. She didn't care: she leaned into Jack's shoulder and looked up into his eyes. Her heart ached with the sweetness of the moment.

"Mae," he began, "some stuff has changed, and I need to explain it to you. First off, I found out I'm going to Peru in January, for two years. I'll be working with an agricultural program up in the mountains, pretty remote. I figured they'd want a two-year commitment, but what I didn't count on is that I can't come back at all during that time."

Mae tried not to shiver, but she felt like she was freezing right to the bench. She'd never seen Jack so grim.

"So, Mae, I can't come back in June, you understand?"

Immobilized by apprehension and the cold, she couldn't even nod, but her mind flew about uncontrollably, wildly, like a bird trapped in a room. *The wedding? Nora's caution. Four more years of school. Occasional letters. Alone again.* The pain spilled out of her eyes, tears freezing in her eyelashes, some splattering on his jacket sleeve.

"No, Mae, listen!"

Mae tried to quell the din in her head, to pull back to him, to the gazebo. Here, where she was shivering so hard that even her head was shaking. *Don't throw up.* Jack brought the tip of his nose to hers, tried to fill her with his eyes. "Mae, I can't come back, but you could go there. You could join me after graduation, if you'll stay there with me, work with me. See, we could get married in Peru, maybe on a mountaintop. You and me."

Mae's gut was still shuddering, but the pressure of his nose, pressed to hers, quieted her head. She could feel her nose running, her lashes sticking, but she couldn't move her mouth, even shape her lips. Jack pulled away and eased a tiny velvet case out of his left pocket, pushing the lid up with his thumb. The ring held a light-blue stone, an oval, with a diamond chip on each side. They both stared down at it, reverently.

"The first time I met you, you said your favorite color was blue, so I got a blue topaz, and a diamond for each month since then, for each perfect month since then. The jeweler said a plain band can fit right up to it, but someday, Mae, someday I promise I'll get you a band that's a ring of diamonds all the way 'round, 'cause every month will be perfect."

Mae was on a warm mountaintop, in a gauzy white gown that ruffled in the breeze. A halo of wildflowers crowned her head, and long sky-blue ribbons trailed down her back. Mama and Michael would be there. The sun would be strong, bright. Her voice came out weak, frozen: "Jack?"

Jack pressed a gloved finger against her lips and swung around, dropping onto one knee. "Mae, would you do me the honor of marrying me?"

Mae no longer shivered, although the moment felt frozen: frozen time, frozen marble, frozen branches, frozen lashes, a perfect crystalline stillness. She didn't want to disturb it, puncture it with any sound, but Jack tugged off his glove and then hers and wiggled the ring up her finger. "Please?"

Mae leaned forward, nose to nose once more. "Yes." She barely touched his lips. "Yes."

♦ ♦ ♦

"No." Calm but firm enough to fill the dorm parlor. "I forbid it." Uncle Nick stood square, resolute. His silvery hair looked like steel. His black eyebrows were knit together.

"But, no, please?" Mae beseeched Aunt Sophie and then turned to Mama: *Please understand!* "Just listen, we have it all figured out."

Aunt Sophie pressed her lips tight, shaking her head, teary.

"If you'd just meet him..."

"No need." Uncle Nick was unbending. "This is a family matter."

"Mama, please! I love him. My whole future happiness is with him. I know if you talk with him, you'd see. I could call him. He'd be here less than an hour. He would've been here if you'd told me you were coming. Mama? Let me call Jack. Meet him?"

Mama was silent, her expression cryptic. Mae pressed her: "He's such a good person, and look, look at the ring, Mama." Mae held out her hand. "Isn't it beautiful? Please, this means everything to me."

Slowly, Mama took Mae's hand, squeezing it as she peered into Mae's eyes. "I know, Maisie, but Nick is right."

No. This can't be happening. Confusion, dread, resentment all colored Mae's voice. "You're on his side?"

Mama's face pinched tight. "It's not about sides, Mae; it's about your future, and you're too young to make such important choices."

"I'm almost eighteen. Jack's already twenty-one! I'm old enough to know I love him!"

"You're seventeen with your first serious boyfriend, but you haven't even finished high school, much less college. Mae, for your own future, before you think of engagements and wedding gowns." Mama's face softened. "Sweetie, don't you know we want your happiness?" She stroked Mae's hair.

"Then trust me, Mama," Mae urged, trying to preempt her mother's consciousness, make her forget about Nick and Sophie and whatever discussions had filled their drive down here. "This is what'll make me happy, incredibly happy, I promise."

"I understand, Mae, I really do. I was only nineteen when I married your father."

Relief washed through Mae, and she closed her eyes for a moment, gripping her mother's hand. *It'll be okay: Mama sees.*

"But, Mae," Mama's tone was taut. "Sweetheart, I'm saying I understand how important this feels right now, but it would be a mistake. Just look at how hard it's been for us because I didn't have enough education to support you and Michael."

"Listen to your mother," Uncle Nick interjected. "Think how hard it's been for her. She wants something better for you."

Mae stared at him, incredulous, unable to form the words. *How hard it was for her? Don't support her. Send Michael off in one direction, me in another, now you're noticing it was hard on everyone?* Her hands clenched into tight fists; her eyes glittered.

"Mae," Aunt Sophie tentatively added, "college first. Just a few more years..."

Mae didn't respond, didn't even look at Sophie.

"Maisie," Mama's voice was low but unyielding, "if it's meant to be, he'll wait for you."

Mae shot back, "So we're supposed to stay engaged for four whole years, no wait, four and a half?"

"No, no engagement," Uncle Nick pronounced. "You may not be engaged before you are twenty-one."

"Are you deaf?" Mae's voice shook. "I'm engaged *now*!"

"You must return the ring." Uncle Nick was clearly displeased by her tone.

"Nick." Aunt Sophie rose from her chair, moving toward his side. "Maybe a long engagement? As long as she still goes to college?" Sophie looked to Mama for support. "Ellie, maybe allow the engagement? Four years to plan, and if it's meant to be?"

"No!" Uncle Nick insisted. "She'll return the ring."

"The hell I will!" Mae sputtered, jumping to her feet. "I'm eighteen in a few months, and if I have to, I'll hitch to Peru to be with my fiancé. Jesus H. Christ!"

Silence. Uncle Nick's eyes narrowed to slits. He took two long menacing steps toward Mae, shaking Sophie off his arm. "What?" He towered over her. "What did you say?" he demanded.

"You heard me," she retorted.

"You take the Lord's name in vain?"

Mae smiled defiantly, seeing that he was as confused as he was angry.

"This is the way you talk, despite the training of the sisters, despite the example of your mother? What, what's this 'H'? What does that stand for?" he bellowed, just inches from her face.

Mae squeezed her fists even tighter. She'd made him lose his composure. "Don't know, don't care."

His right hand flew up and hovered, ready to slap her. Aunt Sophie gasped; Mama cried out, "No!"

Mae didn't blink. "You think you could hurt me more?" she taunted. "And you don't think I could say something worse? You're talking about initials, and I'm talking about my whole future. Not that my happiness has ever been of much interest to you. When's the last time you visited me here, huh? Eighth-grade graduation? Yeah, your concern for my well-being's just overwhelming. Go on, take your best shot if you think you can top the last seven years."

Nick lowered his arm, wordlessly pointing to sit down. "Not another word. This is done. You are not engaged. You may not be engaged until you are twenty-one. You will return that ring. You will not go to Peru. You will graduate this June, you will attend college in the fall, and you will earn a degree before we ever have this discussion again."

"No." She dug her fingernails into her thighs: the pain helped her feel strong.

"Yes, Mae." Mama forced Mae to meet her gaze. "Uncle Nick is right: you *will* do as you're told. You're seventeen, not as mature as you think, and you won't defy us."

"No," Mae repeated, almost whimpering. Her mother looked pained but immovable. Mae turned toward Aunt Sophie, questioning. Sophie, grey with the strain, shook her head, mustering a quavering, "I'm sorry, sweetheart."

The three unbending figures surrounded her. Mae studied each face as if they were unfamiliar and then dropped her gaze to her lap, escaping into the bending blue light of her ring. *My ring. Mine.*

"You are ruining my life," she stated dispassionately. "And just so you know, I will never forgive you. Never."

♦ ♦ ♦

Jack sounded determined. "It'll be okay. We can work this out."

Mae's lashes were sticky with tears and mascara. She shook her head fiercely. "You don't know them. They'll never budge. My mother caved into him." *Again.* Tears surged out both corners of her eyes. *Hate them, I hate them all.*

"No, don't. I can fix this, I promise." Fumbling for a Kleenex, Jack dabbed at her eyes. "Have faith in me."

Mae snatched the Kleenex and twisted away. Sighing, she tipped her head back on the car seat, closing her eyes, taking a shuddering breath. *No more tears. They aren't worth it.* "Look," she explained, turning back toward Jack, prying lashes apart with the dry corner of the Kleenex, "we'll never have their permission, or their blessing. They're impossible. We're on our own here." She shivered, sniffling.

"You cold? Want to go in the lobby? Or back to my dorm?"

"No, not private enough. Just keep the engine running so there's heat."

"Look, I'll call your mom, or should I call your uncle? Tell me who, and I'll drive to Chicago this weekend. We can go together."

"He won't see you, I know him." *God! Just want to be happy. They're ruining it.*

"Maybe start with your mom, then. Maybe she's the one to approach. I mean, my folks weren't exactly enthusiastic, but I think my mom understands more. Maybe your mom will too."

Mae stared at the glove box. "Great, your parents haven't even met me yet, and they don't like me already."

"No, it's not about you, I told you that. It's just the situation: they think we're rushing, afraid I won't go to med school when I get back. They just want a longer engagement, that's all."

"He won't even let me be engaged. I hate him!"

"C'mon, Mae, he can't stop us from being engaged, not if we know we're waiting for each other. So you don't wear the ring. So what?" He kissed the top of her head. "You'll know. I'll know."

"But I love this ring, and I'm gonna wear it. I'm not giving it back!"

"Good, 'cause I won't take it back. Look, don't fight about wearing it: just tuck it in your jewelry box when you go home for the holidays and then wear it at school."

"They'll find out, somehow they will." She covered the ring with her hand.

"Nope, look, got a solution. See?" Jack reached into his jacket pocket and pulled out a long gold chain, so delicate it barely caught the light.

"At school you wear it 'round your neck, and the ring will rest right over your heart. Like so." The clasp gave him a little trouble, but he finally got it around her neck. "The ring isn't on there yet, but it should lay right around…here." He unzipped her jacket enough to duck his head and kiss her blouse, right over her breastbone. He looked up, grinning. "Feels right to me." He kissed her again, more on her left breast.

Mae pulled his mouth onto hers. *Yes, this was how to feel, not that other crap.* She pushed him back enough to lock eyes. "Hell, let's run away. Today. Get married. They can't do anything about it. Finish school, don't finish, couldn't care less, just be together."

Jack touched his hand to her mouth. "Nah, Mae, I know you're mad, but we gotta do it right: talk to parents, your uncle, make it a family thing. I mean, what if you can't come to Peru with me? I'm committed, and I can't have you cut off from your family when I'm so far away. We can persuade them. Trust me."

Mae's lip quivered. *They never listen to me. You don't know how they've never listened to me.* "They just have to let me go with you," she whimpered.

Jack nodded. "I know, honest, Mae, how could I go two years without seeing you? Two weeks sounds impossible." He kissed her, then pulled back to study her face. "I don't know how I'll go if it's without you. But if I got to wait for you, somehow I will. If we have to, we'll do it."

"Not me; I'm not waiting, not two whole years. If I have to, I'll follow on my own. I'll squirrel away anything Aunt Sophie sends me, 'n' borrow from Nora, take a set of buses to Mexico…"

"Whoa, hold on! Not a good plan, not safe. You don't speak Spanish!"

"Maybe a boat," Mae puzzled aloud. "Maybe catch a boat from, like, San Diego?"

"No, this is crazy. You'd never find your way, and even if you did, you're seventeen, so your uncle could have it annulled."

"I'm almost eighteen, so doesn't matter what they think. Once I'm eighteen, what can they do with us so far away? Or have a baby right away, then they'd never break us up." Mae tugged on his sleeve. "Really, I know them. Let's do it. Who cares if they're ticked off?"

"Me. What would we come back to, Mae? Have you thought that far? I want my parents to love you, not look at you like some schemer."

"Schemer?" Mae gasped. "So now I'm a schemer!" She covered her eyes with her hands but could hear the gravity in Jack's voice.

"Think. Of course not, but from their point of view, it'd look like you forced the issue. Be realistic. You really think they'd be happy for us? Love you the way I do?"

Mae squeezed her temples. "Doesn't matter what it looks like or what they feel."

Jack's tone was not conciliatory. "It matters to me. A lot."

Mae was silent, stony.

"Mae." Jack tried to pull her chin closer, but she jerked it away. "Mae, think."

"So," she summed up frostily, "what your parents want is more important than what I want."

"No, no, I never said that." He paused. "It's not an either-or thing."

"The hell it isn't," she responded quietly, with great certainty. She turned back toward him, insistent. "Fight to be with me. I need you to fight for me. No one ever does."

"I'm trying to!"

"No, I mean *fight*, really *fight* to be with me, no conditions: you, me, period."

"Look, Mae, I love you, gonna be with you, but I guess I can wait for you if I have to, if that brings our families along: be engaged, come back to you, to a wedding and a whole future together, the right way. I can wait for you. Can't you wait for me?"

"No."

Jack's pained, incredulous expression pierced right through her breastbone, but there was no compromise, no middle ground.

"No?"

"No." She wriggled the ring off her finger and held it up for him.

"No!" Jack sounded frantic. "What're you doing? No, Mae, you can't mean this. You can't." He grabbed her hand and pressed her fist around the ring.

"Will you help me join you there? Yes or no?" Her voice sounded hollow, disconnected.

He moved her hand to his heart. "No, Mae, you need to trust me and know I'll wait for you, for two years if I have to, and you'll wait for me, right?"

Mae tugged her hand away, uncurled her fingers, and watched the ring drop into his lap. It bounced once and then rested on his thigh. Jack stared down for a moment and then picked it up, took her hand back, and pried her fist open. He pressed the ring deeply into her palm and forced her fingers closed around it. He looked up at her, shaking his head. His eyes glistened with tears, but his voice wavered with anger. "No. We're engaged. And you have to keep this ring. And we'll work this out, because I love you."

Mae pulled back, clutching the ring. As she uncurled her fingers, she could feel the sharp edge of the setting pushed deep into her palm. Mae dragged the embedded edge toward her thumb, drawing a bloody line over an inch long. Groping for the door handle, Mae clambered out. "Not enough," she replied, letting the ring and a drop of blood spill between her fingers. "Not enough." She slammed the door closed.

Chapter Seven

Red Sugar

Christmas Eve, 1963

Mae licked her fingertip, pressing it against the counter to pick up the red sugar sprinkles, adding to the faint trail of pink blotches on the Formica. *Kinda pretty.* Picking up the spatula, she slipped it barely under the edge of a cookie. Yes, they were cool enough now to transfer into the cookie tin. This whole batch had red sprinkles. Next, green sugar and then maybe chocolate jimmies.

"How'd they turn out?" Mama called from over by her sewing table.

"Fine, Mama: they look good." Mae popped a cracked one into her mouth.

"Hey, broken ones for me, too!" Michael was fanned out on the living-room floor, awash in wrapping paper and ribbon.

"Michael, she'll share. Finish up those packages for Uncle Nick and Aunt Sophie. Get them under the tree. I like knowing we're all set for Christmas. Then just a couple of cookies, though: not all that long till supper."

"So tomorrow's dinner at Uncle Nick's?" Michael snipped the ribbon with a flourish.

"Yes, sweetie, but a quiet Christmas morning all to ourselves. Nine o'clock Mass and then scrambled eggs and ham and half the afternoon to relax, maybe play some more rummy."

"Sounds good." Michael twisted up his mouth as he fumbled with the tape.

"Fourteen, fifteen, plus a cracked one for Michael." Mae lifted the spatula, waving to her brother. "There's one here for you."

"Only one?" Michael scolded. "You could break more if you tried."

Mae grinned. "Can I help it if I'm a good cook? Perfect little cookies; come see how neat the stacks are."

Michael sprang up and sauntered over to inspect. "Not bad, not bad." The cracked cookie crumbled as he picked it up.

"Mae's a fine cook, isn't she?" Mama put down her needle, easing the lace smooth.

"Ma, you made the dough!"

"Yes, but Maisie is slicing and decorating them and watching them bake. That's the real work."

"Hmph." Michael's mouth was full.

"And," Mama continued, "by the time the last batch bakes, I'll be finished with this gown, Michael will have taken care of gifts, and our work will be finished for the day!" She held up the bodice, studying the lace edging.

"Let's see, Mama." Mae craned her neck across the counter. "Ooh, that's pretty."

Mama nodded. "It is, isn't it?" She shook it out gently, easing the lace at the neckline a little more. "Someday, Maisie, I'll make you the most beautiful wedding gown you've ever seen."

Mae beamed. "Like yours?"

Mama laughed softly. "If you want, 'though mine was not all that formal, what with it being a morning wedding. I didn't have a train."

"Oh, but it was fancy!" Mae knew the picture well: Papa laughing, his hands completely enveloping Mama's, while Mama smiled up at him through the edge of her veil. "I get your veil, right?"

Mama got out her tiniest scissors to trim threads. "Yes, safely packed away for you someday."

Michael searched for sugar on the counter. "Just the crumbs," he moaned. "The story of my life."

Mama clucked, "Ah yes, such tragedy." Then, more seriously, she added, "But you know, Michael, I do have your father's ring and his best cuff links for you, when you're older."

Michael ducked his head, flushing. "Aw, I was just joking..."

"I know, sweetheart, but I want you to have something of his to help you remember him."

"I remember him fine!" Michael sounded edgy. "Not like I was a baby." He reached toward the cookie tin. Mae moved to stop his hand, but he glared at her, snatched two cookies off the top, and then turned away.

Mama rested the gown in her lap. "All I'm saying is that I wish I could've saved more for you, but we did need to pare down a little now that I'm in a smaller apartment."

Mae slowly unrolled the stiff waxed paper, keeping the cylinder of frozen cookie dough as symmetrical as possible. "It looks nice here, Mama, nice and cozy." *Next batch, green sprinkles.* Mae hummed, "Oh Christmas Tree," and started slicing, slow and even, arranging them on the cookie sheet: *four, then three, four, three.*

"Well," Mama allowed, "I kept our nicest furniture, and your favorites, and then the odd pieces that I sold paid for the new sleeper sofa for Michael."

Michael began rolling up the ribbon. "Yep, I've got the biggest room all to myself."

"Yeah, well, I like having Mama for a roommate: at least she doesn't snore!"

Michael wadded up a scrap of wrapping paper and whipped it straight at Mae's forehead. "I don't snore. And look who's talking: the drooler."

"I don't drool, and don't mess up my cookies." Mae flicked the paper ball off the counter.

"Do too drool, and you talk in your sleep."

"As I was saying," Mama interrupted, "this place is smaller, but it's cozy. Just a bit crowded now, but that's because of our little Christmas tree and the decorations. You'll see, after the holidays, it will feel roomier. Just one bedroom less, otherwise it's a lot like our old place."

Mae frowned, picking up the knife. "But what about next summer, and next year, when we're both home?" She sliced another cookie from the roll and then looked toward her mother.

Mama's eyes were locked on the threads she was trimming. She seemed not to hear Mae. Then she answered, flatly, "Let's wait and see. We'll manage."

Michael crumpled another paper scrap and aimed at the Zenith. The ball bounced off the center of the screen and right back to him. He scooped it up, turning his back to Mae and taking aim at the delicate angel on the top of the Christmas tree.

♦ ♦ ♦

The café table was set with a lace-trimmed cloth and matching napkins. Mae turned over the edge and inspected the stitching. Yep, hand appliquéd, Mama's work. No wonder it seemed familiar, yet they'd never had a round table before. Mae ventured a puzzled, "Mama?"

Mama looked up from the stove. "Recognize it?" She sounded proud.

Mae moved the flatware and unfolded her napkin: ivory colored, with a lace corner. "Huh. Is it...oh, is it from our old dining room?"

Mama grinned as she carried the bowl of dilled carrots over to the table. "Yes, and I must say, it turned out even better than I'd planned. I was able to cut the length so that there was enough left to make a half dozen napkins." She smoothed the tablecloth with one hand.

Mae refolded her napkin. "It's pretty, Mama. Michael, come see." She rested her fork back on top of the napkin.

Michael lumbered over. "What?"

"The table. Mama made the tablecloth."

"Oh. Nice." He plopped into his seat, sniffing the carrots.

Mae slipped in next to him. She gave him a poke. "Cooties!"

"Don't," he muttered, very definite, not taking his eyes off the carrots.

Frowning, Mae ducked her head, tried to catch his eye, but Michael just stiffened. *C'mon, Michael, we're home; don't wreck it.* She pushed back her chair. "Want me to serve, Mama?" She started to get up.

"No, sit! It's not often I get to have us all together. Besides, it's three steps to the table." Mama flitted back and forth, first with relishes, then with hot biscuits. Pots clattered as she arranged the chicken and dumplings on the dinner plates.

Mae studied Michael. Normally she'd leave him alone when he was grumpy, but he was going to upset Mama. Mae kicked his ankle and got an angry, sideways glance. "Just don't," she whispered.

"Don't what?" Mama balanced all three plates, a trick from her waitressing days. She slid the plate with a half chicken breast down in front of Michael and then the other half down for Mae. Her own plate had three dumplings and extra gravy.

Michael looked from plate to plate and protested, "Ma, you need some. We can share."

"No, thanks! For some reason, meat hasn't agreed with me lately." Mama was all smiles. "This is perfect for me. Now let's say grace and eat while it's hot. Bless us, O Lord, and these, Thy gifts, which we are about to receive, from Thy bounty, through Christ our Lord. Amen." She made the sign of the cross and reached for her napkin.

"It looks really good, Mama. Doesn't it, Michael?"

"Yeah, thanks, Ma." Michael gave Mae a slight nod. *He knew.*

"Well," Mama began, passing the biscuits, "I don't know how it got to be Christmas already. The busy weeks just fly by, don't they?"

"Mm-hmm." Mae nodded, her mouth full of olives.

"Well," Michael drawled, "I, for one, will need to sleep a whole lot in the next few days to recover from all those busy weeks." He arched his eyebrows, challenging, "Do not step into the living room before ten o'clock!"

"Ten!" Mama shook her head. "No, Mass is at nine. I think seven thirty."

Michael heaved a sigh. "Seven forty-five, but that's it."

"What?" Mae jumped in. "Need your beauty sleep?"

"Yeah, that's it." Michael was trying. "It's just that muscle building takes so much outta you." He flexed his biceps.

Mama played along. "You must admit, Mae, your brother is taller and stronger every time we see him."

"Correct," Michael intoned. "And don't you forget it." He wagged his fork at Mae.

"Oh yes, sir!" Mae responded, cowering.

"That's better." Michael pointed his fork straight at her. "Now eat."

"Sir, yes, sir!" Mae picked up her fork and knife. Michael stuffed a whole biscuit in his mouth.

"Michael!" Mama protested halfheartedly.

He shrugged, mumbling, "Hungry!"

♦ ♦ ♦

"Mae, that's enough for tonight. Relax a little before bed."

"Just one more batch: red pinwheels."

"If you want...Michael, cards?"

"Nah, kinda tired."

"That's fine, sweetie. Shall we prepare your bed?"

"Not yet." He stretched out on the nubby carpet. "I'm good."

Mama hooked her left foot under the embroidered footrest and pulled it closer. She slumped lower in her chair, crossed her ankles, and picked up McCall's. Mae sliced just under a quarter inch to get a few extra cookies out of the roll. The spirals of pink and white dough looked psychedelic on the cookie sheet.

Michael rolled onto his back. "Do we have to go to Uncle Nick's tomorrow?"

Mama looked up with pursed lips. "We always do."

"Yeah, well, let's not this year."

"Why not? Think how disappointed Sophie would be."

"Yeah, but he wouldn't care. He doesn't care."

Mama plopped her magazine onto her lap. "Of course Uncle Nick cares. He loves us."

Michael flipped back onto his stomach. "Not enough."

Mae stopped slicing; she looked up to see her mother wagging a finger. "Michael Jerome Panos, such talk! For all that your Uncle Nick's done for us!"

"Yeah, well, what's he done for you, Ma?"

"Well..." Mama blushed, a pink blotch on each cheek. "I'll, I'll tell you what he's done for me: he's providing a fine education for my children."

"Yeah, yeah," Michael pressed, "but that's me 'n' Mae. What about you, Ma? Why isn't he helping you more?"

"Michael," Mama corrected, "that is helping me. That's just Uncle Nick's way: he's...he's old world. He takes care of his brother's children."

"But, Ma," Michael was dogged, "old world is just your nice way of saying stingy!"

"Supporting you is hardly stingy! He takes his responsibilities for his blood relatives very seriously. He, he has no responsibility to support me, just an in-law."

"But if he helped support you, then he'd be helping all of us 'cause then we could stay home with you."

Mae couldn't resist. "Michael's right: we could've been home this year." She let the knife drop gently onto the dough, her eyes fixed on her mother's face, but Mama let her head drop slightly, and a thick strand of ash-brown hair spilled out from behind her ear, shielding her eyes.

"Ma, you gotta admit—"

"Enough!" Sharp. Then, quietly, "No more. Uncle Nick cares for you both, and you should be most thankful. You only have one aunt and uncle, who are more than generous." Mama tucked her hair back but didn't look at them.

"Ma, still—"

"Michael Jerome, end of discussion." Mama opened her magazine. Mae resumed slicing. After a moment's silence, Mama added, "You know, Uncle Nick has already arranged for next year's tuition, for both of you. Hundreds of dollars. Hundreds."

Mae's hand slipped, and the knife tip dug into her thumb. Blood welled up and spilled onto the cookie, muddling the clean lines of the spiral. Mae pressed her thumb to her lips, staring at the messy cookie and then at Michael, who stared grimly right back at her. The clutter of the tree, the presents, dissolved away, and all that remained was a small living room, a sewing nook, a modest bedroom. Room for one. *One. No!* She gaped at Michael, struggling to breathe.

He barely shook his head, at the situation, at how dense she was. *Dummy.*

Mae sucked in a little air and looked down at the bloody cookie. *Maybe...but, but next year's tuition, Mama and Sophie must've known...* Her eyes stung but not with tears, no, stung from the pressure behind them, like concrete, weighing her head down. *Idiot, telling everyone it was temporary, but she said, she let me think...I'm such an idiot.* With a shudder and then a firmer breath, Mae gingerly transferred the bloodstained cookie next to the others on the sheet and tossed some red sprinkles on top. She sliced four more, very deliberately, and slipped the cookie sheet onto the top rack of the oven. The waxed paper crackled as Mae sealed up the rest of the dough.

"All finished, Mae?" Mama called.

Have to answer. "I'm putting part back in the freezer for tomorrow. Gonna go to bed as soon as this batch is done."

Mama moved to stand up. "I can finish for you, if you want to wash up."

"Nope, I'll finish. Besides, I have a special cookie just for you."

Chapter Eight

The Phone Call

Christmas Eve, 1970

"Come sit down." Mama set two mugs of tea on the café table. Her face was tinged, her eyes ringed, with gray fatigue.

Mae tugged at the chair across from her mother, pulling her cup of tea over. Even sitting opposite, even slumping back, she felt too close, wished the table was bigger. Mama leaned forward—*since when did she ever put her elbows on the table?* Mae folded her arms.

"Mae." Mama frowned. "When will this stop? Week after week. You spoiled Thanksgiving with your sulking; now you're going to ruin everyone's Christmas too?"

Mae tipped her head back and fixed her gaze on a small crack in the ceiling. "What do you want? Pollyanna?" She flashed an overly toothy smile.

Mama's eyes narrowed, sparking irritation. "Watch your tone, young lady. If you think this behavior convinces me you're mature enough to be engaged, you're sorely mistaken."

Mae refused to look away from the ceiling. "I'm not engaged, remember? We established that. I'm not arguing. Not whining. But for the record, I'm starting to hate Christmas as much as Thanksgiving, so sorry if I'm not bubbly enough to suit everyone. Happy holidays, my ass."

Mama shook her hands in frustration, then wrapped them gingerly around the hot mug. "Oh, Mae." She dropped her head. "Sweetheart, look, I'm not insisting you be bubbly. Just don't make it awkward for us all. Can't we have a nice Christmas with Sophie and Nick? It's bad enough Michael isn't here. Can't we make the best of it?"

"Ah, make the best of it. Yes, that *is* your solution to everything, isn't it? Just make do, just take your lumps, but don't make a peep, don't upset anybody else! And look how beautifully it's worked out for you!" Mae swept her arm grandly, gesturing across the kitchen and living room. "You must be so proud."

Silence. No, Mae was not letting her off that easily.

"Mother, how can you stand it? Really?" Mae shook her head. "Have you ever fought for anything in your whole life? Ever?"

Mama stared into her teacup.

"That's what I thought." Mae oozed scorn. "Pretty pathetic if you ask me." Mae savored her mother's silence.

But then Mama looked up, unblinking, and replied, "You know, I do the best I can." She stiffly rose from her chair, disappearing into the bedroom.

Mae flinched. *Shit, shit, shit. God, if only Michael were here. Michael, come home. Need you, need time with you...what time is it anyway?* She glanced at her watch: almost six thirty. *Huh, he usually called by now.*

Of course, that was not helping: Jack calling every single evening, wanting to talk. And every single time, Mama telling him, "No, I'm sorry, but no, Mae won't come to the phone. Mae's asked you to stop calling. Sorry but no, please don't call back..." At first Mae would ask, what did he say? What did he tell you? Now she just shook her head, didn't want to know. And Mama would look sorry, purse her lips tightly, and go back to whatever she was doing before. One of these days, he'd stop. Soon, hopefully. But normally he called by now. Mae shifted uneasily in her chair. *Huh, almost six thirty.*

Mae's eyes flicked aimlessly about: the curve of the table, the curling steam from Mama's mug, the glint on the edge of the spoon. A second wisp of steam from her cup. The crack on the ceiling...*six thirty. Just as well. Needed to face facts eventually.*

"Just as well," she announced to the forlorn tea mugs, sitting untouched, abandoned. Mae pushed away from the table and climbed over the back of the love seat. She pulled her knees up tight to her chin and checked the clock. *Six thirty-one. He wasn't going to call. God.* She stared at the blank TV screen. *Nah, not worth getting up to turn it on. Jeez, wish Michael were here. Michael knew, knew her like nobody else.* She lost herself in the blank screen again, the cool dark screen.

♦ ♦ ♦

The radiator clicked on: Mae blinked at her reflection in the opaque TV screen and then turned to check the kitchen clock: six fifty. *Stop it, Mae, forget it. Find something to do. Could, could mend the nightgown, the tear on the right seam, near the hem. Oh, but Mama's in the bedroom. So's the nightgown. Crap.*

The phone rang. Mae didn't move, didn't exhale. It rang again. Mama emerged, strode to the kitchen wall, picked up the receiver, with a steady, pleasant, "Hello?" A moment of hesitation and then she almost shouted, "Michael! Sweetheart!" Her voice, her expression sparkled. "Michael, where are you?" She strained to hear. Mae twisted around, on her knees, pressed against the back cushions. Mama looked a little muddled. "Where? Still? But they let you call? Are you all right?" She smiled at Mae with a relieved nod and made the sign of the cross. "Oh, honey, good... yes, that's the best gift, to hear your voice...uh-huh...yes...and Merry Almost-Christmas to you, too, sweetie. Uh-huh...no, that's fine; don't you give that a second thought, because we'll be thinking of you on Christmas Day. What? I'm sorry, can you repeat that?" She squinted, as if that would help her hear. "Oh yes, yes, except at Mass, otherwise we'll be here... um-hmm...what...? Oh, surely...wait, don't go anywhere!" She waved excitedly to Mae. "She's right here, hang on." Mae hurtled over.

"Michael?"

"Maisie, how are you?"

"Fine, what about you?"

"Okay. Just thought I'd call now 'cause the lines'll be so jammed tomorrow."

"I suppose. But you're good?"

"Sure. Listen, got your last letter, about breaking things off, really sorry. You hangin' on okay?"

"Yeah, not much choice." Mae turned away from her mother, pulling the phone cord tightly across her back and upper arm. "Sure wish you were here, though."

"I know." Michael sounded so faint. "Me too."

Couldn't find the words. "So, Michael?"

"Yeah?"

"You still on the same schedule for, you know, when your tour's over?"

"Far as I know, Mae, so don't worry 'bout that, okay?" *Was he hesitating, or was it static in the connection?* "Look, Mae, you gotta take care of yourself till I get back there. And Ma, too, Mae. Sorry, but it falls on you; you gotta take care of Ma for me, just for a little bit. Can you do that?"

"But," she wavered, "you don't get. I mean, it's—" *Silence.* "Michael? Michael?"

The line was dead. *Crap.* Mae slowly uncoiled from the phone line and handed the dead receiver to her mother. "Guess we got disconnected. Sorry." She somberly watched Mama put the phone to her ear, then hang it up. Mae headed into the bedroom.

"Wait, Mae, what did he say?" Mama trailed after her.

"Not much else," Mae tossed back over her shoulder. "Just Merry Christmas and that he wanted to call when he could." She snatched up her nightgown and inspected the seam: yep, a small tear. *A stitch in time saves nine*, she noted, brushing past her mother to find a needle at the sewing table.

"And he sounded well, didn't he?"

"Think so." *Had the needle, now for some light-yellow thread, more like a cream.* She started flipping through the thread drawer.

"Can I help you? What do you need?" Mama was at her elbow.

Mae shrank back. "No, don't."

"Really, let me help."

"No, Mother, please!"

But Mama's hand crawled insistently across the fabric, and Mae abruptly stuck her with the needle. Mama pulled back with a confused cry; Mae dropped the nightgown and fumbled for her mother's hand.

"Oh no, did I prick you? Jeez, I didn't mean to. I'm...so clumsy. You're not bleeding, are you? Maybe I'm just too tired to do this now. It can wait till tomorrow. I'll just get to bed, okay? I'm, well, sorry."

Mae gave her mother a hasty peck on the cheek, scooped up the nightgown, and rushed into the bathroom. Locking the door, she pressed her cheek against the doorframe. *Oh God. Crap, crap, crap. Michael, sorry.* She tugged on the nightgown and washed her face with trembling hands. Taking a careful breath, she cracked open the door to peek out. Mama sat at the sewing table, caved over.

Mae slipped through the doorways, hoping her mother wouldn't look up. She didn't. Mae's sheepish, "Good night," went unanswered. Under the covers it was a little better, even though she wasn't at all sleepy. *Couldn't be much past seven, maybe five after. And Jack—well, guess that was that.*

Mae lay there, helpless against the snippets of images washing though her. *Jack's lips. Old Spice. The gazebo.* She tried to force her mind elsewhere. *Michael, imagine Michael drinking coffee, looking over his schedule. Michael opening a chart, getting ready for—*

The phone rang. Mae gasped and shot up straight. Mama picked up right away. "Hello?" She sounded tentative. "Yes? Michael, you're back! Mae said you got disconnected. What? Oh, no matter, such a treat to talk more. So what time is it there? Uh-huh...and who will be with you for Christmas?"

Mae curled back onto her pillow. *God, she'd love to talk to Michael, but no, this was Mama's call.* May listened to the bright tone in her mother's voice. *Didn't seem right, lying there with the shadows, not asleep, but Mama wasn't making a move to call her. Mama missed Michael but not like she did. So not fair.*

Mae fell asleep with her little finger hooked through the hole in her seam. When she woke the next morning, she was sure she hadn't had a single dream, and she sighed perplexedly when she found a bigger tear in her nightgown. Christmas Eve and no Michael, no more Jack. Another shitty Christmas.

♦ ♦ ♦

"Please," Mama muttered as she rang the doorbell. "For me?"

Mae didn't answer, just listened to the approaching clack-clack of Sophie's heels. *No, not for you, for Michael. Only for Michael.*

The weighty eight-panel door swung open. Sophie beamed, as if surprised by their arrival. "Ellen!" A quick kiss on the cheek. "And Mae!" Another, more deliberate kiss. She took in Mae's face. "Look at you, Mae. So lovely tonight! But where are my manners? Come in! Come in out of the cold." She waved them into the foyer.

Dorothy, in her black dress and white apron, scurried up, with a shy nod for a greeting. "May I take your coats?"

Mae glanced around, unsure of where to put down the gifts she held. Sophie caught her eye, and Mae abruptly pushed the packages toward her. "Here, Aunt Sophie, these are for you." *For Michael.* "And Merry Christmas," Mae added, forcing the corners of her lips up.

"Thank you, sweetheart, and Merry Christmas to you, too," Sophie responded, now surprisingly subdued. Her quicksilver shifts in expression were a bit unnerving, so Mae focused on the buttons of her dress coat. Dorothy lightly gripped the shoulders as Mae slipped her arms out of the sleeves. As Dorothy disappeared wordlessly with the coats draped over her arm, Mae called after her, "Thank you!"

"I wish I'd known Dorothy would be here," Ellie whispered to Sophie. "I'd have brought her a little something, too."

Sophie shook her head, wrinkling her nose. "No need. I'll be sending her home with a whole bag of treats, beyond her Christmas bonus. You know Nick." She shook her head again. "It just wasn't worth the quarrel, and Dorothy didn't mind, so I guess tonight we are ladies of leisure!" Sophie turned toward Mae. "Come with me, Mae. I believe Nick was just opening a bottle of wine for dinner." She led them into the living room.

"Did we delay dinner?" Mama fretted. "We're a bit late."

"No!" Sophie insisted. "But when you called, I suggested to Nick that we forego cocktail hour and just start with wine, and we'll just carry it to the table with us for dinner. Then I needn't keep Dorothy late, and we can open gifts after dinner instead."

Sophie turned to Mae. "Your mother mentioned on the phone you needed a little extra time to get ready." She smiled generously, her teeth snowy white against her red lipstick. "I remember spending so much time on my hair and makeup when I was your age. I guess some things never change. And, Mae, I just can't tell you how pleased we are that you're here." *Now wistful. Thank God Sophie was holding the gifts—she looked like she wanted a hug.*

Mae turned toward her mother. "You told her I was making us late?"

"No," Ellie corrected. "I told Sophie we were *both* running late this afternoon."

"That's true!" Sophie jumped in, sounding alarmed. "And anyway, we're all here now. Nick, look who's here! Isn't this nice?" Sophie set the gifts on the end table and patted Mae's shoulders.

Mae leaned back against Sophie's hands as Uncle Nick stepped close and muttered, "Merry Christmas," brushing a kiss on Mae's forehead. He turned, adding, "Merry Christmas, Ellen," taking Mama's hand and brushing another kiss on her cheek. *So massive, he made them all feel so dwarfed.* Mae could feel Sophie's hands trembling. *Take care of them. For you, Michael, only doing this for you.* Turning toward Sophie, Mae forced a reassuring smile.

Sophie blinked a few times, teary. "I'm so glad you're here," she repeated.

♦ ♦ ♦

Mae folded her hands in her lap, watching Dorothy place a long silver platter of crème puffs and chocolate éclairs between Sophie and Nick. "I'll have coffee in a moment," Dorothy promised as she handed the silver tongs to Sophie.

Sophie nodded her thanks. “Ladies first! Ellen, crème puff, éclair, or one of each?”

“Well, it is the holidays: one of each, please!” Mama was the most relaxed one at the table and also the most flushed. She was halfway through her fourth glass of wine. Mae had never seen her mother tipsy, and was observing her with an arched sense of superiority. Mae, on the other hand, was pointedly controlled, speaking only when spoken to, responding in monosyllables, maintaining a polite tone that clearly signaled the effort required.

Nor was it lost on anyone. Uncle Nick was even more reserved than usual, occasionally responding to Sophie’s overtures but frequently allowing his unsmiling gaze to settle heavily on Mae. Mae alternately ignored him or returned the same unfriendly stare. Sophie and Mama provided most of the chatter, keeping lulls at bay with mundane commentary on the weather and the holidays. At one point a more earnest discussion centered on Michael: his assignment, his training, his anticipated return. For a few precious minutes, maybe only ten in all, a truce spontaneously occurred, and all four shared their feelings and worries about Michael, unguarded, as a family. But as doubts got voiced and speculations dwindled, the unspoken reasserted itself, leaving Mae and Nick to grow stony, Sophie to prattle desperately, and Mama to drink.

“And, Mae, how about one of each for you?” Sophie suggested.

“Fine,” Mae agreed flatly. Dorothy poured coffees.

“Nick?”

“One éclair is plenty.” He turned to Mae. “So what are your plans for college?” he demanded.

“Nick!” Sophie cut in. “Not tonight!” She turned toward Mama. “Ellie and Mae will have plenty of time to discuss plans before Mae returns to school, right?”

Mama nodded, extending her sip.

“On the contrary,” Nick asserted, “I would think most of her classmates have already applied for next year.” He zeroed in on Mae. “Haven’t they?”

Mae felt her cheeks reddening. *Michael, remember Michael.* "Guess so." *Don't start with me*, she mentally telegraphed Nick.

He knew, but he persisted. "Your roommate?"

"Her name's Nora. Same as six years ago."

Uncle Nick somehow grew taller as he leaned in toward her. "Has Nora applied to colleges?" His eyes, nearly black, burned.

Mae stared back in silence.

"Oh my, Nora!" Sophie jumped in. "I meant to ask about her earlier. How is she? Is her family well?"

"Has she applied?" Nick repeated forcefully.

Michael.

"Well," Mae choked out, "her parents want her to stay to attend college at St. Mary's, so she's got plans, if that's what you mean."

"That's what I mean."

"Mae," Sophie ventured, "have you thought of continuing there as well?" Despite Sophie's apparent good intentions, Mae needed this conversation to end. *Now.*

"I haven't decided what *I* want to do yet," Mae pointedly addressed Sophie. *Michael.* "But I guess I'll have to pretty soon." Mae refused to look at Uncle Nick, but in her peripheral vision, she saw Mama raise her hand to her temple.

"Oh dear," Mama warbled. "I'm afraid I have a migraine coming on. And I haven't had one in so long...you know, sometimes even a little bit of red wine is enough to set it off." Her cheeks were draining of color even as she spoke, her eyelids fluttering.

"Dear, want to lie down?" Sophie offered.

Mama barely shook her head. "I'm sorry, but I'm afraid I need to get home before it gets worse. I'm sorry, after such a lovely dinner..." A tear rolled down her cheek.

Sophie patted her arm. "Don't be silly, can't be helped." Sophie turned to Nick. "Ellie shouldn't drive. You'll need to take them home."

Nick nodded, folding his napkin.

"No," Mae demanded. "I'll drive."

All eyes turned to Nick. He soberly assessed Mae and then nodded. "Yes, the roads are clear. She can take care of her mother."

Sophie took charge. "Ellen, just sit there while I pack up gifts. You and Mae open them tomorrow, when you feel up to it. Mae, find the keys and bring the car right up to our walk. Nick, have Dorothy wrap up some of the pastries while you get their coats. And, Mae, don't you go out without your coat—wait for your uncle."

Mae and Nick exchanged wary glances, agreeing to a détente. He rose without a word as Mama propped her head up with both hands, shrinking down with pain.

The stiff paper of the Marshall Field's bag crackled as it filled up with Sophie's wrapped boxes. "Mae, why don't you take these to the car, and Nick will bring the sweets out with your mother?" Sophie stopped herself for a second, looking Mae squarely in the eye. She gently cradled Mae's face with both hands. "Thank you, Mae. You're a good girl." Sophie transferred a kiss from her finger to the tip of Mae's nose. "Now button up, bring the car around." Sophie returned to Mama, and Mae turned to find Uncle Nick holding up her coat. She slipped it on and picked up the shopping bag and both purses. Mae waved the keys.

"Nick, make her button up!" Sophie called from the dining room table.

Mae hesitated, but Uncle Nick simply tipped his head toward the front door.

Barely nodding, Mae yanked the door open and felt slapped by the damp chill. She hustled across the street to where the Chevy was parked. *Crap, so cold! Gifts in the trunk, start the ignition. Oh, brrr.* She buttoned up while the engine warmed for a minute and then, seeing no traffic, made a tight U-turn at the first intersection and pulled up in front of Nick and Sophie's. Their front door opened, and Nick eased out, one hand on Mama's elbow, the other hand balancing a pastry box. As they crept toward the curb, Mae threw the heat on full blast, flinching at the initial shot of cold but then smelling a trickle of heat as her mother reached the car.

Nick placed the box on the hood, then guided Mama onto the front seat. “All right?” he checked. Mama nodded, tipping her head back, keeping her eyes closed.

He slipped the box between them on the front seat. “All right?” he repeated, this time to Mae.

Just close the door. “I need to go.”

Nick nodded. “Very well.” He closed the door. Mae pulled away.

Chapter Nine

A New Mixer

January 1971

Mae brushed the tips of her hair impatiently. Some strands curled, others stopped short midwave. She shook her head, trying to get them to blend. *Nope.* "I give up." She tossed the hairbrush down. "Good enough."

Nora glanced back through the reflection of the dresser mirror. "No, not really. Want me to straighten the back for you?"

"Nah." Mae studied her own reflection. "Guess I'm going au naturel." She hesitated, eying her makeup bag. "Except for lipstick, eye shadow. But no blush, no mascara. No prom look."

"I'd take the prom look over the pothead look."

"There *is* no pothead look, it's 'natural.'"

"Look, I like the frosted apricot lipstick, but it's not exactly natural." Nora tipped her head as she looked Mae over. "You know, Mae, you're pretty enough to pull off the earthy thing, but don't be sloppy. Let me fix up the tips with a curling iron."

Mae ran her fingers through the thick waves. "Nah." She slipped on her long beaded earrings from Bangladesh and then three heavy rings: a Mexican topaz, a thick silver band, and a narrow turquoise pinkie ring. Brushing her hands nervously down the front of her thighs, Mae smoothed her jeans. "Too much? Like I'm trying too hard?"

Nora shrugged. "No, you look good—y' know, peacenik."

Mae beamed. "Really?"

"Yeah, just wish you weren't so hung up on impressing that crowd."

Mae stiffened. "That crowd? Sounds snotty."

Nora raised an eyebrow with a dry, "Hm. Look, you wanna hang out with them—cool—but you're spazzing about fitting it."

"I fit in fine. You just don't get it: it's about peace."

Nora twisted open her lipstick. "Right. Nobody gets how nice peace would be except you guys. And smoking dope will help end the war sooner."

"We're protesting; we're antiestablishment. At least we're trying to make a difference."

"Wonder how Michael would feel if he could see you."

"Shut up," Mae growled. "I know him a helluva lot better than you do."

"If you say so," Nora muttered.

Mae whipped around so fast that her earrings slapped her neck. "Look, don't need your hassles. Back off."

Nora raised her hands in surrender. "Fine, I'm not your mother." Nora brushed past Mae and out the door. "See ya tomorrow."

Mae didn't answer except to silently flip her off. Then, hesitating, Mae worked her fingers through a couple of tangles. There were so many.

♦ ♦ ♦

"Don't walk away from me, okay?" Mae whispered as Emma pushed the front door open into a bunch of guys standing just inside. Emma tugged her embroidered tunic straight, tossed back her dangly earrings, and pushed harder.

"Hey, guys!" Emma called out. "Room for us?"

"Hey, Em, c'mon in." Some guy with a military-type buzz and glassy eyes grinned. He shoved the guy next to him to open the door wider, waving the girls in and sloshing his beer in the process.

"Hey, Dave, thanks." Emma blew a kiss toward him. "How are ya, babe?"

"Groovy. Glad you made it."

Emma tossed her hair. "'Course I did! I brought Mae this time: this is Mae."

Dave nodded. "Hey. Beer, guys?"

Emma's pale eyes flicked across the room. "Nah, not just yet. Ooh, chem lab over there?"

Dave chuckled. "Go, Emmie! Straight to it! Yeah, at Thursday's biochem Al bogarted some more tubes." He nodded approvingly.

Emma snatched Mae's hand and pulled her over to the card table tucked in the corner. "C'mon, you'll love this. See how pretty?" Emma's hand hovered over racks of dozens of test tubes, each filled about half full of liquids in varied shades of golds, greens, and reds.

"What are they?" Mae frowned.

Emma's hand hovered a moment longer and then plucked a mint-colored vial from the very middle. "Booze, all kinds: it's a mystery. Just pick one ya like!"

"Okay." Mae selected an orange-tinged tube.

"No, hang on!" Emma clutched Mae's arm. "You take two 'n' mix 'em. That's why they're not full. Pick another to pour into this one." Emma snatched a pale yellow and added it. "See? Far out!" With an appreciative swirl of the now emerald-green drink, Emma tossed it back in one gulp.

Mae licked her lips. "Okay, well...this one I guess." She blended in an amber-colored one and gulped it down her throat. Her eyes teared up from the burn. "Whoa!" she gasped.

Emma giggled. "You should see your face! Good?"

Mae nodded, her throat still fiery.

Emma tossed her hair and smoothed Mae's bangs with both hands. "*Now* it's time for beer. Oh, look at those pink cheeks! Pretty, all flushed like—oh, wait!" Emma dug into her back pocket and pressed a small red packet into Mae's hand. "Here, for later, just in case."

Mae's jaw hung open as she eyed the condom. She pressed it back into Emma's hand. "No, I can't—I don't—it's a sin."

Emma burst into giggles. "You crack me up! Once you're screwing, pretty sure you're past the whole 'sin' part!" Emma pushed it into Mae's jean pocket. "Just a Trojan—won't bite you!"

Mae blushed fiercely.

"Oh," Emma grimaced, lightly rubbing Mae's arm. "Not yet? That's cool too; don't worry 'bout it. Just for...whenever, okay?"

Mae nodded, trying to look more nonchalant. She tossed her hair like Emma. "Sure, cool. Um, look okay?"

"Fab!" Emma winked. "C'mon, let's go find the guys."

"Hey, how about another round of chem lab first?"

"Ha, knew you'd like it—that's my Mae! Sure, which ones?"

♦ ♦ ♦

"You bored? I'm bored." Emma pouted.

Mae shrugged—too buzzed to tell. "Dunno. What, you wanna find a different party?"

"Nah, too much work..." Emma brightened up. "How 'bout a game?"

"Game?"

"Gimme a dare, a dare for some guy we don't know. Like those guys over there. Gimme a dare to do something with one of them."

The girls eyed a huddle of guys near the kitchen doorway. One was a full head taller, with a heavy mustache. Mae nodded at him. "Okay, the tall one. Put your hand on his butt right when you meet him."

"Aw, no, a real challenge."

Mae hesitated. "Then, instead, stick your tongue in his ear." *Challenge, huh? Fat chance you'll do that!*

Emma evaluated him for a moment. "Okay, watch me, but you come with me." She took Mae's elbow as they snaked their way toward the kitchen door. "Hey!" she exclaimed to her target. "I gotta secret! Wanna know?" She crooked her finger to come closer.

He sized her up with a smirk and leaned in. "Sure, what's your big secret?"

Emma rested her hands on his cheeks, pulling him closer, and then swirled her tongue in his ear and fell back in a peal of giggles. He shook his head, laughing, wiping his ear with his sleeve. "Crazy chick!" he pretended to scold.

Emma grabbed Mae's elbow again and pulled her back into a huddle. "Your turn!"

Mae caught her breath. "Shit, really?"

"Hell, yes, fair's fair!" Emma insisted, her eyes roaming and then settling on a different bunch of guys. "That one, reddish hair. Walk up and really plant one on him, no explanation, and then turn around and walk away."

Mae gulped. *Fair's fair.* Inhaling deeply, she marched up, so deliberate that all three boys stopped talking. Somehow up close the redhead was not so cute, so Mae turned to the slender guy to his right, reached up to capture his blond curls on the back of his head, pulled him down toward her, and French-kissed him. She released him, turning to go, but felt him grab her arm.

"Hold on there! What was that?" he demanded, chuckling.

"Dare," she stammered, pulling back.

He laced his fingers in her hair and drew her mouth onto his. Her knees buckled a little as he released her.

"Hey," she protested breathlessly.

"Dare!"

"From who?" she whispered, trying to pull up taller.

"You." He tapped her nose.

Mae shook her head, stepping backward on Emma's toes.

"Tommy! Naughty boy!" Emma teased, grasping Mae's hand to keep her there. "You be nice to Mae!"

"I was! It was nice, right?" he asked Mae.

Mae nodded. "I guess." *Holy shit, yes! No, Mae, be cool.* Mae tossed her hair. "So I'm Mae."

"Tommy." He turned to Emma. "Em, there's action in the kitchen." He tipped his head.

"Two chem labs!" Emma squealed. "Love it!"

"Actually, no, it's hash oil, and chem lab's by the front door."

"Yeah, we already saw—did—that," Mae interjected, flashing her dimple.

Emma focused on Mae. "Well, Maisie, chem or kitchen?"

Mae hesitated. "Kitchen. Sure, why not?"

Emma beamed. "C'mon. Guys?"

"Right behind ya, Em." Sandwiched between Emma and the redheaded guy, Mae shuffled through the kitchen door.

♦ ♦ ♦

"Wanna try it?" Emma slumped against her, surprisingly heavy.

"Haven't seen you do it," Mae tried to joke.

"Oh, I will. I've done it before." Emma nodded wisely. "Just watch Ed."

Ed slipped his whole face into the gas mask. Most of the hair on the top of his head disappeared too, leaving a funky-looking blond fringe spilling from his ears to his shoulders.

"Ready?" Joey asked into the other end of the tube. "Here it comes…" He connected the tube to the bong and fired it up.

Ed's chest expanded broadly.

"Whoa, man, slow down!" Joey coached him. "Just regular breaths. You'll feel it in a sec."

Ed rested his elbows on his knees and breathed more deliberately. Two, three, four and then he fumbled to pull off the mask. "Oh man," he mumbled thickly. His eyelids fluttered. "Good hit."

"It's true," Emma urged Mae. "You'll be so spaced, good for hours."

"Hours?" *Budweisers and hash brownies weren't making much of a dent so far.* "Okay," Mae agreed, "I'm game."

Emma crowed, "Hey, guys, Mae's gonna take a hit."

The bong guy, Joey, looked Mae over. "Ever done this before?"

Mae shook her head.

"What's the strongest stuff you've done? Midol?" he snickered.

"Hash oil."

Joey raised one eyebrow in approval. "Okay then, but you're little, so only three, okay?"

Mae shrugged. "Cool." She slipped onto the couch, right next to Ed, who was half gone, a big puddle of bliss. Mae picked up the bulky gas mask and plopped it on. It smelled like burnt rubber. The weight bent her neck forward. "Ouch!" she cried involuntarily. She heard some sniggers.

"All right in there?" Joey's voice rattled up the hollow tube.

"Yeah, yeah, just didn't know it was this heavy." Mae shifted the mask a little.

"Somebody pull the strap tighter for this chick," Joey ordered. Mae felt a cinching motion across the back of her skull. The mask closed all around her. She gripped both knees, waiting.

"Okay," came Joey's echoing voice. "Just breathe regular. We'll help you get it off."

Mae nodded. She tried to pull her mind away from the thought of the thick plastic sealing her face off from the oxygen in the room. She tried to think about her fingers, relaxing her fingers. *First the thumbs: don't clutch. Okay, index fingers, breathe, middle fingers, whoa*—she was breathing smoke, that familiar, burned, sickly sweet smell. Her eyes stung as she inhaled harder, trying to find oxygen. Someone was holding her hand, but between the white smoke and the tears in her eyes, she couldn't see out. *Trust them, trust them,* Mae ordered herself, holding up two and then three fingers with each subsequent breath. Immediately someone tugged at the strap in back, tearing her hair roots, but she didn't care. The cumbersome mask lifted up and forward, and cool air washed over her cheeks and eyes. She gasped and hacked out some of the residue in her lungs. *Blurry.*

Emma squeezed her hand. "Buzzed?"

Mae nodded, managing a thumbs-up. Her eyes burned and teared up at the same time. *Feels like my lipstick's melting...huh, my fingers are buzzing.* She felt a loopy grin ease across her face, out of her control. She could feel her body, observe it, but somehow she was disconnected, just encased in it.

"Sit back," Emma whispered, gently pushing her down.

Mae nodded while her body rolled back, melting into the cushion. Yeah, that was better, with the cushion smooshed up all around her, holding her steady while her mind floated up, dissolved into vapor, tiny particles drifting away, growing faint. *So buzzed, so buzzed.* "Good hit," she murmured, her eyelids drooping. Someone brushed her hair back. Someone else stroked her arm. *Ah. A blur, a very, very, very good blur.* She tried to say, "Good hit" again, but she couldn't find her mouth. Someone touched her neck, or was that her breast? Arm, thighs. *Yeah. Very, very, very good.*

♦ ♦ ♦

"Lord, I hate Valentine day!" Mae announced loudly as she walked alone down the hallway. She was directing her complaint to the big blackboard off the foyer, which was filled with two and a half columns of names today, announcing who had flowers waiting for them at the front desk. Never, her name had never been there, so she refused to look directly at the long list. "Bullshit holiday, invented by florists," she grumbled, taking the first flight of stairs by twos, feeling the inner corners of her purse for her key, for its hard zigzag edge. But the door wasn't locked: Nora was at her desk with several sheets of notes and four or five open books on the floor, circling her chair like sharks. She looked almost that freaked.

"Hey." Mae climbed onto her bunk.

"Hey." Nora bent over to read out of a book on the floor.

"Research paper?"

"Yeah."

Nora's tense voice. She got so uptight about papers, had to be just right. Should probably leave, but yuck. Maybe a nap. The old springs groaned as Mae rolled onto her side. Even lying still, she was probably bugging Nora. She tried to be extra quiet.

"Knock, knock!" Melina's voice. "Hey, Mae, let's see!"

Mae rolled over slowly, frowning. "See what?" Mae looked from Melina to Nora, who'd twisted around to see what was going on.

"Your flowers; where are they?" Melina peeked around the room.

Nora looked as startled as Mae felt. Mae ventured, "Me?"

Melina nodded. "Your name's on the board. I can't believe you didn't see it!"

"You sure?" *Didn't feel right.*

"Jeez, Mae, get off your butt and go see!" Melina popped out of view.

"Yeah, go on," Nora seconded.

"You just want me outta the room, but fine, I'm going." Mae rolled to the floor with a pointed thud.

"God, go already." Nora turned back to hunch over her work.

Mae eased down the stairwell, reluctantly approaching the blackboard. *Jeez, if Melina got this wrong, she was in deep shit.* Mae scanned down the first column of names: Lisa Gale, Monica Jenson, Madonna Tully—well, of course, Donna, she got flowers almost every week. Let's see, Lisa, Monica, Donna, Vicki, Mary Kay, Ginny, Catherine, *Mae Panos. Honest to God, near the end of the first column, so they must've come this morning. What the hell!*

Mae approached the front desk: Judy was on duty. "Hey, Judy," she tried to sound nonchalant. "Guess I got flowers."

"Oh yeah? Lemme check." Judy ran her finger down her list. "Okay, over by the alcove, under the St. Patrick window. Those yellow roses with the babies' breath? Those."

Mae stared, didn't move. "You sure?"

Judy rechecked her list. "Yep!" She grinned. "Who're they from?"

"No clue..." Mae muttered.

"Hoo, a secret admirer! Neat! See if there's a card."

Mae took one step and then looked up in distrust.

"If you don't want 'em, I can take them off your hands," Judy goaded.

Mae tossed her a sideways glance. "Thanks, I can handle it." Mae strolled toward the alcove, slowly, trying to look blasé despite her heart banging against her ribs. *Jack, it could only be Jack. But how'd he pull this off from so far away?*

Her left hand was trembling so hard that she shoved it into her pocket. With her right she reached for the envelope: *Mae Panos* in a scratchy male script. Mae frowned, hesitating. Jack? Did she even know what Jack's handwriting looked like? All those hours of talking but no notes, no letters. Huh, nothing in writing, no evidence they were ever together, except her ring. Wherever that was. Her heart tripped, banged again. *Flowers now?*

Peeling open the miniature envelope, she pulled out the card. *What would there be to say now?* The card was upside down: she rotated it haltingly. *Thinking of you, Tommy.* Mae flipped the card over: blank back. Mae scowled and reread it. *Thinking of you, Tommy.* Wrong card. Maybe switched with another order? No, the heaviness in her gut told Mae she did know a Tommy. *Somehow. But Tommy who?*

Mae swiveled around slowly, absorbed in the card. *Tommy.* She headed toward the stairs.

"Mae!" Judy called after her. "Your roses!"

Mae flushed, backtracked. "Right. Guess I'll take them too."

Judy chuckled as she drew a line through Mae's name. Mae snatched up the vase and took off for her room.

She entered silently; Nora was still absorbed in her writing. Mae set the vase heavily on her dresser, hoping Nora would look up. Nora did.

Nora moaned, "Gorgeous!" She looked at Mae, questioning. "Yellow roses. Wow!" Clearly Nora was being careful, wouldn't ask.

"From some guy named Tommy."

"Who's Tommy?"

"Good question."

Nora stepped over the books on the floor to sniff the roses appreciatively. "So you have a secret admirer, Mary Panos!" She barely touched the babies' breath. "My, my..."

"Yeah." Mae ducked her head down. "So you don't know who he is?"

"Nope," Nora responded absently, adjusting the arrangement. She rotated one rosebud carefully. "Keep them on top of your dresser. With the reflection in the mirror, it will look like two dozen!" Nora turned toward Mae. "So who could this Tommy be?"

Mae shook her head. "No idea."

"Huh." Nora picked up the card. "'Thinking of you.' I guess he could be admiring you from afar...but kinda sounds like he knows you. Can't place him?"

"Not really."

"Unless..." Nora grinned. "Is Tommy a stoner? But then again, do stoners even observe Valentine day? Kinda bourgeois, isn't it?" Nora was obviously enjoying this possibility.

"No," Mae muttered, increasingly uneasy, thinking back three, four weekends. *Who was there? Emma, Sandra, Ed, Joey, Denise, who else? Man, that night was a blur. Fumbling, hands fumbling with her belt buckle.* "No," Mae repeated. "And for your information, love and peace go together, so there."

"Ooh, good comeback." Nora wasn't going to debate her. "Okay, so Tommy is just a mystery guy. You're pretty, someone's noticed you." She glanced back at her desk. "Man, guess I should get back to this stupid paper." The tension was back in her voice.

"What's it on?" Mae didn't really care, but it seemed polite.

"Post-Civil War immigration to the US: you know, the Irish, the potato famine, all that." Nora plopped down at her desk chair. "Fifteen pages, double spaced, typed, for Sister Ann Marie."

"Yuck," Mae sympathized.

"Yeah." Nora sighed heavily. "Gonna be up till midnight easy." She clutched the auburn hair at the nape of her neck tightly.

"Want me to type for you later? I'll start typing while you write the end—save you a couple of hours."

"Would you?" Nora tipped her head over the back of her chair, catching Mae's eye upside down. "But you did last week too…"

"So?" Mae shrugged. "No big deal. How 'bout I come back in an hour and start on what you got?"

"Wow, thanks." Nora smiled and flashed a peace sign and then sat up again, looking at her notes. Mae returned the peace sign feebly, to the back of Nora's head.

"Okay, see you later. Headin' over to Emma's."

"Thanks, Mae," Nora called after her.

♦ ♦ ♦

Emma's room was so, well, Emma. She'd taken down the closet door and hung pink strands of beads in the doorframe. Her bedspread had some Marrakech-style pattern, kind of gently psychedelic. Somehow she found pink lightbulbs that gave her room an exotic, shadowy mood. Emma was very into pinks and roses, because Rose was her middle name. She even had a little rose tattooed right where her thigh met her butt. And Emma was really sweet, in a spacey, strung-out kind of way. Just seemed to love everybody. Never locked her door, even though her dresser was covered in a tangle of jewelry: beads, silver bracelets, five or six rings, even more dangly earrings. Guess she just didn't worry about anyone stealing them. *Trusted everybody. Incredible.*

"Mae!" Emma sounded thrilled, as if they'd been apart for years. She threw her arms open wide. She wrapped herself around Mae as she plopped alongside on the bed. "How are you?" She gave a squeeze.

Mae didn't fight the embrace. "Oh, fine, just...wondering, you know, about that party last month."

"What about it?" Emma patted her shoulder, hanging on.

"Well, who were we hanging out with? You know those guys a lot better than I do."

"Well, let's see...Eddie, Dave, me, you...Steve and Jimmy, and...and a few others. Awesome, wasn't it?" She squeezed Mae again.

"Yeah, awesome. But I can't remember a lot of it, like..." *Wasn't sure how to say it.*

"Oh!" Emma gave a gentle shove. "You can't remember after the bong." She laughed lightly. "Yeah, you were pretty far gone, but don't worry, you were having fun, just trippin' a little—you were fine."

"Were you with me?" *Again, that dull weight, low in her gut. Remembered running her fingers through really blond, white blond hair, so soft, while his lips were on her neck...*

"Hm." Emma tipped her head back, trying to remember. "For a while, yeah, you 'n' me with Eddie, we were crashed on the couch. And then, let's see...I kinda remember you with some other guys in the kitchen, and then I sorta lost track of you after I took a hit off the gas mask...I swear that was laced with something." Emma squeezed her eyes to concentrate: wasn't capable of frowning. "Let's see, I remember you with…oh!" She shoved Mae, giggling. "Is this about Joe? You know, Tommy?"

"What? Who?" Mae couldn't even think in a straight line. "Joe who? Tommy who?" She clutched Emma's arm.

"Chill out! He's a great guy. You were cute together! Very into each other."

Mae cringed. "Who? Tommy or Joe?"

"Mae, Tommy *is* Joe, remember? Joe Thomasini, but everyone calls him Tommy 'cause Joey's his roommate. You know: Joey's the really dark one, from Long Island, and Tommy's from like Dayton or Cincinnati or something. Blondish, kinda tall. Remember?"

Mae nodded. *The dare guy.* "So I was, well, with Tommy?"

"Well, I kinda remember you guys rollin' around in the Passion Pit, you know, those mattresses off the den. But not anything too heavy. Mae, don't psych yourself out." Emma planted a kiss on her cheek. "So you made out a little. No big deal."

Mae mustered up a crooked smile. "Right, no big deal."

Emma wrapped both arms around Mae's shoulders. "Mae, you had a good time. You were happy. Don't worry, kiddo, I'm telling you, he's cool."

"Must be," Mae pondered. "He sent me flowers for Valentine's Day."

"Far out!" Emma squealed. "See, Mae, he likes you."

"Guess so." Mae felt muddled, as if her thoughts were scattering in six different directions at once. She needed to be alone, try to think. "In fact, he sent me roses, yellow ones."

"Oh!" Emma beamed. "I love roses!"

"Yeah, well, know what? I told Nora I'd start typing for her, but I'll bring a rose down to you in a while. How would that be?"

"Really!" Emma clasped her hands, bracelets dancing. "You're so sweet!"

"No big deal." Mae stood up. "See ya in a bit, okay?" She headed through the door decisively.

"Thanks, Mae!" Emma called behind her. "I do love roses!"

"I know, Em, I know.

Chapter Ten

Pressed for Time

March 1971

"Ooh, he's here!" Emma poked Mae in the ribs. "Bet he's hoping you made this scene."

Mae's eyes tracked right along with Emma. The room was crowded, but Emma was right: that was the back of his head, a couple of inches above most of the others. *The long hair, really thick, a little wavy, the color of dark honey; yeah, remembered that...remembered heavy for such a slender guy. Heavy on top of her so she rolled—don't, Mae, just don't.* Mae studied him intently, thankful he was facing the other way, so she could stare. And she did stare, frowning in concentration.

"Mae, you worry too much," Emma whispered, her lips touching Mae's ear.

"Who's worried?" Mae countered, her eyes still fixed on Tommy.

"Mellow out. Plus, you're not as pretty when you're all uptight. Let him see you're even prettier than he remembers. Pretty, pretty Mae, the hot-looking chick he sent flowers to." Emma shook her head back and forth, her earrings jingling crazily. "No worrying: you look perfect. Tommy's gonna dig you. So you want to walk up to him or let him find you?"

Mae hesitated, acting as if she could consider either possibility, although she knew her legs would melt from under her if she even tried to cross the room. *Remembered his hands stroking the insides of her thighs.* Mae shook her head, trying to shake away the memory. "Let's stay for now, okay?"

Emma gave Mae's hand a cheery squeeze. "Cool." She sniffed and turned to the right. "Something's happening over here. C'mon, follow me." Mae clung to Emma's hand as they wove into the crowd.

♦ ♦ ♦

"You're here." His voice sifted down from behind her head, settled on the surface of her hair, a mist. Mae caught her breath. *Mae, be cool.* She eased around.

"Oh, hi there." *Good, sounded about right, not too much.*

"Was wondering if you'd be here tonight." He was smiling down at her, just a trace of a grin but gentle, nice.

"Oh sure, Em dragged me along…" Mae glanced around but couldn't spot Emma. *Where the hell did she go? Don't look rattled, Mae.*

"Yeah, Emma, saw her a couple of minutes ago. That's when I figured I'd check it out, see if you came too."

He came looking. Mae dropped her head, blushing. *Damn. Say something.* She forced her chin up, locked in on his eyes: blue like cornflowers. "You here every weekend?"

He barely shook his head and took a sip of beer. "Nah, but probably most. But you've been here a few times now. Like these guys?"

"Yeah, good as any." *Crap, didn't come out right.* "I mean, they're cool, and beats the school dance scene, you know?" Flashed her most knowing smile.

"Oh, so you guys are from the academy. Was wondering."

"Senior, just a few more months." Mae pulled up taller. "So guess you're a Domer?"

"Just finishing freshman year. Mechanical engineering."

"Wow." Mae nodded appreciatively. "Engineering."

"I like it. I'm thinking maybe bridges."

Mae frowned in confusion.

"Building bridges. Or maybe skyscrapers, like the Sears Tower."

"Oh right!" *Damn, couldn't read his expression.* "Kinda stoned," she offered with a one-sided smile, hoping he'd notice her dimple.

"So...?" Tommy ventured.

Mae squinted, puzzled. "So...?"

He cleared his throat. "So you got my flowers?"

"Oh!" Mae grimaced. "Shit, yes. I mean, thank you. They're gorgeous, and...and that was really sweet, a real surprise."

"Good, glad you liked them. But, really, you were surprised?"

Mae started talking faster. "Well, yeah, I mean we just met and all, and I never got flowers for Valentine's Day before, so of course I wasn't expecting anything. I mean, we hardly know each other." *Shut up, Mae, shut up! You sound nervous.* She took a long sip of beer, tried to settle down.

"Well, yes and no..."

"Yes and no what?" she demanded. *Damn, too much edge in her voice. Calm down!*

"Just..." He frowned, staring at her while he took a sip of beer. Then, a little gravely, he offered, "Look, we were both pretty messed up that night, and after, I was worried that you, well, I just wanted you to know I dig you, and it was nice."

"Oh," she whispered. Couldn't blink. Felt a flush creeping across her cheeks.

"Is it, are we, we're cool then?" His tone was earnest, unnerving.

Mae shuddered and then flipped her head back and shook out her hair, forcing a smile. "Oh, definitely. Cool."

Tommy sighed as he gently guided one of her wayward curls behind her ear. "Awesome. Another beer? I'll get you one."

Mae tossed down the last mouthful and handed him the empty cup. "Sure." He put his hand over hers and let it rest there a moment, before taking the cup and heading off. Her hand felt so empty as she watched him thread his way through the crowd.

"Thanks!" she called after him.

Tommy glanced back over his shoulder and nodded that he'd heard. Mae ran her fingers through her hair. *More tangles. Crap.*

♦ ♦ ♦

"Have you finished your note cards?" Nora was all organization these days: lots of projects in the month before finals. Each corner of her desk held a neat stack of note cards on top of books on top of folders and loose pages. Her voice was businesslike.

Gonna be hard to live with. Mae sighed.

Nora shook her head. "Guess that means no. Mae!"

God, don't scold, Mae begged silently, pulling her pillow over her head. *No energy for this crap.* She pushed the pillow aside. "Look, Nora, I'm planning it in my head. I'll take a nap and then start writing stuff down. Nothing's due for a few days."

Nora shook her head. "You're tired all the time, Mae. Must be run down. Jeez, maybe you got mono. Really, you look like hell."

"Thanks a ton."

"Check if you got swollen glands, like this." Nora pressed her fingers along her jawline to demonstrate.

"No! I don't need to check my glands! I look like hell 'cause I drink too much, and it's making me pale and puffy. And I am not going to any parties for a while, *okay*, Mother?"

"Fine!" Nora shot back. "Excuse me for being concerned." She hastily transferred the stack from the back left corner of her desk into her book bag. "I'm heading to the library, so I can concentrate!" She stomped off, slamming the door behind her.

"Yeah, bye!" Mae shouted after her and then rolled to face the wall. *Ick. A nap, probably better after a nap.* Her body was so tired, but her mind was jumbled, active. Focus, focus on something...Michael, next letter to Michael. *Sorry it's been so long, but the last few weeks have been crazy. I just need to get the hell outta here, can't wait for graduation so I can leave this place, even if it's just to cross the avenue to the college.*

The doorknob was turning. Nora was back. "Forgot something," she explained, frosty, checking her top drawer.

Guess I'm a St. Mary's lifer, but new classes, new teachers, just need a change so badly.

"Mae?" *A weirdly conciliatory tone.* Mae didn't answer, but she rolled over to look at Nora.

"Look, I'm kinda spazzed, don't wanna freak out on you, but obviously you're not..." Nora was oddly tentative, licking her lips. "Could you... maybe you should go to the infirmary and get a...well...get checked out." She was watching Mae closely for a reaction. "I'll go with, if you want. You know, just someone to walk over with you."

She's not here because she forgot something. Mae averted her gaze up to the springs of the top bunk. Could still feel Nora looking at her, so Mae closed her eyes. "My mother says everything seems worse if you're tired," Mae murmured, pulling the satin edge of the blanket up to her lower lip. "I'll feel better after a nap, really. And then I'll get to work. Thanks anyway." *Go, please go. Don't ask, don't remind me. He was so heavy, pressing down, so heavy.* Mae kept her eyes closed.

The desk drawer scraped closed. "Okay, well, if you change your mind, I'll be back in maybe an hour. I'll turn off the lights as I leave."

Mae rolled over with a muffled, "Yep." *Could still feel Nora's eyes on her.* A long moment later, the lights switched off, and the door clicked closed. She was alone. She was afraid to open her eyes. Searching with her hands, as if she were blind, she fingered the rows of tiny springs supporting the top bunk, until she found the familiar one with the jagged tip and then pressed, pressed her thumb against the point until she felt the skin pop and the blood well up. *Better.*

♦ ♦ ♦

Michael—I'm pregnant. God help me, I'm pregnant. There, said it twice to you, and I can't even figure out how to say it once to anyone else. By the time you read this, I'll have told Mother, but I swear I just can't watch Sophie tear up and Uncle Nick get all grim with me...oh, why aren't you here? I know you'd help me figure things out. Not that there are many choices. I guess Mama will help me raise the baby. No college, just living back at home. It's hard to picture, except that maybe you'll be back by then. I could stand it if you were around too. You will *come back to Chicago, won't you? My due date (oh GOD) is November 10. Does your tour still end in October?* Please *come back the minute they'll let you. I'm begging.*

It was only once, Michael, honest, just once at a party, and I was stoned, he was stoned, nobody really thinking. At least there's only a month left till graduation, and I can split. I think Nora realizes, but she's not saying anything. Maybe I should tell her. Maybe that'd help me know what to say to Mama. Or wait till I get home, so there are fewer months left. Crap, I don't know.

Okay, I tell you, then Nora, then Mama...then Tommy. Shit, we haven't even had a date or anything. And he gets to go and do all the things he's planned while I go live with my mother and be reminded daily how much of a disappointment I am. I've made a mess of things. If only I were brave as you, I'd move to another city, like St. Louis, and let them think I'm a war widow. Sorry, that's a shitty thing to say to you, but you know, at least then people would feel sorry for me instead of whispering with their Christian condescension. Will they even baptize the baby at St. Ignatius? They have to baptize a baby if you ask, don't they? They can't condemn her soul just because her mother's a mess, can they? You know, I know it's a girl, know it for sure. Don't ask me how. Michael, I pray for you every night: you better pray for me now too. Just please stay safe, please come home, because that stupid war is going to drag on with or without you, but in about six months everything changes for me. Please hurry home, Michael. xo Mae

♦ ♦ ♦

"I'm late, I'm late," Mae fretted, barreling down the stairs, grabbing the railing to keep on her feet. "Shit, shit, shit, late." Lurching to a stop on the first floor, she brushed her hands down her blouse and skirt, breathing deeply and pulling tall, then yanking open the heavy fire door to march down the hallway to the reception desk for Sister Mary Anthony's office. Tiny Sister Leo, probably ninety years old, was organizing mail as Mae stopped pointedly to catch her eye. "I have an eleven o'clock appoint—" Mae began as Sister peered up through horn-rimmed glasses and silently pointed with the letter opener to go ahead. "Thank you, Sister," Mae whispered, smoothing her blouse and skirt one more time as she stepped up to Sister Mary Anthony's door. Mae raised her hand to knock even though the door was slightly ajar, but hearing the tone in her mother's voice, she grabbed the doorknob and pushed the door open to join them.

Both women turned to focus on Mae: Sister Mary Anthony looked grave, composed, but Mama looked...weird, confused. *What in the world?* Mae glanced quickly behind the door to check, but no Nick, no Sophie. *Good. But what had just been said for Mama to look so—*

"Take a seat, Mary Therese," Sister nodded toward the chair pulled next to Mama's. "And close the door." Sister sounded concerned, not too frosty. *Could be worse. But what's been said?*

"I apologize, being late, didn't mean to be late," Mae offered as she circled over to her chair, perching on the edge of it. "Oh." She leaned over to give her mother a peck on the cheek. "Was your train ride all right?"

Mama looked positively grieved as she nodded a little yes, her lips pinched tightly together. "How are you feeling, Maisie?"

"Okay, but what...?" Mae turned with a questioning look to Sister.

"Your mother and I were just discussing your, well, situation. This situation has come up before here at the academy, but of course, it is always difficult." Sister's mouth settled in a grave line as she eyed Mae expectantly.

Mae nodded, trying to remember what she'd prepared. *Blank.* "Yes, well, I'm very sorry for, all this, I realize...the serious consequences, and I, I'll do my best to be responsible...now." *Sound like an idiot, Mae.* She turned to her mother for help.

"Sister," Mama implored, obviously back to whatever had been interrupted, "it's just one month till graduation, and Mae is not showing, if anything she looks thin." Mama turned back to Mae. "You look too thin. And pale. Are you eating?"

"Yes, Mother," Mae responded, instantly regretting the edge in her voice. "Yes," she reiterated more gently, "I am. I've been tired, but otherwise I'm fine."

Mama nodded, unconvinced, and then looked back to Sister Mary Anthony to implore, "One more month, Sister, after all these years? Please? Just one month so she could graduate. I can let out her skirts, if needed: it wouldn't show; no one would know."

Sister Mary Anthony leaned across her massive desk toward Mama, nodding her head. "I understand. I feel for you, and I understand your request. But no, Mrs. Panos, as I said, Mae must return home with you tonight. Our policy is that students in her situation must withdraw from the school immediately. If we don't hold to this very high standard, what are we teaching the other young women here?"

"Wait, what?" Mae interjected. "I'm out? Just like that?"

Sister leaned back into her chair as she assessed Mae. "Yes, Mary Therese. You need to go home with your mother."

"But we are practically up to finals! Graduation practice is in, like, three weeks!"

"Mae, who knows?" Mama demanded. "Who've you told? Nora?"

"N-no!" Mae stammered, thrown off by Mama's fierceness. "She, I think she suspects, but she hasn't really asked, she wouldn't say anyth—"

"You see, Sister?" Mama interrupted. "No one knows, no one need know. It is so important that she graduate, so that after, maybe even by the January term, or certainly by the next fall, Mae could return and resume, even if she is a little behind her classmates. Go to summer school each year then, to catch up."

"Wait!" Mae protested. "What? How do I—I'm not coming back to school—what, leave the baby behind with you? How would that work?"

Both set of eyes locked on Mae. The silence pressed down on everyone. Mae frowned at her mother and then at Sister, then back to her mother. *Wait a minute. No, no, what—*

"Mae," her mother began, slowly and firmly, "if no one knows, then I am asking Sister to permit you to stay to graduate, then you return home, and after, well, after the baby is safely delivered and you have recovered, you would return to begin college. You would be behind, but you could return."

Wait a minute. "You think I am giving up the baby? Like, for adoption?"

Silence.

"Of course you are," Mama pronounced. "Mrs. Tennes, at our church, she works for the Cradle Society, up in Evanston, and she helps unwed mothers. She's a social worker. She'll help us find a good placement, a good home."

"Oh no!" Mae countered. "This is *my* daughter. I'm not giving her up. I'll stay home after graduation and raise her, and maybe I can go to school part time when she is older, but..."

"Are you engaged?" Sister asked pointedly.

"No."

"Is the father—are you close to being engaged?"

Shit, don't blush, don't blush. "No, not exactly," Mae responded tersely. She raised her chin up, meeting Sister's gaze squarely. Sister was inscrutable; Mae was resolute.

Finally Sister broke the silence. "Mary, listen to your mother. Go home, let this child have a normal family, and let your family guide you as you move on."

Mae gulped. "This child is my daughter, and she's mine. Mine. I'd have an abortion before I'd give her away."

Mama gasped and covered her mouth with her hands. Sister's eyes were flint.

"Apologize to your mother. Now."

Shaking, Mae turned to Mama. "I, I didn't mean that. Sorry, Mama. I, it's just I know I'm having a daughter, my daughter, and I'm not giving her up. No. And, and you can raise a baby without a father. I mean, you know that: you did that!"

Mama looked incredibly sad. "But not by choice, Mae. I was widowed: that is entirely different. And even then, you have no idea, no idea whatsoever how hard it would be for you. But I know."

"I can do it."

Sister folded her hands, contemplating them for a long moment, then focused on Mae. "Listen to your mother. Go home with her. You have the next few hours to pack a small bag, and we'll help you both to the late afternoon train. You are to tell no one why you're leaving. If asked, say you've been sick and are going home for a few days with your mother. You've told no one?"

"Just my brother, in a letter."

"Not Nora?"

"No."

Sister turned to Mama, tipping her head pensively. "I grieve for you, for the difficulty of the situation, and I appreciate your concerns for Mary's future. I must uphold the policy of her immediate dismissal. However, I shall consult Mary's teachers to see if there's a way that she can complete the semester from home and receive her diploma, so that she has better options for her future education."

Mama teared up. "Thank you, thank you, Sister, that would mean everything."

Sister nodded and reached across the desk to squeeze Mama's hand. "I'm not promising, but I will try."

Mama nodded, tears running down both cheeks.

Mae watched them, stunned. But then Sister turned her grim attention back to Mae.

"You, young lady, have caused your mother more heartache than you can imagine. To be an unwed mother is selfish, incredibly selfish. You listen to me. Time to grow up. You have only two responsible choices: give this baby up for adoption or get married. Adoption or marriage."

Chapter Eleven

The Wedding

May 1971

"One more, Maisie. Sorry if I'm hurting you," Mama murmured. *Ouch.* Mae kept her eyes closed even though that left nothing to focus on but the tugging and tearing.

"Ow," Mae whispered, the faintest complaint threading out into the atmosphere. Mae felt hands rest on her shoulders. *Sophie.*

"Almost finished, sweetheart. Just keep your eyes closed," Sophie urged.

"Hang tight," Nora added. "You're almost there."

A palpable silence washed around them all, and then Mama eased one last bobby pin in on the left, catching several roots at the base of the tiny rhinestone tiara. Mae felt her mother's hands flutter all about, arranging the veil. "There!" Mama proclaimed. "Open your eyes and see what a lovely bride you've become!"

Mae blinked several times, fake eyelashes tickling the outer corners of her eyes. Blinking rapidly, she focused through the filmy veil suspended just past the tip of her nose. No, not brushing against her cheekbone either, or her ears. Amazing, it floated, enveloped her without touching her, a delicate layer of protection between her and the rest of the world. Her own space, a modicum of privacy. She smiled in relief.

"You're pleased then?" Mama ventured.

"What?" Mae was still lost inside her veil. *Oh, facing a mirror.* "Oh!" Mae gasped at the reflection of a young woman, not a seventeen-year-old girl. Tall and slender—the extra height of the shoulder-length veil, the fitted lines of the silk suit, two extra inches from the pumps, dyed the same ice pink—together they created the illusion of a mature woman. The padded bra balanced the more pronounced curve in her hips, and the suit jacket skimmed just below her waist. Even her belly looked smooth, sleek. Mae turned slightly left, then right. *Yes, really good.* She turned further and craned to peek over her shoulder. *Not bad.* A shy smile crept across her face.

"Don't twist, sweetheart: no wrinkles!" Aunt Sophie smoothed the jacket with her hands. "I'll save my kiss for after the ceremony, so I don't smudge your makeup. Promise a kiss later?" Mae nodded, her throat catching.

"I'll get your bouquet. Back in a sec." Nora winked her approval and then slipped through the doorway, her full satin skirt rustling with each step.

Mae turned toward her mother, eyebrows raised in a question. Mama nodded, wistfully smiling. "Beautiful sweetheart, just so, so grown up, and really, really beautiful."

"Thanks," Mae choked out, turning back to her reflection. The extra makeup: *too much?* Or was she flushed? Did she really look more mature, or like a little girl playing dress up? Snapshots of times, years ago, lifetimes ago, parading around the apartment in heavy, layered gowns, trains dragging like anchors when she tried to pivot. Stiff, scratchy beading brushing against her neck, her fingertips. Gowns of other brides, those gowns her mother labored over, adjusting seams, adding ruffles to peek out of the bustles: those gowns would be her closest brush to being The Bride, the vision of white silk and lace and pearls and petticoats. Hers was a paler vision, an elegant but understated, not-quite-white, not-too-fancy-under-the-circumstances vision, pretty but not the gown she'd expected in her future. Didn't know at nine years old that she had already had her moment as the fancy bride, the take-your-breath-away bride. *Oh well*, Mae sighed. Her chin dropped, but no tears: *not so much sad as to be expected.*

"What?" Mama's tone was not that confused: she probably knew the answer. "Mae, do you feel all right? Do you want to sit down?" *Don't ask about something you can't fix, Mama.*

"No, don't want to wrinkle my skirt. I'm fine, really." Mae's tone was equally unconvincing. Mae hit on a kind lie, not even a lie, really. "Just wish Michael were here."

"Of course you do, Mae, we all do." Sophie squeezed her hand. "But he is here in our hearts today, and God willing, home again in just a few more months. I'm sure you're in his thoughts today, sweetheart."

"Maybe he'll be able to call." Mae offered a reassuring smile.

Sophie nodded. "He knows the reception is at the Cape Cod Room, and Uncle Nick sent the phone number to him, so we know he'll try, right?"

Mae shrugged. "If he can, he will, and if not, soon, I'm sure."

Sophie smiled appreciatively. "That's our brave girl! Mae, we just want this to be a happy day for you, you know that."

"I know, thank you. And thanks again for the pearls." Mae touched the strand lightly. "They're elegant."

"You know?" Aunt Sophie squinted. "I can't tell if they're picking up the hint of pink from the suit or if they have a bit of a blush tone of their own. No matter! You're a vision with or without pearls, but I'm glad you like them."

Mae lifted the veil to kiss Sophie on the cheek. "I love them." She let the veil drop again. *Yes, better behind the veil.*

Nora bustled in. "His family's here, Mrs. Panos. And Mae, your flowers."

"Oh!" Mama stepped close to peek at Mae through the veil. "I should go greet them. Are you all right for a few minutes, Mae?"

Mae waved her toward the door. "Fine."

"I'll stay with her, Mrs. Panos. Don't worry."

"Thank you, Nora. Sophie, join me? Nick is probably out there already."

"Certainly. Let's get Tom's family settled in. Girls, we'll be back in a few minutes."

"We're fine," Nora repeated.

Nora was careful to close the door softly behind Mama and Sophie. Turning slowly, she pressed her back against it, an unspoken pledge of protection. "So." She peered into the veil. "How are you?"

Mae shrugged. "Hangin' on."

"Really." Not so much a question as a challenge, albeit a gentle one.

Mae shrugged again. "What am I supposed to say?"

"To them? That you're fine, you're excited, you're a little nervous. But to me...the truth."

"I...too weird, like it's not quite real, you know?"

Nora nodded somberly.

Mae started to pace. "They were right, you know: that I was too young to get married right after graduation, to Jack." Her eyes darted about the room, not really seeing anything. "Too young at eighteen, but here I am now, seventeen, before graduation, and they want me married off, all signed, sealed, and delivered before I'm one inch wider." Mae turned to Nora for an answer but, getting none, sighed and slumped onto the edge of a chair, shaking her head. "And they hate me, you know."

"Who?" Nora countered. "Your family? No, they don't! Mae, they thought giving up the baby would've been better, but they're trying."

"No, *his* family."

"Oh. Well, you don't really know that," Nora suggested. "Anyway, it's not that simple. They're just upset about, the circumstances, and that he's moving so far away from them, you know, by coming to Chicago."

Mae reiterated grimly, "Nah, they pretty much hate me. Probably think I did it on purpose, to catch me a Domer husband. And wanting that paternity test—"

"Which Tommy nixed, and even if he hadn't, clearly your uncle was ready to tell them to go to hell—"

With Tommy in the passion pit, Mae rolling on top of him. But also a snatch of a memory of Ed, kissing Ed, playing with his white-blond bangs. Giggling at Ed licking her toes.

"Hey," Nora startled Mae. "Who knows what they think, and really, what difference does it make? You guys are making the best of a tough situation, so screw the speculation and get your head on straight, Mae."

Mae's whole face tightened. "This your idea of the maid-of-honor pep talk?"

Nora's right eyebrow shot up. "Yeah, as a matter of fact, it is. You know, Mae, this is gonna be as good or bad as you make it. You. Ball's in your court."

Mae studied the tips of her pumps. "Ah, so it *is* all my fault."

"Oh, come off it. You know I didn't say that." Nora got right in Mae's face. "Mae, you know full well I'm talking about how you get all snippy, and, pardon my French, bitchy when you get feeling sorry for yourself. Now I don't know Tommy all that well—"

"Me neither," Mae added darkly, amused by her irony.

"That!" Nora pounced, poking her finger right into the veil. "That's the bullshit I mean, Mary Panos! He's taking a chance on you, and from what I can tell, he's going into it with a pretty positive mind-set, so maybe you could muster up the same." Nora dropped the accusatory finger, but her eyebrow remained arched.

"Cool it! I get it!" Mae raised her hands in surrender.

"You'd better get it, Mae. This time it's important." The eyebrow relaxed. "Okay then, take these." She handed Mae the bouquet. "Stand up straight. Lemme take a look." Nora assessed Mae from head to toe, then drew a little circle with her hand. "Now turn around."

Mae sighed in exasperation. "Turn!" Nora commanded. Mae complied.

Two sharp knocks interrupted them. Mae hesitated as Nora held up one hand. "Don't move," Nora directed. "I'll see what's up."

Nora pulled the door open a few inches, then more with a gracious, "Oh hi, come on in." His sisters marched in, Jenny and...the younger one. *Laurie? No, Lizzie, that's right, Lizzie.* Mae spun back to face them. "Hi."

Lizzie smiled. "Don't you look pretty." A little forced but polite. Jenny hung back, snapping the elastic band of her wrist corsage. Mae pressed the bouquet more tightly against her waist. Silence.

"She does, doesn't she?" Nora jumped in. "You must be Tommy's sisters. I'm Nora." Perfunctory smiles, introductions, company manners.

"Um, so, Mary, we brought this for you." Lizzie handed her a small box: under the clear plastic case was a delicate garter, with sky-blue ribbon and ivory lace. Lizzie added, "That covers something new or something blue, whichever you need."

"Oh," Mae whispered, blinking back a surge of tears. "Wow, how sweet. Thank you."

"Whoa, Mae, no tears, your makeup!" Nora pressed a Kleenex into Mae's hand. She held the veil up for Mae to dab at her lashes. "It's really pretty," she added, correcting her own manners.

"Well, you know," Lizzie stumbled, "we just want to say welcome, welcome to our family, and good luck and all…" As her voice trailed off, she turned to Jenny.

"Yeah," Jenny added flatly. "Joe wanted to come up, but we told him no: been enough bad luck already." She frowned. "You know he got the job in the hardware store?"

Mae nodded. "Yeah, he told me. Seemed pretty happy about it."

"Right," Jenny noted dryly, "except that he's wanted to be an engineer since he was ten."

"Look, that was his idea, not mine," Mae countered. "And for that matter, Chicago was his idea too. He thought I needed to be near my family."

"And what about him needing to be near his family?" Jenny grumbled. "What about his career? Now he's not in school!"

"Obviously. Neither am I."

Jenny shook her fists. "He had a scholarship at Notre Dame, dipshit."

"Jen, don't!" Lizzie held up a hand in warning. "Jen, please?"

"And out of school means he could get drafted! That ever occur to you? Or were you too busy picking out flowers and baby names?" Jenny turned to Lizzie. "She thinks it's all about her, can't you see that?" Anger gave way to anguish in her voice.

Lizzie took her sister's arm. "Stop, Jen! This won't help. All this, it'll just upset Joey." She gestured toward Mae. "This is hard on her too. Don't make it harder."

"Drafted?" Mae choked out. "If," she turned to Nora, "then, then how would I—"

"Oh my *God*!" Jenny erupted. "Is there anything that is *not* about you? Let's get out of here, Liz, now, or I swear I'm gonna punch her out."

Lizzie and Nora instantly stepped between Jenny and Mae.

"C'mon." Lizzie took Jenny's elbow. "You're right, we should go. Sorry," she called over her shoulder as she pushed Jenny through the door. "Oh hi!" she added, too brightly, to someone in the hallway. "We're on our way to the chapel now!" The quick clicks of their heels on the tile receded as Sophie peeked in. "Ready?" she asked expectantly, twisting her head to try to glimpse Mae behind Nora.

Nora switched on a smile. "Just one minute. I'll bring her to you, okay?" She did not move for Sophie.

Sophie hesitated, her eyebrows knotted in concern. "Well, then come to the vestibule."

"Great," Nora oozed. "We'll be right there." She watched Sophie close the door and then turned slowly to face Mae. "Man," she wondered out loud, "what was that?" Then, lifting the veil, she asked, "You okay?"

The veil tried to dance as Mae shook her head. "No, not really..." Then, pulling up tall, she squared her shoulders and motioned to let the veil back down. "Oh well, let's go."

Nora hesitated. "Okay. It'll be okay, Mae." Nora gave the veil one more desultory adjustment. "It'll be okay," she echoed, even as they both shook their heads.

♦ ♦ ♦

"Gorgeous." Nora flicked at the tips of Mae's veil. "Perfect." She gently nudged Mae's arm a bit higher, positioning the bouquet. "You'll take his breath away, Mae." *Such a sweet smile. Such a good friend.*

Music. *So loud!* The organ made the whole church tremble. Nora turned, gliding ahead, the practiced procession.

Uncle Nick started to offer his arm, then pulled it back. He turned to face her. "Ready?" *Really asking.* Mae met his gaze: serious, not angry. *Maybe dutiful, yes, his duty, her duty too.* She nodded. He nodded back. *Okay, together.* He bent his left arm; she slipped her hand into the crook of his elbow. *On my side. Okay.* Eyes forward, lifting her chin, she sensed he lifted his chin too. *Parallel.*

Patient, he waited for her, didn't step until she did. Right, pause, left, pause, head steady, petals fluttering. *God, help.* Mae leaned more heavily on his arm. He rested his right hand over hers: even steps left, pause, right, pause. *Oh God. This tiny side chapel, how can the aisle be this long? Too many people looking.* Last pew, bride's side, three old ladies nodding and smiling, lost in their own bridal memories. *Who...? Oh, Mrs. Tennes, and Mrs. Sexauer, and...oh, Mrs. Reynolds. There for Mama? No, just love a wedding. Everybody loves a bride.* Mae offered a trembling smile. They beamed.

Everyone else clustered in the first two rows: Mama and Sophie, Mr. and Mrs. O'Toole. *Oh, Michael, I need you.* Nora pivoted at the railing. Mae stepped past Tommy's family: the sisters, a brother, his dad's arm tight around his mother's shoulders. She's sobbing. *Don't look, don't look, eyes forward. God, help me. Focus on the priest.* Father Langan peering through Coke-bottle glasses, the black rims too heavy for his shrunken face. Absolutely ancient but still, beckoning, nodding kindly.

Tommy. His curls looked bright blond against his black suit. *New suit.* So still, taking Mae in, his unwavering gaze pulling her toward him like a tractor beam. Nick's arm, Tommy's eyes: Mae was propelled the last few steps, couldn't feel her feet, just the vibrations of the organ reverberating in her bouquet. Uncle Nick lifting the veil, kissing her cheek, guiding her hand into Tommy's. No more steps. Mae looked up at Tommy, confused. Were they where they were supposed to be? He pulled her in closer, a strong grasp, but he looked away to Father Langan.

Father's words spilled past her, bouncing off the gray stone floor. His monotone was steady, the words older than he, and the prayers settled under the pews, in cracks and corners, and slowly filled the chapel like a dusting of snow. The sacred space felt smaller, cleaner, and Mae fixed her eyes on an altar candle, watching it flick bravely. *Slight little dancing flame, glowing. For them.*

"I do." *Tommy!* Mae gasped.

"And do you, Mary Therese, take Joseph to be your lawful wedded husband? Do you promise to love and obey him, forsake all others unto him, in good times and in bad, in sickness and in health, until death do you part?"

"I do." Mae blinked in surprise: the words were past her lips before she could even think, even control the inflection of her voice. But the words were clear, the voice was hers, propelled by a breath she never felt.

"Then repeat after me," Father intoned to Tommy. "With this ring, I thee wed."

"With this ring"—Tommy wiggled the band up Mae's finger—"I thee wed." He looked closely into her eyes and, for the first time, smiled. *Oh.*

"And, Mary," Father repeated. "With this ring"—Nora handed her Tommy's band—"I thee wed."

"With." Mae fumbled, pushing it awkwardly to his first knuckle. "With this ring I thee wed." She slipped it into place and looked up at Tommy, appreciating his smile but not having one to return.

Father Langan etched the sign of the cross in the air between them. "Then, by the power vested in me, I now pronounce you man and wife." With a slight bow toward Tommy, he added, "You may kiss the bride."

With one finger, Tommy tipped Mae's face up toward him and touched his lips to hers. *Oh.* Mae just could not kiss him back, but when he straightened again and opened his eyes, she found a smile for him. He squeezed her hand. *Maybe he understood.*

Chapter Twelve

Not Yet

September 1979

Just another minute or two. Mae glanced again at her watch, tapping her foot to mark the seconds, swatting at a pesky bee. Stupid bees, so aggressive this time of year. She'd read somewhere that they reacted to the shorter days and the cooler nights, and especially to the dwindling flowers: knew what was coming, sort of. She absently waved off another bee and then hesitated as another mother, closer to the school steps, waved back. *Shit, I didn't mean you.* But she smiled back. *Be polite; it's just for another minute.* Mae brushed her bangs back toward her ears as she strolled up.

"Hi," the other mom began.

"Hi." Perfunctory chatting time. "Who are you waiting for?" *Pretend to be interested.*

"My son, Robbie, third grade. You?"

"Kristy, in second. Mrs. Campbell's class."

"Oh, she's great, super energetic! We had her last year. You'll like her."

The afternoon bell rang, and seconds later the heavy aluminum doors swung open, spitting out a swarm of banging elbows and book bags and voices shrill with the pent-up energy of the last hour of school. Boys and girls tumbled past, most threading their way to a particular bus in the long yellow line humming at the curb. Older kids brushed past them, automatically dropping their voices near adults, sharing sly glances. Robbie's mom tried to continue. "By the way, I'm Mitzi, Mitzi Williams."

"Mary. Oh, there's mine!" Mae held out her hand toward Kristy. "Nice to meet you," she called over her shoulder, weaving her way toward the bottom step.

Her beautiful girl, skipping up, starting to look like a colt—*when did those legs get so long?* Kristy got some height and streaky blond hair from her dad, but it was all Panos in her face: freckled like Mae, and the same eyes, same almond shape, now hazel, somewhere between brown, blue-gray, even a wash of green in the right light. Changed like the waves of Lake Michigan, depending on the light and the force of the wind.

"Hi, Mom." Kristy sparkled as Mae laced their fingers together.

"C'mon, peanut, let's go," she directed in her best Mom voice.

"Okeydoke," Kristy agreed, swinging her mom's arm with her skip.

"So good day?

"Mm-hmm."

"Hey, Kristy!"

Kristy spun around: Annie was hanging out of the number-two bus window, almost out to her waist. "Remember to bring the Chinese jump rope tomorrow!"

Kristy waved. "I know! I will!" she called over the revving bus engines. Bus number two lurched forward, and Annie had to grab tight, shrieking and laughing as another girl tugged her back in. Mae tried to continue, but Kristy resisted her pull.

"Mom?"

"What?" Mae knew.

"Maybe Friday? Could I take the bus home Friday?"

"Maybe. We'll see."

"Oh, Mom! That means 'no'!"

"No, that means 'let's see how the week goes.'" Mae started forward again, and Kristy followed, minus the skip. "Anyway, you'd have to spend almost a half hour on the bus, when I can walk you home in ten minutes."

"But it's fun on the bus. I'm like the only one in second grade not on it. Laura's on it; Nattie's on it; Trish and Sue and Roseann and Frannie..."

"I get it, I get it! It's just—watch the curb—Kristy, honey, you don't know how lucky you are that I take you to and from school. A lot of those kids, their moms can't because of little brothers and sisters at home, or some of their moms work."

Kristy nodded. "I know, I know" signaled that she knew this conversation by heart. She stopped, squinting up at her mother. "It's just..." Her scrunched-up, earnest expression made Mae stoop down to listen.

"What?"

"Next year, you know, I'll look like a real baby."

Oh. "Kinda dorky, walking with your mom?"

Kristy nodded.

"Hmm, right." Mae mulled over this new complaint. "So guess by next year, we'd better get you on the bus, at least most days, huh?"

Kristy brightened. "Really?"

"Yeah, but here's the deal: you're still my baby, just won't show it 'round school, okay?"

Kristy nodded. "Promise. Girl Scout honor." She raised her right hand, three fingers up.

"You're not a Girl Scout."

Kristy grinned, her Michael grin. "Not yet!"

Mae groaned. "Lord, help me!" Mae pointed her daughter toward home. "You, young lady, are pushing it! Now walk!"

"Left, right, left, right..." Kristy swung on her arm, tugging and skipping in her own erratic, exuberant way.

"Slower! I want to hear about your day!"

Kristy slowed but stayed very bouncy. "Like what?"

"Good day?"

"I guess." Kristy sidestepped the fire hydrant, gliding around it like a swallow. "Oh! Guess what! Mrs. D.'s having a baby!"

"Who?"

"Mrs. Douglass, my music teacher. Told the whole class today."

"Ah, exciting. Watch: curb."

Kristy bounded the curb and tugged forward. "I'm hungry."

"We're almost back. You can have a snack but just a little one—we'll eat early. Any homework?"

"Nope."

"Okay, then cartoons for a bit, but you set the table by five."

"Daddy gonna be home by then?"

"No, just set for the two of us: he's late again with work, so we'll go ahead and eat."

Kristy's stride lost a little spring. "Can't we wait for him?"

"Nope, don't know how late he'll be." Kristy stopped swinging her arm. "Look," Mae added, "you'll probably get to see him before bed."

"So I can stay up?"

Mae steered Kristy up the front walk of their brownstone. "We'll see."

Kristy sighed as she plopped up the crooked concrete steps. A city bus lumbered up to the corner, whining to a stop. Kristy waited while Mae unlocked the mailbox: Thomasini #2, just to the right of Beihl #1.

Mae flipped through the bills, snapped the brass box back closed, and fumbled for the security-door key. Yanking the heavy door wide, she shooed Kristy up the short flight to their front door and offered a key to Kristy, watching Kristy successfully jiggle the sticky deadbolt and twist the tarnished doorknob. "Good job, peanut."

"Thanks," Kristy responded, automatically tucking her book bag and shoes into the front hallway closet.

"Wash up!"

"I know! But I *am* hungry..."

"Right. Milk and cookies, or peanut butter and apples?"

"Anything else?" Kristy called back.

"Well, juice and crackers. Want peanut butter crackers?"

"Yeah."

The chair grated against the linoleum floor as Kristy climbed up, wiggling fingers as Mae placed grape juice and a plate of peanut butter crackers on the plaid placemat. Kristy launched into the crackers; Mae watched, amused. "Really were hungry, huh?"

Kristy shrugged. "Told ya," she mumbled through cracker crumbs.

"God, you on another growth spurt?"

"Dunno. Can I have more?"

"That's 'May I have more?' and yes, you may, but only a few. Dinner at five thirty."

"Can't we just wait for Dad?"

"No. Supper and bath, and then you can hang out with him if he's home before bedtime." She set a few more crackers on the plate.

"Mom," Kristy fretted, "nobody goes to bed at seven thirty. Even Eunie—and her mom is psycho—even Eunie stays up till eight."

"Yeah, well, your psycho mom says seven thirty 'cause I want you healthy and strong, and if you're on a growth spurt, you need the sleep."

Kristy grew quiet, inscrutable. Her eyes narrowed. "Gonna be taller than you, you know."

"No doubt," Mae allowed, frowning at her daughter's tone. "Why, is it a contest?"

"Maybe," Kristy arched one eyebrow and stuffed another cracker in her mouth.

"Well, think I'm safe for another year or two. Finish up, then you can watch, what, *Scooby-Doo*?"

"Yeah." Kristy stacked her cup and plate in the sink, and then padded off to the living room. Mae heard the click of the T.V. She stood there, arms folded, unsure what to do next.

♦ ♦ ♦

The deadbolt clicked. "Home!" Tommy announced.

"Shh!" Mae gestured from the couch as Tommy glanced about.

He made a face: "Kristy in bed already?"

Mae nodded. "It's almost eight."

"Hi, Daddy!" Kristy called from her room.

"Jeez, you woke her!"

"Nope!" Kristy's voice sifted through the crack below her bedroom door. "I'm not sleepy yet! Can I come out?"

"No!" Mae quickly retorted, pointing at Tommy to agree.

"No," he echoed, "but I'll come tuck ya in."

Mae rolled her eyes. "Don't get her more awake."

"I know. Just a good-night kiss. Back in a sec." He opened the bedroom door just enough to peek his head in. "You in here? Where are you? Can't see!"

"Right here, Daddy!" He mostly closed the door behind him.

Mae heard the creak of the mattress. "Stay in bed!" she ordered.

"She is," Tommy called back. "Man, there's barely any room for me to sit on the edge anymore. You're *enormous*!" he exclaimed, and Kristy squealed.

Their chatter grew quiet, but he stayed in there awhile. Mae flipped off the TV, brushed a little dust off the glass table, and arranged the magazines and TV guide into neat stacks, with the candle positioned between them. She glanced around: pretty tidy. The chairs were parallel, the pillows plumped; the figurines on the mantle were symmetrical; the beige carpet had fresh vacuum tracks; the kitchen all cleaned up from dinner. She perched on the arm of the couch, listening to the hum of the voices in the other room while she picked at flecks of lint. When he still didn't come out, she reached in the drawer of the end table and pulled out matches and the joint in the back. She lit the sandalwood candle and then the joint off the same match and settled into the sofa, enjoying the commingled scents, the bittersweet smoke.

Tommy pulled Kristy's door closed behind him. "Jeez, Mae," he whispered. "C'mon!"

"Ready for dinner?"

"She's not even asleep yet."

"She's not getting out of bed. Relax. Want some?" She offered a toke.

"No, and I wish you wouldn't, at least not when she's home."

Mae shrugged. "I lit the candle first: she only smells that. Just my dessert."

Tommy loosened his tie. "So you ate already?"

"Yeah, but there's a warm plate for you in the oven." She started to sit up, but he gestured for her to stay.

"Never mind. I'll get it." He headed into the kitchen as she took a deep drag. She licked her fingers and pinched off the rest, laying it gently on the table top as he returned with a napkin, plate, and fork.

"There, put it out already, okay?" She pointed.

"Fine." Tommy started on his mashed potatoes. "So how was your day?"

"Good, I guess. You?"

"All right, 'though didn't expect to be this late. Thought seven at the latest, but Bob needed me, and I'm sure I'm on the short list for a manager position, so I stayed."

"Good."

"I'll try to get home a bit earlier tomorrow. Then maybe we can eat together."

Mae grimaced. "I dunno."

"Why? How early? Six thirty?"

"Five thirty."

"Aw, come on, no way I can make that. How 'bout six thirty?"

Mae tucked the joint in the very back of the drawer. "Hate to mess with the routine. Routines are good for kids."

"Look, if I get one of these manager positions that're coming up, I can be home close to six most days, so we can have six thirty as a new routine."

"We'll see." Mae slumped back into the sofa, closing her eyes. She felt a little spaced out but could hear Tommy chewing. *Annoying.* She tried to listen for other sounds: a bus, anything. Finally, the chewing stopped. She heard the plate rest on the table with a quiet clack.

"You know...?" he ventured.

Do not like the tone of his voice. She opened her eyes.

"I was talking with Bob, and sounds like if I get the promotion, it'd probably be at the other store, further west on Touhy Avenue, you know, by Park Ridge."

"Well, that'll be a longer commute. No way you'd be home six thirty."

"Right. Or"—Tommy leaned forward—"we could move that direction."

Mae stiffened.

"We've been saving. Plus, I'll have a raise, so we could afford a nicer apartment."

"I keep this nice!"

"Yes, you do, but that doesn't fix the neighborhood. Mae, you wouldn't have to hover over her so much."

"I don't mind."

"I know, but she's getting older, and she's gonna want to run around with her friends. You wouldn't be much further from your mom, and it's not like we got lots of friends 'round here we'd be leaving."

"I'm friendly with Mrs. Beihl."

Tommy sighed. "Come off it, Mae, one eighty-five-year-old neighbor doesn't count. You know you haven't tried to make friends here."

"Mrs. Beihl," Mae reiterated.

Tommy looked skeptical. "Grandma Nazi?"

Mae grinned despite herself. She swatted at him. "Don't call her that."

"Fine. You made friends with a Holocaust apologist. I stand corrected. We'll invite her for pork roast and sauerkraut once a month, okay?"

"Stop!" Mae laughed, trying to wipe the smile off her face. "She's a nice neighbor, and she's, she's all alone. She needs a neighbor. So maybe she minimizes what the Nazis did..."

"Minimizes? I bet her son's middle name is Adolph," Tommy deadpanned.

"Stop!" Mae protested but hoping he wouldn't: felt good to goof around together.

Tommy gave a Nazi salute. "Heil Beihl!"

Mae rolled on the sofa, giggling. "Stop," she whimpered.

He slouched back, grinning, surveying the damage. "You're such a mess, lightweight."

"Stiff."

"Yeah, yeah." Tommy's expression grew more thoughtful. "But back to my original point. What do ya think?"

In a flash, the spark was gone. "I think you shouldn't be making plans without me." Even Mae was surprised by the razor edge in her voice.

"I'm not making plans without you. What are we doing right now?"

"You've obviously thought about this a lot already."

"Could be a good idea. Michael thinks so too."

"Wait, you discussed it with Michael before me?"

"No, not like that!" Tommy backpedaled. "Just came up: I mean, he's a realtor, so he knows about the schools and property values."

"Do *not* go behind my back, especially with my own brother. *My* brother, not yours."

"Didn't go behind your back, and he didn't mind me asking." Tommy sounded grim.

"I mind!" Mae shot back.

"You're gonna wake up Kristy," Tommy warned.

"Tough!" Mae growled.

Tommy looked down, then leveled a stony gaze at Mae. "You're, hell, no point discussing this now." He stood up.

"Oh please," Mae baited. "I can't have an opinion because I smoke a little?"

"A little?"

"I have it totally under control, you know it. Didn't I quit while I was pregnant?"

"Eight years ago, a real saint. Where're you getting it anyway?"

"Oh, you know, I put out for it at the Howard Street bus station."

Tommy shook his head. "Nice, Mae, class act."

"Not nice enough? Guess I fit the neighborhood." She whipped the matchbook at him.

"You said it, not me. Going to bed."

"Yeah, do that," Mae called after him, punching the sofa pillow.

♦ ♦ ♦

Mrs. Beihl carefully split the can of Mountain Dew between two glasses brimming with ice. The tremor in her hand made the soda dance as it splashed over the cubes. Using both hands to serve Mae, she smoothed the lace placemats before bringing her own glass over. Mrs. Beihl gestured toward the Hydrox cookies arranged on a small china plate: "Have one."

Mae gestured for her hostess to sit. Mrs. Beihl stiffly lowered herself onto the chair, shifting her broad hips to the center of the seat and brushing back yellow-gray wisps across her visible scalp. Mae offered her a cookie.

"Yes," Mrs. Beihl agreed, transferring two to her own plate. "But the real treat, das is the Mountain Dew. Thank you for bringing from the store. Heavy bottles for me. You keep bringing me my treat!" She savored a long sip and smiled, deep wrinkles radiating like sunrays from the corners of her sunken eyes. "Ah. So little Kristy likes her new teacher?'

"Yes, likes school."

"Important. Smart little girl, yes?"

"I think so." Mae bit into her cookie. "But really, not just me, her teachers say so, and her grades are all A's and B's."

Mrs. Beihl's head bobbed up and down. "Gutt. Her opportunities, they will come from a gutt education. And, of course, her family. She has a mama to look after her, and a poppa who works hard, I think. Hmm?" Her eyes were sharp as she focused on Mae.

Mae shrugged. "Sure, he works hard. He's up for promotion."

Mrs. Beihl bobbled more approval. "Is gutt he's ambitious. Money helps."

Mae sighed, sipping on her Mountain Dew. "Sure, we could use more money, who couldn't? But he works such long hours, might as well be divorced."

"No!" the old lady scolded. "Not gutt for Kristy, not for you! You are lucky to have a hardworking husband. I did too. He was my teacher: taught me to read, and my numbers. Said I was his best student, and he only taught me when I was not working the fields, just for I was smart. Paid with a loaf of my mama's bread, when she could make extra. Was all he wanted. Well," she allowed, her smile crinkling out to her ears, "except later he wanted me. But proper, to marry, and I say yes and Poppa say yes." Mrs. Beihl traced the edge of the pine table with the tips of her dry fingers, gone for a moment. "But," she snapped back, "he worked hard, me too, so later we can pay, eh..." she frowned. "Bribes, for visas, to come here. Took a long time," she pronounced, "but we did it." Her icy blue eyes penetrated: "Maybe you are bored? Not enough work for you?"

Mae leaned back in her chair. "No, I'm busy enough. I'm sewing a new bedspread for Kristy, with white eyelet ruffles on the side, wide ones." She showed the span with her hands. "Then I'll make matching curtains, after a Halloween costume."

"You like to sew?"

Mae nodded as she sipped.

"Your mama, she teach you?"

"I guess. Picked up the basics from her."

"Me, only sew enough to mend. I mostly worked in fields, you know, and big gardens. Everyone had gardens. You see my pots?" Mrs. Beihl popped up, waddling toward the back door.

Mae had seen them many times but obediently followed. "How are your plants doing?" In back, four clay pots perched in equal intervals along the edge of the freshly swept porch floor. The tomato and pepper plants, sagging with fruit, were staked to old bamboo. The bean plant, snug in the corner, had several loops of string guiding its tendrils up around the railing. The concord grapes draped heavily over a short trellis stabbed into the dark potting soil. Bands of sunlight, defined by the wooden slats of the railing, created a decorative overlay across the leaves, the dirt, the clay brims. Like the shadowy stripes embedded in a quilt, Mae noted, appreciating the symmetry of light and shade.

"Best garden in the neighborhood," Mae offered, patting the curve of her neighbor's back.

"Maybe you should have pots next summer. I help you start them."

"Maybe."

"Here, two tomatoes for your dinner." Mrs. Beihl bent over cautiously.

"Oh no, you keep them."

"Every week, you carry heavy cans and bottles from store to me. Take a tomato!"

"Okay, okay, one for dinner tonight. Thank you."

"Come." Mrs. Beihl waved her back inside. "More Mountain Dew. We can share."

"Oh no!" Mae protested more forcefully. "I'll have a sugar buzz for days. I don't know how you can drink it with cookies. Don't you ever have milk instead?"

Mrs. Beihl shrugged as she flipped the top on another can, measuring more into each glass. "No, never liked milk. The taste, the, the texture. I never had it until I was five, maybe six years old, could barely swallow it, tasted so strange. Mama made me drink it whenever we have some, but lucky, we did not have often, just if Mama could bake for a lady in town, then she'd pay Mama with milk, maybe a little meat for stew, or a good soup bone sometimes." Mrs. Beihl wrinkled her nose. "Never liked it."

"But as a baby?"

"Mamas nursed their babies, but not long, they needed to work the crops. So the older babies had weak broth, you know, from cooked roots, or bones, and tea, weak tea. Bitter drinks, thin, so the milk seemed..." She waved her hands, trying to snatch at a word. "Too, you know..." She gave up. "Thick. Strange."

"Huh." Mae tried to imagine a child preferring bitter broth over sweet milk.

They nodded their heads and sipped the Mountain Dew. Mae glanced at her watch. "I should get going. Need to pick up Kristy at school."

"I see you walk with her, keep her safe. When I was a girl, I learned to hide whenever the soldiers came by. My poppa taught me to run into the cellar. Those soldiers, they sometimes took young girls from their families, even little girls if they were pretty..." Mrs. Beihl looked far past Mae, far past the safety of her kitchen table. "Take girls and ruin them, they could never come home, no one would marry them. And once they shot my dog for no reason, just laughed. I heard the yelp, but Mama stood on the cellar door, wouldn't let me out. By the time the soldiers left, he was already dead." Her eyes pinched, almost disappearing into the deep folds. "I wanted to kill those soldiers." Her gaze returned to Mae. "Cruel, bad men."

Mae wriggled. "I'm sorry. So those were the Nazi soldiers?"

"No!" Mrs. Beihl exclaimed, grabbing onto Mae's arm. "Those were the police! It was the Nazis who were strong enough to stop them."

"Oh, I see." Mae patted the old lady's hand, hoping to loosen the bony grip. "The Nazis made it better for you." Mrs. Beihl's hand relaxed.

"Yes, better, see?" Mrs. Beihl asked plaintively.

"Well sure, you needed help."

"Yes, they helped us. Our lives got much better. Not so hungry, not so scared."

"Well sure," Mae repeated, debating if she could make another move to leave just yet. "I mean, those were tough times."

"So hard." Mrs. Beihl looked at Mae expectantly. When Mae simply returned her gaze, Mrs. Beihl nodded, gathering up the remaining cookies in a fresh napkin. "You go, but take these."

"No." Mae waved her hands in protest. "You keep them. I have the tomato."

"Yes." Mrs. Beihl pressed them into Mae's palms. "You take these upstairs before you go get little Kristy. A treat from me, you tell her."

"All right, thanks. I'll run them upstairs now, so I can be there on time."

"Gutt, and next time, you bring Kristy too, yes?"

"Sure," Mae lied. "Next time."

The old lady hobbled to the door. "Manage all right?"

"Yes! Thanks for the goodies." Mae scurried up the stairs. "Talk to you soon."

"You are a nice neighbor." Mrs. Beihl stayed in her doorway, waving, as Mae fished for her key at the top of the landing.

"Bye!" Mae called down as her door clicked open.

"Bye!" Mrs. Beihl called up. Both doors closed with the same thud.

Chapter Thirteen

Ready or Not

October 1979

"The bartender's now on duty!" Michael announced. "Your pleasure, madam?" He bowed low to match Kristy's eye level.

"Let's see..." Kristy puzzled. "How is the Coke this evening?"

"Ah, the barkeeper's specialty: cherry and orange slice, or two cherries?"

"Two cherries, please."

"But of course! And for your lovely companion?" He turned to Mae as he straightened.

"Any wine opened?"

"Red?"

"Red, sure."

"Be right back." As he turned sharply on his heel, Mae flinched. She hated any reminders of his military days.

Tommy moved to join him. "I'll pour ours. Jack Daniels?"

"Yep, not too many rocks."

"Got it. Oh, what about Ellie?"

"Ma!" Michael hollered in the direction of the kitchen. "Wine?"

"Surely!" she called back. "Be out in a minute, getting the dumplings started." Ellie emerged a moment later, wiping her hands down her apron. "Twenty minutes till supper's ready." She accepted a glass of wine from Tommy. "Thanks, sweetheart." She surveyed her brood, smiling. "Everybody got what they need?"

"I'd like an extra grand in the bank, but otherwise I'm good," Michael panned.

Ellie countered, "Well, I have a twenty in my purse."

Michael shook his head. "Nah, twenty just won't cover it. Maybe I should sell Miss Kristy. She'd fetch a pretty penny." He wiggled claws at her.

"Daddy!" Kristy shrieked, ducking behind her father. She clutched his knees from behind.

"Whoa!" Tommy's drink sloshed. "Don't worry: I can take out Uncle Michael if I have to."

"Sure of that, are we?" Michael struck a warrior pose, while Kristy muffled giggles in her father's pant leg.

Mae observed their play with a too-familiar uneasiness. Felt unreal, or maybe not to them, but she felt on the fringes of it all. Like a family but not *her* family. *A TV family.* She drained her glass of wine.

"Thirsty!" she called out, waving her glass in Michael's direction.

"I'll get it," Tommy offered, gesturing to Kristy to release her grasp. Kristy shook her head, pig tails dancing, so Tommy started toward the kitchen counter, dragging her like an anchor on his right leg.

"Kristy!" Mae barked. Kristy immediately let go. Mae softened her tone. "Don't make Daddy spill on Grandma's carpet, okay? Not the time to be silly."

Michael pulled Kristy up. "Don't listen to her," he stage-whispered. "It's the perfect time to be silly."

Mae watched them exchange an intimate, sly wink. *Grown-up Michael winking at the female version of eight-year-old Michael. Took her breath away.* "I give up!" Mae relented, letting Tommy fill her glass. "Be silly. Just don't spill."

"Okay, Mom!" Michael mocked her. Mae stuck her tongue out at him. At least now she was part of it.

"Look at your mother," Mama observed to Kristy. "Sure she's a grown-up?"

"She just pretends." Kristy stuck her tongue out in return.

Enough. Mae took a long sip. "Twenty minutes still, right? I'm going to get a little air." Mae brushed past them toward the back door. Her cheeks felt warm. *Just the wine.*

♦ ♦ ♦

Mae rested her forearms on the porch railing, exhaling slowly, savoring the bitter smoke, hoping some trace would cling to her tongue and teeth when she had to return inside. The sun was dropping almost to the skyline. Soon the light would dim, and without it the October air would turn chilly. Right now it was perfect, barely cool against her cheekbones and the tip of her nose, as if she'd just washed her face. *Should go join the others, help put the salad on the table.* Mae took one more drag, not too deep, to save the little she had. Smoky warm inside, a hint of a breeze ruffled her hair, the air tracing the curves of her ears. *Almost perfect.*

The screen-door hinges whined, and the door slapped sharply against its frame. Mae deftly covered the joint with her free hand as she glanced back. Michael. "Hey." She smiled.

"Hey there." He leaned on the railing next to her, sniffing the air appreciatively. "Smog?"

"Want some?"

"Nah." He lifted up, bracing just his hands on the wood, focused on the sunset.

"You sure?"

"No, reminds me of 'Nam. Got whiskey inside."

Mae shrugged, took one last toke, and put it out with licked fingers. "Sorry if the smell bothers you." She waved one hand back and forth broadly, trying to clear the air around them.

"No big deal, just not that appealing. Huh. Look at those colors." The clouds were starting to reflect the sunset with ribbons of tangerine and violet.

"Pretty," Mae concurred, staring off for a moment. Then, pinching the joint to make sure it was out, she slipped it in her pants pocket.

Michael nudged her lightly with his elbow. "At Mom's?" he goaded.

"She's not coming out here. I hear her fussing around the table."

"Yeah, should get back in, I guess."

Mae sighed. "Suppose so."

"You okay?" Michael quizzed.

"Oh, sure." She tried to flash a bright smile straight at him, but he was too close, and the smile twisted on itself. Mae looked up at the clouds. "Brighter oranges: look!"

"You seem uptight," Michael insisted.

"Nah, fine. I just, you know, I got a nice routine going for Kristy, school and all, and Tommy wants to change things."

"And?" Michael was looking at her, but she kept her eyes on the clouds.

"And it's too much. I mean, the promotion is great, good for him, but I think we should keep everything else the same for now."

"'Good for him?'" Michael leaned in front of her to catch her eye. "Isn't it good for all of you?" Mae double-blinked: his face was too close.

"Of course," she capitulated, turning to face him. "But it's my job to take care of Kristy, and moving, changing schools and all..." She shook her head. "Too stressful."

"For you?"

"No, for her! I'm taking care of her!"

"Tommy's trying to, too."

Mae pushed her brother back. "You're on his side? Thanks."

"'His side'? Jeez, Mae, you stuck in seventh grade?"

"Hardly. I'm being a mom."

"Right, I get that. But how 'bout what's best for your whole family? Mae, Tommy's got the right idea. Huge step for you guys if you snatch one of those starter homes. Huge. And, yeah, Kristy'd change schools but into a great school district. Kids everywhere on those blocks. She'd settle in, no time at all." He was scrutinizing her. She leaned further away.

"Look," her voice softened. "I get it, I do. Just want her to be happy, you know?"

Michael nodded, and Mae relaxed back onto the railing. Mae rested her hand on his arm, taking in the streaky skyline. Now reds were in the mix: poppy red and blood red.

"Mae?"

"Hmm?"

"I want you to remember something—no, two things." His tone was kind, but Mae shrank back anyway, dropping her head. *Here we go.*

"One, Kristy's already a happy kid. You're a good mom. She's a good kid, a happy kid."

Hot tears surged up. "I, I hope so. I really am trying."

"It shows. She's fine. You worry too much."

Two tears splattered on the wood as Mae nodded. "So what's two?" she whispered, her voice clutching.

"Two: you got a good husband. Bend a little, Mae, meet him halfway. Last time I checked, he was on the same side as you."

"I know."

"Do you, really? 'Cause here's three: Kristy's crazy about her dad, and that doesn't take away from you."

"I know that!" Mae protested.

Michael just looked at her, wordless, inscrutable.

"I know that!" she repeated, irritated. *Hard to read him now. Didn't like this kind of quiet.* "Is there a four?" she offered, trying for a baiting tone.

He shook his head, lifting one eyebrow. "Nah, three's your limit. Four 'n' your head would probably explode."

The old grin. Thanks, Michael.

He straightened his belt buckle. "Inside?"

Mae stretched. "Sure. I should be helping."

"Yes, you should, and I should be drinking."

"Fix one for me?"

"Well, I guess one with dinner but with plenty of ice, lightweight."

"Not a lightweight."

Inscrutable. "Time will tell."

"Mae, Michael!" Mama's voice trailed out.

"Coming!" Michael called back, holding the door open. Mae swept past with a royal nod, and he let the door clap closed behind them.

♦ ♦ ♦

"Can we go home now?" Kristy slumped in the back seat.

"Yes, time to get back. It's a school night," Mae seconded.

"C'mon, guys, it's not late. Just one more stop." Tommy took an extra sharp turn to topple Kristy over in her seat. She squealed her approval even as Mae poked him.

"Cut that out!" Mae demanded.

"No, again!" Kristy yelled.

"Gotta admit, that perked her up!" Still, Tommy caught Kristy's eye in the rearview mirror. "Ever heard of a seat belt? Buckle up 'n' I just might try it again."

"Okay, okay," she acquiesced, groping in the crack of the seat for the straps.

"Bad example," Mae persisted.

"Lighten up, would ya? We're celebrating."

Mae sighed. "Yes, nice dinner, nice to see the new store, and now we should get home. Kristy's bedtime."

"I need to show you guys one more thing." Tommy executed a very slow, smooth turn. "Better?"

"Sure." Mae frowned, scanning the block. "Where are we going, anyway?" She didn't recognize these side streets.

Tommy didn't answer. He eased up to the curb and turned off the engine. Mae's eyes swept across the tidy rows of bungalows and small Cape Cods lining the street. In a flash, the hairs stood up on the back of her neck. Turning, she peered at Tommy, but he didn't return her gaze. "What have you done?" she demanded in a low, grim voice.

"What's happening?" Kristy ventured, studying her parents' faces.

Tommy turned his head slightly but continued to look past Mae as he responded to Kristy. "See that house over there, pumpkin? With the two-oh-three on the column? Well, guess what? It's ours," Tommy announced.

Kristy shrieked a delighted, "No kidding! Cool!" Tugging the seat belt off, she scrambled out the back door as Mae stared at Tommy in disbelief.

"Whoa!" Tommy called after Kristy. "Hang on, get back here. It's not ours yet. Not for another month."

"Can I stand here and look?" Kristy sang out from the curb.

"Yeah, but stay put."

"Okeydoke." Kristy jumped up and down, fingers wiggling in spastic delight.

Mae could hardly blink. "You bought it?" she choked out.

"They accepted our offer today. Michael's confident it'll close by the end of the month."

Our offer? Your offer. Mae just stared.

"Michael says we got it at a great price, that we'll get a great return on it."

Mae remained silent.

Tommy sighed, turning to face her. "Look, you're probably mad, but I had to move on it, Mae. Be fair: how many times have I tried to broach this with you, and you shoot it down for no good reason?"

"Take me home now." Mae almost strangled on the words. Couldn't even look at him. *Hate him, just hate him.*

"No, Mae, look at this neighborhood. Everyone keeps up their yards. Mature trees. And I want you to see the school, just two blocks. Kristy can walk. Tons of other kids here."

Mae rolled down her window. "Kristy, come back. Time to go home."

"Aw, already?"

"Now, young lady!"

"Mae," Tommy muttered, "you're mad at me. Don't yell at her."

Don't even...

Kristy yanked the back door open and crawled in.

Tommy started the engine but let the car idle. He looked soberly at Mae, then twisted around to look at Kristy. "Wanna see the school? Just around the corner. Take two minutes." He shifted into drive and pulled forward. Mae glared at him, speechless, as he continued to explain to Kristy, "See, turn at this corner...there, see it? When the weather's nice, you can walk to school, and I'll walk to work, and Mom can have the car."

"Cool!" Kristy crooned. "Can I go on the playground? Just five minutes?"

"Sure, scoot." Tommy parked, and she clambered out, running toward the swings.

"You can have the car," he reiterated quietly, rubbing his hands on his thighs.

"For what?" she snarled.

Tommy pounded the steering wheel. "For whatever you want, dammit! Errands, carpools, to visit your mom, visit Nora for a change. How many times have you brushed off Nora when she tries to meet up? Anything, Mae. I don't care!"

Mae shrank down at his raised voice. *Hold your ground, hold your ground.* "Obviously you don't care, since you did this all without me."

"Mae!" he shot back, shaking his hands at her as if struggling not to slap her. "Jesus!" He covered his face with his hands and took a slow, sober breath, turning sideways in the seat to face her, pale and discouraged. "Mae, I try to talk to you, but all you do is tune out. So you tell me. You give me one rational reason against this move and I'll pull out. Screw the earnest money."

It hurt to look at his face, pulled tight, eyes flat with exhaustion. Mae closed her eyes. *What about me? Me?* She turned her face away. Her throat would barely let air through, much less words.

"Mae? Look at me."

Tears burned as she opened her eyes. She brushed them away with the back of her hand.

"Mae? Please talk to me."

"No point. You decided without me. Nothing to say," she wheezed. "What good would it do?"

"It would do us good as a family, and God knows we haven't been doing that great. But think, Mae: now we've got more money, more time together, a chance to make friends with other couples, finally act like a couple. That'd be good for us, Mae."

"No, good for you, and I'm sure you think it's good for Kristy, but don't suggest it's good for me. I already said what's good for me."

Tommy rested his forehead on the steering wheel. "Us, Mae. You and me."

Mae stared out the window, shaking her head. "It's done, nothing more to say," she pronounced, resolutely wiping the last of the tears. "Guess we're going to do what you want. But right now I want to go home." She rolled down her window. "Kristy! Back in!" Mae was silent as Kristy tumbled into the back seat.

Just looking at her parents' backs, Kristy froze. "What?"

Neither responded, and for a moment, suspended in a fog of uncertainty, they sat.

Then, Mae commanded, "Seat belt."

♦ ♦ ♦

"I'm hooked," Mae admitted. "I'm a Mountain Dew junkie."

Mrs. Beihl chuckled in agreement. "Gutt, no? I have one, sometimes two, every day. You pour, okay?" She pushed the can toward Mae, tracing a wobbly path across the tabletop. *Huh, her tremor's worse. Too bad. Don't stare.*

Mae popped the tab, easing it over the two glasses of ice, watching the fizz spray in random arcs. A sickly color, that bilious greenish-yellow, but the sugar and caffeine was a comfortable lift in the lull of the afternoon. *Oh, she's still shuffling around.* "Can I help you with something?"

"No, no, can do this much!" Mrs. Beihl turned slowly, both hands clenching a Corning ware plate mounded with sugar wafers. She stepped closer, concentrating on holding her treats steady. Mae had a momentary flash of Mrs. Beihl as a young girl, thin brown braids and sagging woolen stockings, helping serve supper. Mae smiled wistfully.

"Ah, a smile!" Mrs. Beihl set the plate down. "So pretty when you smile."

Mae dutifully pulled her smile broader and then let it drop: too much effort. "Sorry if I seem down lately. I guess packing has me bummed."

"Oh?" Mrs. Beihl dropped into her chair.

"Well, it's all happening so fast."

Mrs. Beihl nodded as she grasped a pink sugar wafer. She nudged the plate closer to Mae, who picked up a brown wafer. "This move worries you?"

Mae shoved her cookie in her mouth, using the crunching time to find the right words. "Not worried, exactly," she mumbled through the crumbs. "More bugged."

"Irritated?"

Mae shrugged as she picked up another chocolate wafer and snapped it in half. "Well, yes, because I, I like how we're situated now, but I feel kinda outvoted by everybody. My mother, my brother, my aunt and uncle, even Kristy thinks it's great, but she's too young to understand all the, you know, implications: new school, new neighborhood." Mae popped part of the cookie in, crunching nervously.

"Well," Mrs. Beihl pondered, "she's a confident girl. She'll make friends. And you"—she patted Mae's forearm with a palm scratchy with calluses—"such a nice neighbor, the way you check on the old lady below you. I will miss you, but you make friends with other mamas." She nodded emphatically as she squeezed Mae's arm.

"I'll miss you too," Mae sighed. "Who's going to get your groceries? Or drink your Mountain Dew?" She offered a feeble smile.

"Why, you!" Mrs. Beihl proclaimed. "You come when Kristy is in school. By end of next month, I start my Christmas baking, and I'll have rum balls, maybe even sugar stars started. I'm a gutt baker. Mama taught me."

"I remember," Mae agreed. "Tommy still wants me to learn to make your kuchen."

"There!" Mrs. Beihl tapped the table twice for emphasis. "We bake together if you like."

Mae nodded unenthusiastically.

"Or," the old lady added gently, "I make extra for you to take home."

Mae flinched in embarrassment. "No, lessons would be great. I just might not be your best student ever."

Mrs. Beihl shook her head, smiling. "I was not gutt cook at first. Mama only give me little jobs because sugar was too expensive for me to spoil a batch. Once I let all the molasses cookies burn... oh, she was so mad!" She gazed out the window. "And the fancy jam cookies, for to pay our doctor—his wife not a cook—Mama wouldn't let me touch those, not ever." She peered at Mae. "I'm glad to teach you. I have no one to give Mama's recipes to." Her face drooped slightly.

Oh no. "But what nice times you had with your mother, learning from her." *Not sad, please, not sad stories.*

Mrs. Beihl let her trembling hands jiggle the ice in her glass. *Too late, the old stories were inevitable now.* Mae settled into her chair, prepared to listen. She'd do that much for the old lady. Who would listen to her after they moved?

"Yes," Mrs. Beihl began haltingly, "yes, blessed with a fine Mama. Papa too. So brave but mit so little..." She clasped her hands, interlaced fingers so knobby and scarred that they looked like tangled roots. Mae dropped her own hands into her lap, suddenly embarrassed by her Daylily Pink nail polish. Mrs. Beihl, however, had already drifted past hands, past sugar wafers, past the scratched tabletop. "Yes," she repeated, "blessed with gutt parents in a bad time, a terrible time. Police, so brutal, just taking and taking, and if you resisted..." Her voice grew steadier with anger as she looked through her ragged fingernails. "Before, they would round up all the boys, bring them to the square, and say they can choose to enlist. They ask each boy, not their mama or papa, each boy one by one. Some say yes and go climb on the truck. Some say no, so they stand to the side.

Then"—she winced—"they take the, the baling wire, and wrap around all the boys who refuse, and make them step together, all bound together, to the edge of the river, and they shoot one in the head and push them all in, in the river." She covered her eyes with shivering hands. "Those boys, they slip under so fast, and mamas screaming and papas diving in, but no, no, cannot reach them, and those, those men, laughing, boasting that they do so much with one bullet..." Mrs. Beihl's head sunk deeper into her spreading fingers, her tremor extending down her forearms, her elbows rolling on the table. "Those boys, I knew those boys. They wanted to be mit their families, help feed their brothers and sisters." Her head bobbed up, her eyes round and bright with fury. She locked onto Mae. "Damn police, damn brutes."

Mae nodded, afraid she looked more uncomfortable than sympathetic.

"Damn police," Mrs. Beihl repeated. "When the Nazis came, they knocked them straight to hell, where they belonged. The Nazis didn't hurt us. Sure, they wanted the boys to join, but the boys wanted to, they had good education, been in youth groups, wanted to be part of Germany's recovery. You see? Not so bad as people think," Mrs. Beihl fretted. "They protected our families, gave us doctors, teachers. One winter, they brought warm coats for everyone, a mountain of coats in the back of a truck; everyone took one."

"Where did the coats come from?"

Silence. *Oh.*

"I don't know," Mrs. Beihl murmured. "All I know, they saved us. Not the monsters people think—no, our saviors." She blinked erratically, brushing one hand along Mae's arm, the other across the table, trying to pull herself back into her kitchen. "They saved us," she repeated gravely, reaching for Mae's hand.

Mae enclosed the gnarled hand in both of hers. *Some funky tangle of fingers.* Patting the hands smoother, Mae resolutely cleared her throat. "Those were hard times," she observed gravely. "Very hard. Complicated."

Mrs. Beihl's eyes softened, shiny with tears. "Complicated," she echoed. "Yes." The two women nodded, teary, trying to understand the pain, but words couldn't explain it enough, couldn't sort through it and settle it, so all they could do was silently bear it together. Be sorry together. That was the best they could do. That would have to be enough.

♦ ♦ ♦

More boxes coming in, two or three at a time. Mae the traffic cop. "To the bedroom with that one." She pointed Michael, who deliberately bumped her as he went by. Then, moving men. "Oh, those go in the kitchen. Careful! See, they're marked 'fragile.'"

They trudged away, one muttering to the other, "Almost every box is marked 'fragile'!" Mae shook her head. *Ignore them. Just get this over with.*

With no one on the doorstep, she took a moment to assess the living room. *Keep the sofa there, but those chairs…? And the dining room: maybe a dining set by Christmas. Hm.*

"Mom!" Kristy startled her. "Can I have the rocking chair in my room?"

"Huh?" Mae reoriented. "No, sweetie, not till I see how the rooms set up." Mae caught Kristy's downcast eyes. "Tell you what, maybe, okay? Ask again in a couple of days, once this stuff's unpacked." Mae tapped the tip of Kristy's nose; Kristy tugged at her hand.

"And remember," Kristy persisted, "you said my bedroom gets painted first!"

"Yes, before the month is out."

"Pink!"

Mae wrinkled her nose. "You sure? What, like seashell pink?"

"No! Hot pink, really, really hot!"

"Oh, honey, that's too much in a little room. Maybe hot-pink accents: you know, pink pillows with the white bedspread?"

"Mo-om," Kristy whined, dropping to her knees without letting go of Mae's hand. "You promised."

"Where do you want these?" Tommy held a lamp in each hand.

"Oh, lemme see. Pottery base, our bedroom, and the brass one in the living room."

"Mo-om!"

"What's wrong?" Tommy asked Kristy.

"Nothing," Mae answered for her, tugging Kristy to her feet. "Later, okay? Start to unpack the stuff in your room? That'd be a big help."

"Can I play outside?

"That's 'May I,' and no, honey, too hectic right now."

"What if she stays right in front? I'll keep an eye on her," Tommy offered.

"Okay then, but stay where Daddy can see you!"

"Promise!" Kristy scooted out the front door.

"And out of the way of the workmen!" Mae called, pretty sure Kristy was gone.

"I'll watch," Tommy promised, brushing past and through the door with a quick duck and weave to avoid another moving man with three small boxes on a bent dolly.

Mae gestured left. "Kitchen." He nodded and veered off.

"What's next?" Michael was at her right elbow. "Car's unloaded. I can do something for another hour, but then I gotta split. Got showings this afternoon."

Mae sighed. "What's next? I wish I knew...master bedroom!" she called out to the movers.

"You okay? We okay? I'm-okay-you're-okay?"

Mae shook her head, swatting him with the papers she held. "I should be so mad at you," she warned Michael. "But what's done is done, so gotta make the best of it."

"Now there's a life philosophy."

Mae shrugged. "What am I supposed to do? Kristy and Tommy are dancing around like it's Christmas. No point bringing them down. And this place?" She scanned the room. "Has possibilities, I guess."

"Yes, it does. 'Bout time you caught on, Maisie."

Maisie. Had to smile at that—hardly ever got called that anymore.

"Oh my God, she smiles! She still knows how to smile!"

"Shut up." Another swat. "Like I'm so scary."

"Nah, more like grim."

"Am not."

"Right, Little Mary Sunshine. So, Ms. Sunshine, gimme a job. Not so good at being decorative."

"Jeez, Michael, there's a ton to do. Gotta wash down the kitchen shelves with Pine Sol before I can unpack dishes."

"Well, they already look clean to me, but I can wipe them down for you. Unskilled labor's my specialty."

"Really? Would you mind?" Her voice lifted with relief.

"One good sport deserves another. I'll just—hey, Ma!" he yelled out toward the front stoop. "Sophie! Thought you guys were downtown."

The ladies wobbled in, swaying under the weight of bulging shopping bags in each hand. "Hi, sweethearts!" Ellie motioned kisses in their direction as she toddled toward the kitchen. "Sophie and I brought lunch." Her bags hit the kitchen counter with a soft thud.

Sophie detoured to kiss them properly. "Just lovely, Mae!" she exclaimed. Mae rolled her eyes, pointing to the jumble of boxes. "No matter!" Sophie insisted. "I can imagine when you're finished, you with your eye for decor."

"Sophie, bring the sandwiches in here," Ellie's voice floated around the corner from the kitchen. "We'll set up a little buffet, and people can eat when they want."

Sophie reached for her bags, but Michael intercepted them with a quiet, "Got 'em." He sniffed as he walked. "Ham salad?"

"Yes," Ellie answered from the doorway, twisting open a tall silver thermos. "And egg salad, chips, a thermos of coffee, and a few Cokes for those who want a cold drink. Ready for a Coke?"

"Gramma, Gramma!" Kristy burst in. "Didja see my room yet?" She pulled Ellie's hand. "Come see. Aunt Sophie, come with?"

"Your new room! You take Grandma upstairs, sweetheart, and I'll follow once I set up lunch for your mother. How's that?"

Mae couldn't resist peeking into the bag. "Gee, thank you. I was going to send Tom to McDonald's, but this is much nicer. Here, let me help."

Michael had already emptied one bag. "I got it. Love egg salad!" He tore open the Ruffles.

Sophie pulled out paper plates and napkins. "And nothing to wash at the end. It's a day to keep things simple."

Mae nodded and then pointed another mover upstairs. "Master bedroom, please," she called up the stairs, rubbing her brow. "Not much about this is simple," she confided to Sophie.

"I know, sweetheart, but it will seem worth it once you're settled in."

"I suppose," Mae allowed. "But I'm not moving again for another twenty years."

"Well, just get through this: no point worrying about the next move."

"Hey!" Mae scolded Michael. "Other people like egg salad, you know."

"There's enough for lunch and supper," Sophie assured her.

"Is Kristy in here?" Tommy strode up, glancing all around. "Hi, Sophie." He pecked her cheek.

"Upstairs with her grandma," Sophie responded.

"Keeping an eye on her?" Mae elbowed him.

"Sorry." He shrugged. "I started to assemble the jungle gym and—oh, what kind of sandwiches?"

Mae shook her head, groaning. Sophie took her hand. "Mae, you're so busy. Ellie and I want to take Kristy downtown, for the whole afternoon and dinner. Then you don't have to keep track of her, Tom can set up her bed, and I'd love to get her an outfit for her first day at the new school. Please?"

"Oh, that's nice, really, but it'll be such a long day..." Mae could hear the lethargy in her protest.

"No," Sophie insisted, "my driver's coming in thirty minutes, and we'll go door-to-door. Kristy will be entertained, and you'll have one less distraction. We'll bring her back just in time to tuck into bed. Please?"

Tommy joined them. "What?" he asked through egg salad on rye.

"They want to take Kristy for the afternoon."

"Great, we could get a lot done." Seeing Mae frown, he added hastily, "Okay with you?"

His addendum caught Mae like a slap. "*Now* you ask my opinion?" she growled with unmodulated hostility. Sophie froze like a rabbit. Tommy squeezed Mae's hand.

"Mae." His tone was a warning. *Careful in front of Sophie.*

I know, I know! She telegraphed right back, digging her nails into his fingers to loosen his grip. "Tell you what, Aunt Sophie: go tell Kristy, get her to eat a bite before you leave?" Mae's smile was polite and artificial, and the tense circles around Sophie's eyes and lips barely eased.

"Of course," Sophie responded. "I'll bring everyone down in a few minutes." She backed up two steps, glancing between them, and then turned toward the stairs.

Mae locked onto Tommy. *Wait*, his eyes signaled. *I know, I know*, she shot back. They both listened for the creak of the step at the top of the landing.

"Lady?" a mover quizzed. Mae pointed upstairs.

Tommy waited, then challenged, "Go on, say it."

"Don't you pretend you care about my opinion in front of my family. Don't you dare." She squeezed once more with her nails before she let go.

Tommy flinched a little and rubbed his hand. "Fine. I deserve that. What else?"

Angry static muddled the words in her head. "You—don't you—look, I'm making the best of this, but if, if you *ever* make a big decision about my life again, I'm outta here."

He studied her face gravely. He nodded, and she felt she had somehow won. Mae started to turn away, but he clamped onto her wrist. "Wait," he commanded. She turned back toward him, confused by his tone. "Our life, Mae. *Ours*. I'm tired of being the only one who thinks of it that way."

Mae shrank back. *More static, no words.*

"I understand you. You understand me?" He seemed so tall.

She nodded as he relaxed his grip. Suddenly he looked as flummoxed as she felt, and she was glad he was still holding on to her. *Oh God, tears in his eyes. Oh God, they would drown in this static together.* "Don't," she pleaded. Couldn't look, so she buried her face in his chest, felt it shudder against the tears. "Don't, we're okay. We'll be okay." He caved in against her, making them both stagger. "We'll be okay," she repeated, not sure it was true, but those were the only words she could find.

Chapter Fourteen

Maybe This Time

"Yoo-hoo, knock, knock!" someone chirped at the front door. Puzzled, Mae stacked one more bowl on the shelf, then peeked from the kitchen. *Huh.* Three women were filing in, all holding dishes. All three were blond: the tallest one had frosted hair, short with dark roots, but the other two sported taut ponytails. The one with the jogging headband cocked her head, flashing a bright smile at Mae, repeating, "Knock, knock!"

"Come in." Mae waved them further into the room. "Hi." Mae wiped her hands on the front of her jeans. "I'm Mae."

"I'm Debbie, and I'm your neighbor four doors down," the headband blonde replied as she brushed past Mae to put her casserole down on the kitchen counter. She spun back and offered her hand. "Debbie Connolly." *Wow, firm handshake!* The other ladies stepped closer: frosted hair had a sweet face and other ponytail had dark-blue mascara and moved more stiffly. Headband Debbie gestured to frosted hair: "And this, if you can believe it, is Deborah, who lives right around the corner, and have Debz, with a *z*. Isn't that just too kicky? Oh, and she lives across the street from Deborah. So you've got Debbie, Deborah, and Debz," Debbie punctuated her review with a bobbing head. "Three best friends, all within a block, all the same name, and we're here to welcome you to Brophy Street." As if on cue, Deborah and Debz held out their dishes to Mae.

"Goodness, how nice! Um, please come in. Oh, let me take these." She took Debz's salad bowl, while Deborah lined up her pie plate next to Debbie's dish.

"So we have your dinner all taken care of!" Debbie continued. "I made spaghetti casserole, Debz has her famous tossed salad, and Deborah baked an apple pie. We hope that makes your day a smidgen easier."

"Goodness!" Mae realized she was repeating herself. "Aren't you sweet. What nice neighbors!"

The ladies beamed at her assessment. "Well, we just want to welcome you to the neighborhood," Deborah echoed. "We know settling in and unpacking's a huge job."

Mae gestured apologetically toward the boxes. "I've been at it all day, but you'd never know to look at this."

"Oh, you've made a great start!" Debbie reassured her, tugging open the refrigerator to put her casserole inside. "Look, ladies, how clean!"

"And how empty," Mae added.

"Listen, everyone understands!" Debbie countered. "And getting it organized well is important, so do it right the first time, that's my motto!"

Debz noted, "Debbie is an organizational whiz! If you're not sure how to set something up, just ask her. Why, she even alphabetizes her soup!" The three ladies chuckled.

"Well, once I actually buy some soup, I'll just have to give that a try," Mae added, trying for a light touch of sarcasm.

Debbie's eyes narrowed and glittered brightly. "Don't knock it: save a minute here, a few seconds there, not having to hunt around for things; it all adds up! This time of year, it's worthwhile to keep your apples sorted, too, you know, each variety: baking versus eating."

Oh wow, she was serious. Say something, agree. "Oh, I like things tidy." Mae pointed to the symmetry of the dishes unpacked thus far. "I'll get the kitchen in order and then move on to each room until it's just so. I like my home orderly." She nodded emphatically, and the ladies' heads bobbed in unison.

"And there's not much to do in the yard now," Debz noted. "But after Halloween—oh, neighborhood trick or treating is from four until dusk—then you'll see everyone starting their Christmas decorations. No doubt you already heard we're known for our decorating: we've won the Park

Ridge Candy Cane Lane contest two years in a row, so everyone spends the month of November decorating their houses, and then the day after Thanksgiving, voila! All the lights go on for a Christmas fantasy." Her voice squeaked gleefully.

"Wow," Mae tried to sound appropriately impressed. "Two years straight!"

"Do you have decorations?" Deborah interjected.

"Well, no... I mean, we have some lights, of course."

"Well, everyone has lights, but you know, cut-out Santas or carolers that light up, that kind of thing," Deborah pressed.

"No, but we'll get some. In fact," Mae added for good measure, "my husband's the new manager of the hardware store on Touhy Avenue, so I'm sure his store carries decorations."

"Great! So your husband, is he here? Can we meet him?"

Mae bristled, sure Debbie shifted her shoulders back and thrust her breasts out as she asked. *I don't think so.* "Sorry," Mae responded, her tone tinged with only the faintest apology. "He's up to his elbows assembling bed frames upstairs. Hates interruptions."

"Oh," Debbie responded after a pointedly long pause. "Well, next time then. Ladies, let's leave Mae to her unpacking." She gave Mae an awkward little hug. "So nice to meet you, Mae. Oh, what's your last name anyway?"

"Thomasini."

"Thomasini? Well, that makes sense: you're so dark. You look Italian."

"No," Mae corrected, "I'm not Italian at all, just my husband. I'm Greek and Irish."

"Huh." Debbie waved a dismissive hand. "Ladies!"

Deborah extended her hand. "So nice to meet you."

"You too."

"You might want to put the salad in the frig too," Debz suggested as she shook hands.

"Right, will do."

"Call or stop by if you need anything," Debbie added at the front door. "Oh hi, Cynthia! Mae," she called back. "More company and more food!" She propped the door open for another neighbor. "Smells yummy!"

A petite woman with thick black hair swept behind a wide blue headband stepped in, surveying the group. "Am I interrupting?"

"No, just on our way out," Debbie responded. With a chorus of goodbyes, the various Debbies left, leaving Mae and Cynthia together, looking at each other.

"Okay, well, I'm Cynthia Goldberg, your neighbor straight across the street," she began in a pleasant, matter-of-fact tone. She had the darkest blue eyes Mae had ever seen, darker than her royal-blue headband yet brightened by bristling black eyelashes. And despite her olive complexion, her cheeks glowed pink.

"Please come in," Mae gestured her closer. "I'm Mae, Mae Thomasini."

"Hi, Mae," Cynthia answered. "I waited till all the trucks left but didn't realize you already had guests."

"Oh no, they just stopped by with dinner, you know, to introduce themselves." Mae hoped Cynthia was not holding dinner as well.

"Well, great minds think alike, but mine can sit for a day or two. I brought over some beef burgundy you can pop into your freezer. There is something so depressing about an empty freezer." She laughed with a lopsided smile. "Just save it for a busy day. Guess you'll have one or two of those coming up." *Nice laugh. Sympathetic.*

"Wow, that's great, thank you." Mae placed the large Tupperware container front and center in the freezer. "That's enough for two or three meals!"

"Well, I wasn't sure how big your family was."

"One daughter."

"Really? Me too. How old?"

"Eight. Second grade. Yours?"

"Same! Her name is Sarah."

"And mine's Kristy. So they'll be classmates."

"Yes! I'll have Sarah look for Kristy at recess."

"Thanks." Mae cringed. "Ack, I didn't even ask those other ladies about their kids."

Cynthia shrugged. "Wouldn't worry about it. They were here to find out about you. Soon they'll supply you with tons of details about their own kids. Probably more than you ever wanted to know."

Mae hesitated, and now Cynthia cringed. "Sorry: rude! I shouldn't cut them down. They're fine, and they're being welcoming, bringing dinner and all. It's just, well, they're sort of the self-appointed leaders of the neighborhood, whereas I'm the token Jew, as it were, so I'm a bit, a bit on the fringes. But in fairness, they do a lot at the school, organize a block party every summer, are very into the Candy Cane Lane contest, so don't get me wrong—every neighborhood needs a few moms like that."

"I get it," Mae reassured her. "I'm guessing if we were all in junior high, they wouldn't let me sit at their table either." She floated a wan smile.

"Yeah. But sorry, that sounded bitchy."

"No problem."

Cynthia leaned against the counter, folding her arms. "You know, we get along fine most of the year, but we're coming up on this Candy Cane Lane...thing...and then I get all these hints about decorating our house more, but you know, we're Jewish, so I'm not putting Santa and his reindeer on our roof. We try to meet them halfway, but apparently white lights on the hedge don't cut it."

"What do they expect?"

Cynthia shrugged. "More. I do have a lighted menorah, but I keep that in the back dining-room window, so that's as much as I'm prepared to concede."

"Well, you must be doing enough for them to win two years in a row."

"I guess. Let's let you get unpacked and through Halloween before thinking about Christmas decorations." She glanced about. "Want help? My husband's picking up Sarah after her swim lesson, so I have a little time."

"Swim lessons this time of year?"

"There's a palladium a few miles east of here, edge of Park Ridge. In fact, the next set of lessons starts November first if you're interested."

"Huh, do have a car most days. Maybe Kristy would like that."

"Ah, welcome to the world of carpools!" Cynthia teased. "But really, we could work out the driving, and the girls would get to know each other. Lessons are in six-week blocks. I'll get the phone number to you if you want to call for information."

"Yeah, please do."

Cynthia held out her hands. "So I meant it: can I help with something?"

"Nah, thanks, but I think I need to do it myself, one box at a time."

Cynthia nodded. "That's how I was, too, so I'll get outta your hair for now. But if you change your mind, I'm literally across the street. Want my phone number?"

"Sure!" Mae scanned the counter for a scrap of paper. Spying her purse, she pulled out a pen and her check register. "Here, write it on the last page."

Cynthia scribbled her name and number. "Call if you need something."

"I will," Mae promised, escorting her to the door. "Thanks."

"Bye then!" Cynthia pointed to the white ranch across the street. "That's me!" she announced as she headed down the front walk.

"I'll call soon. Thanks again!" Mae leaned on the front door. *Maybe this would be all right. Just maybe.*

♦ ♦ ♦

Mae cranked up the radio, singing along with Linda Ronstadt as she alphabetized spices.

"Mae, upstairs?" Tommy called down.

"In a sec," Mae called back, straightening the row of glass jars. "Coming!" She scampered up the stairs, glancing in Kristy's room, first on the right. The headboard was tucked neatly up against the wall, centered between the interior corner and the wall with two windows overlooking the back yard. The box spring and mattress were in place: the sheets were already smoothly tucked in, with a Kelly-green blanket folded across the foot. "Oh, you already made the bed? I was going to rewash the sheets."

Tommy rested his hands on her hips, and she stiffened, startled that he was so close. "They're fine; you washed 'em right before you packed. This way she just pops right into bed when your mom brings her home." He slipped his hands around her waist, pulling her closer. "Come see our room."

Now? Are you kidding me? Mae wriggled loose. "I didn't finish her new bedspread yet."

"Come see our room," he repeated, "and tell me where you want the bed frame." He guided her by an elbow down the hall. The bed frame was assembled, but the mattress and box spring were still tipped against the longest wall. "Lemme move it while it's lighter. Which wall?" He pressed his face into her hair, just above her left ear, sniffing her appreciatively. "You choose."

"Wow, a choice?" Mae countered, stepping away from him to survey the room from various angles.

Tommy looked past her, out the window for a moment, pursing his lips; then turning back to Mae, he muttered, "Point taken. But can we not rehash it, Mae? Just tell me where you want the bed?"

Just so the point's taken. "I think centered on this wall, so it's not crowded by the closet." Mae heard her bitchy tone. "Sound okay?" she softened.

He noticed, smiling faintly. "Sure. Will take two seconds." He energetically pushed the frame over, checked for her approval, and then wrestled the box spring and mattress in place.

Mae helped wiggle the mattress straight. "Good," she pronounced. "I'll make it up later, but I want to finish a couple of more boxes in the kitchen." She turned toward the door but then toppled, yanked onto the bed. Tommy rolled partway over her.

"Don't rush off," he murmured, nuzzling the base of her neck. "Let's take a break."

Mae hesitated: Kristy wouldn't be back for hours, after all. Tommy was rubbing her shoulders. *Maybe. Been a while...but so much to do. Man, my neck's stiff. Oh, there, ow, get that muscle.*

"Think it's customary to christen every room of the house," he teased, kneading the knot in her right shoulder. "So we should cover at least the upstairs today. All bedrooms, bathroom, the hallway..."

"Sounds ambitious. Sure you have that kind of staying power?" she bantered back.

"Watch me!" He dove at her, and Mae giggled. He tugged open her first button; she pulled away a few inches. "Wait, I dunno. So bright in here."

He squinted toward the uncovered windows, the late-afternoon sun. "So what?" He went after her next button with his teeth.

"No, wait!" She pushed him off her. "Baby proof?"

Tom hesitated. "Ah, we really need it?"

Well," Mae was calculating the date. "Yeah, probably should. But I don't think I unpacked my diaphragm. Maybe later?"

"Later? No, what if I find a condom?"

Mae shrugged. "Okay."

"Don't go anywhere!"

"Nope, I'll wait here," she promised.

He bounded off the bed and into the hallway. "Two minutes!"

"Fine!" she called back. Hearing a box ripping open downstairs, she rolled off the mattress and stepped into the bathroom. The slanting rays from the setting sun crazy-bounced off the mirror and illuminated the tiny room like a disco ball. *Curtains, curtains before Kristy's bedspread.* Mae tugged open the medicine cabinet and found herself staring at the pink square diaphragm case. *Oops, guess I should tell him.* But then her gaze settled on the plastic tampon holder next to it. She pulled off the sea-foam-green cap, slipped out a tiny Saran-wrap cocoon, and unwrapped a half of a joint. *Man, that's all that's left. I'll have to run back to Rogers Park later this week, when Kristy's in school.* The matchbook was right where she'd tucked it in. She lit up and took a slow, deep drag. She tried to fill herself with the bitter smoke, up into her sinuses, down to the tips of her lungs. Loved that little bit of a sting in her nose, the taste settling on her tongue. She kept her eyes closed, feeling the dark haze seep into familiar nooks.

"What the hell?" Tommy stood in the doorway, glaring at her reflection in the mirror.

Crap. "What?" she replied dismissively. "Just getting in the mood. Relax, it's not like Kristy's home. Here, have some," she offered him the stub of the joint.

He smacked it onto the floor, and now Mae exclaimed, "What the hell!" as she scrambled to collect the spilled weed and burning paper. "Jeez, Tommy, that was all I had!" she cried angrily. "You're such a prick sometimes!"

"I thought we had an understanding you weren't bringing any of that into the new house." "My God, didn't I just say it was the last of it? Getting relaxed for you, for Chrissake."

"Why do you need help to get in the mood? I don't want you that way, all spaced out, hardly there."

"It's worked for you in the past," she snarled. His big hands clamped down on her shoulders, spinning her around to face him. Mae wavered, warning, "Don't you manhandle me!"

"Shut the hell up," he commanded. "You listen to me. We had an agreement, no more pot, and the first fucking afternoon in the house you're getting stoned."

"Be a little uptight, why don't you?" Mae hissed back. "In case you hadn't noticed, kind of a stressful day for me, so what the fuck? I wasn't going to throw out that last little bit, but now you've pretty much wrecked that." Tears stung her eyes, maybe from the smoke, but angry tears too.

"First fucking afternoon!"

"Yeah, well, it's not a fucking afternoon anymore, I'll tell you that!" Mae retorted, twisting away. "You're such a jerk. You're not coming near me." She started to storm past him, ducking under his arm, and then gasped in pain and disbelief as he grabbed her by her hair and pinned her against the wall.

"We're not finished here," he glowered.

"Oh yes, we are. Let go of me!" she insisted, but she didn't pull against his grip on her hair.

The anger radiated off his body. "You're not going anywhere till we have an understanding."

"I understand you're an ass and apparently a bully. Let go!"

"You stoned yet?"

"No, thanks to you, but sure wish I were." She tried to wriggle a little, but the roots of her hair practically screamed, and she had to freeze again. "Would you fucking let go? This hurts!"

"So you can feel something: maybe you aren't stoned after all. Well, Mae, get used to this, 'cause no more getting stoned from this point on. New house, new start, and we're gonna move forward whether you like it or not."

Mae felt paralyzed. His intensity practically sucked the air out of her lungs, but she'd be damned if she were going to let him know. "You don't own me! You can't order me around like a little girl."

"I'm not treating you like a little girl: I'm telling you to stop acting like a snotty little girl!" He pressed into her, too much weight on her, but she dared not move with his fingers clenched so tightly in her hair. *Too weird, he was angry and aroused at the same time; his breathing was so fast, so hot on her forehead. Call his bluff.* She spread her legs a little.

"Want me to act like a grown-up? Here, have at it: I don't care." Mae slowly, gingerly turned her face away from him.

"You think that makes you grown up?" His voice was unfamiliar, a loony mix of heat and disdain.

"As much as I'm gonna be today. Go ahead," she taunted. "Just shove your way in if you can. It's all we got in common anyway. Just don't expect me to come along for the ride, asshole. I'll just stand here and make a grocery list in my head. Sound grown up enough?" His grip lessened a bit, and she smiled triumphantly. She forced her eyes up, wanting to make sure that he knew she had the upper hand. Her smile, though, dropped off her face the instant she saw his disengaged expression. They stared at each other, totally confused. Then his fingers tightened at the roots of her hair.

"Fine," he whispered, pressing so hard into her that she couldn't inhale. His other hand tugged at her belt and ripped her zipper open. *No. Oh my God, no.* Her jeans were twisting down, and she felt the cool wall against the back of her thighs, and now he pressed even harder, lower, so she could gasp in some air, but his hand was a vise behind her head, and she couldn't move, not an inch. *Ow, you son of a bitch! Ow, dammit! Ow, don't cry! Don't you dare cry, Mae! Just, just bread and eggs and milk, and ow, dammit! Ow and, and fruit, apples! Ow, and more coffee, almost out of coffee...*

The air is heavy with the fragrance of coffee. Dorothy pouring more into Aunt Sophie's cup, and the aroma spills over Mae's little egg-shaped cup of cocoa, confusing the smells washing up across Mae's face. Now Dorothy circles to fill Mama's cup. Mama lifts the cup very slowly, not disturbing Michael, who's slumped against Mama's arm with his eyes closed. When she rests her cup in the saucer, she absently strokes Michael's bangs, all the while still looking at Uncle Nick. Michael must have inched his chair closer to hers during dinner, little by little, so now the adults talk over coffee and brandy, and the children must be very quiet, but Michael pretends to sleep, and Mae wishes she could put her head in Aunt Sophie's lap, rub her cheek against the warm and musty silk, but she isn't close enough, and Aunt Sophie would signal to hush, sit up straight, and sip your cocoa. Shh, drink your cocoa, and soon Aunt Sophie will help you swirl the cup three times, turn it upside down, and tell your fortune after it dries. Patience, wait quietly, shh, very quiet.

He was not moving: his forehead was pressed against the wall. His hand was limp, just resting there, no longer clutching her hair. He was almost a statue, except his chest sucked little, erratic breaths. Mae inched away, focused on that hand. Would it let her go? Would it feel her hair slipping through the fingers and clench and rip again? But the fingers were still. Surely they felt her hair slide and swirl away, and when a tangle caught and tugged on his ring, he gently twisted it free, nudged her to keep moving, go on, and so she slipped along the wall and back through the door of the bathroom, closed and locked the door. She pressed her back into the door and slid down to the floor. *Hate him, I hate him.* Felt disconnected from her own body. *Just the cold tile on your butt, the hard door on your spine, feel those.* Jumped a little when he slumped against the other side of the door—*it's okay, it's okay, it's locked*—and they're both very still; both need that door locked.

"Mae?" His voice soft and ragged. "Mae, you okay?"

Shh, be quiet.

"Mae?" He must be listening. "Mae, I, I'm sorry. So sorry."

Mae's eyes cast this way and that, squinting at the last rays of the afternoon that shot almost horizontal across the room. There were a couple of pot seeds behind the toilet: they must've rolled when they spilled. *Maybe could suck on them. No, wouldn't help. Anyway, too tired to move, too damned tired, and they're too far away. Just be still.*

"Mae? Listen, I'll go downstairs, and I'll stay there. I promise to stay there, and so you just, you come out when...I don't know what else to do. I will stay downstairs, I promise." A floorboard creaked as he stood up. She heard him in the hallway, heard him on the stairs. Then she couldn't hear him anymore. Could get off the cold floor, but no, liked the cold. Liked the door. Liked the lock.

♦ ♦ ♦

"Mom!" Kristy's voice, blurry, like underwater.

Kristy's frightened. Wake up, Mae, wake up. Kristy was hanging onto her arm, pulling her under. Mae swatted with her other hand, tried to twist away.

"Mom!"

She's frightened. "What? I'm awake. Okay, let go. I'm awake." She forced her right eye open; the left was too heavy. She blindly patted Kristy's arm. "Just a dream, sweetie. Go back to sleep." Ick, her stomach was icky.

"Mom, can you sleep in your bed? There's not enough room."

No. Mae rolled to the very edge of the mattress, shrinking as small as she could. "Sure there is, honey, there's room." Her right shoulder hung over the edge of the mattress, and her right hand rested on her belly, rubbing it lightly. Ick. *Try to drift off.*

"Mom, I'm squooshed."

"Sweetie, Daddy's snoring too much. Please, just tonight?" *Please, baby, please? I'm sorry I'm lying to you, but I can't go in there.* She lay very still, tried to be very small, take up no space at all.

"It's squooshed," Kristy repeated faintly, her voice dropping off midcomplaint.

That's right, baby, drift off. I'm not here, I'm not really here...

Chapter Fifteen

Nick

The phone ring was too bright, too sharp. Mae dropped the coffee measure, grabbing the receiver, glancing at her watch: 7:02 a.m. Too early. She interrupted the second ring, hoping it didn't wake Tommy or Kristy. *Not ready to see them.*

"Hello?" Her voice was low and husky, almost a growl. She braced against the frig, against the solid, cold metal.

"Mae?" Mama's voice was tentative, weak. Dread tinged with annoyance shuddered up Mae's spine. *Don't—I can't. Don't need something from me.* But 7:02 a.m. could only be bad.

"Mae?" Mama echoed, still unconvinced.

"Yes," Mae responded, her voice raspy, her throat closing. *Mom, just say it. What?*

"Honey, I'm sorry to call so early, but it's—it's Nick. He died last night." Her voice rippled with little waves of sadness.

Mae mashed the back of her skull into the smooth metal. *Nick.*

"Mae?" Mama quavered.

She's shaky. Say something. "Yes," Mae whispered, "Nick."

"I'm sorry to call so early. I wanted to call you last night, but Sophie wouldn't hear of it, insisted we not call you till morning, after a whole day of moving and all."

Wait. "We? Does Michael know?"

"Yes, sweetie, Michael and I ran over there when she called. But it was late, and you'd had such an exhausting day, there was nothing more to do..." Her voice clutched, thick with tears.

"Mother," Mae pressed. *Pull it together. I need you to hold together.* "Tell me what happened."

"Well, I guess when Sophie got home, you know, after dropping us all off, she saw the light on in his study and called to Nick and started to unpack her bags. He didn't join her, so she went to the study and that's"—Mama's voice broke—"I guess that's where she found him, his head on his desk, the phone in his hand." Mama coughed on her tears. "She thinks he tried to call for help, not sure; we're not sure. Poor Nick, all alone." Mama's voice dissolved into sniffles.

Mae closed her eyes, waited.

Finally, "And, Mae, you know what else? Mae, his other hand—"

The picture. Nicky and Alex.

"Was gripping the picture of the boys. You know"—her voice was wet again—"that photograph of them, the one he had on his desk?"

Mae nodded. *The one happiness of that moment, his last moment.*

"Mae?"

"I remember," she responded dully.

"So sad, one hand on the phone, one…"

Mae sighed. *Good-bye, Nick. Not so sad, not really. You wanted to go. Only sad for us, for Sophie. Poor Sophie.* "Um, how's Sophie doing?"

"Well, I'm hoping she was able to sleep a little, after we left, but I don't know. I wanted to stay with her, but she insisted she needed to be by herself. I'd call, but I'm afraid I might wake her if she managed to nod off, so I think I'll just go over there in a bit."

"Okay, good. Do you—do you want me to come with? Maybe I could help." Mae glanced about at the boxes surrounding her. Stacks in every direction. *Crap.*

"No, sweetheart, your hands are full. Not now, anyway."

"You sure?" Mae countered feebly, hoping she was.

"Right now you concentrate on unpacking, and maybe later, when we go to the funeral home? I don't really remember the Greek Orthodox traditions, but they'll know, and Sophie will know. Oh, poor Sophie. I remember the day your father died—"

"Mother," Mae cut in. *No, not Papa. Can't think about that now.* "Listen, you should lie down too."

"Oh, I have, but I couldn't sleep, I really couldn't."

"Well, rest now, so you can help Sophie later. And call me for the funeral home; let Michael go to work. I'm free. I'll pick you both up. Just let me know the time."

"All right. Thanks, sweetie. Shall I call you later then, after I talk with Sophie?"

"Yes. I'll be here, so call whenever."

"Okay, sweetie, thanks."

"Sure. Bye." Mae hung up the receiver with a loud clack and just stood there, holding onto the phone with one hand, rubbing her forehead with the other.

♦ ♦ ♦

"And when did he pass on?" The director's voice oozed sympathy, but his silver pen was poised over a form that signaled just-another-client.

Died. The word is "died." "Yesterday, my uncle died yesterday," Mae announced grimly.

Sophie added, "Late? We're not sure what time." Her eyes were murky, her voice flat.

"I see." He tipped up his elbows to pull back his suit-jacket sleeves and set to writing. "And, I'm sorry—his full name was...?"

Is. "Nicholas Jerome Panos." *Oily. This guy is so oily.*

"P-a-n-o-s? And his birthdate was...?"

Is! "August twentieth, nineteen...eighteen?" Mae turned to Sophie.

"Actually, 1920," Sophie corrected, very gently.

"In 1920," the director intoned as he recorded the date.

He wasn't even sixty? He seemed older; he'd always seemed older than that. Not even sixty?

"A Leo," Sophie told Ellie. "Every bit a Leo."

"I can see that," Ellie concurred. "Like a lion."

A wounded lion. Mae frowned, watching the women smile at each other, apparently at some pleasant memories of Nick. She realized that the director was waiting, pen poised, bushy eyebrows lifted, unwilling to interrupt their moment of relief. *Respectful. Guess this guy's okay.*

"Place of birth?"

"Chicago," Mae replied.

"No!" Sophie thrust her hand out, warning the director not to write. "Sarasota, Florida."

"What?" *Sophie must not be thinking straight.* "Aunt Sophie?"

"Mae, Florida. We met when my parents took me to Sarasota on vacation." Sophie leaned closer, her voice brightening. "He was working as a lifeguard at the resort, and oh, Mae, he was so handsome! It was truly love at first sight, and after we left, Nick wrote to me every week, and at the end of the season, he moved up to Chicago, got a job, and then later your dad joined him. That's how he met your mother here. And they worked so hard, those fellows. Anyway, he got some money in the bank before he asked for my hand." Sophie and Ellie exchanged teary smiles. "Well, Father approved, so we were married in July, and then my father died just a year later, almost to the day, and then my mother just followed him to the grave, after three months, so then it was just Nick and me, and your dad, and of course later, your mother."

"'Followed him to the grave?'"

"Oh yes, Mae, she just died of a broken heart. It happens."

Bewildered, Mae turned to Ellie, then the director, both of whom nodded in affirmation. Now her head was swimming. *How could she know so little about her own family?*

"Other surviving family members?" the director asked Mae.

"Better ask them." Mae shrugged. "Are there others?"

Sophie shook her head wistfully. "No, dear. You, Michael, your mother, your family, me: we're all that's left." She blinked back tears as she grasped Ellie's hand. "And what would I do without you?" she choked out, fumbling for her handkerchief. "How do people get along without family?"

She sobbed into her hankie, curled over, her shoulders bobbing up and down with each painful breath.

Ellie rubbed her back, murmuring, "I know—shh, I know." The funeral director slid his box of Kleenex closer and laid down his pen. Mae slumped back in her chair, her back squeaking against the slippery leather, her thumbs rubbing the carved wooden claws, rubbing where the varnish was worn thin and pale. *What hands had rubbed the same grooves, the same curves? How many more after her? What else could you do? Clutch a hankie, grip an armrest, maybe dig your nails in to hang on. What else could you do?*

♦ ♦ ♦

"Maybe he was confused, you know, maybe from the pain?" the bald man offered, immediately cringing at his awkward suggestion. He snatched at the air, trying futilely to pull his words back.

The darker gentleman looked embarrassed, but Sophie grasped the first man's sleeve, nodding. "I thought of that, too, that maybe he was disoriented, maybe already half, half gone, with the heart attack..." She inhaled deeply with a little hiccup, shaking her head at the mystery. The darker man leaned close to Sophie and murmured something in Greek, grave and perhaps consoling, as Sophie dabbed at her eyes. Mae turned away, leaving them to their sympathetic conjecture. The weight of certainty pulled her away.

"I'm sorry. Please tell Sophie I am sorry." Nick was ashen, his voice raspy, pleading with the little life he had left.

"Sir?" a woman's voice, young, unsure, tinny in his ear. "Do you need assistance? Sir?"

"Please." A shudder as he inhaled, needed to rest his head, impossibly heavy, lay it on the desk. He fixed his eyes on the boys. Coming..."Tell Sophie I'm sorry." An odd, guttural burp popped out of his throat.

Sophie was explaining to someone else: "And the dear girl, the operator, she called me after she saw my name, you know. Sophie's an unusual name. I suppose I was the only one in the obituary notices...She thought she should give me his message, poor thing; she felt so badly that she couldn't do more at the time..."

"Sir, do you need medical assistance?" the girl persisted nervously.

He could not release his grip on the phone; his brain was evaporating, no more signals clear enough to reach to his fingers. No matter: he shoved his whole arm away, let her words bounce off his stony skull, felt the squeezing in his chest start to pass, now a mist of relief expanding and filling the space that had just ached so, filling all the spaces below his skin. No matter. Too, his grip on the boys' photograph held firm, and the pressure of those fingers was the last sensation he could feel, even as his fingertips seemed to dissolve through the wood, the glass, reach right into the yard where Nicky and Alex played, and they darted and shrieked in delight, looking straight out to him, calling, "Papa! Come play, Papa!" He couldn't move his lips to answer, but no matter, they knew he was almost there: Nicky and Alex clutched each other, jumping up and down, jumping as one, their eyes never wavering from his, the purest joy in their cries of "Papa! Papa's here!" Yes, Papa was here.

"Mae? Jesus, here." Tommy was pressing Kleenex into her hand. She peered at him through a thick film of water, blinked, and felt heavy tears roll down her cheeks, following wide, wet tracks. Mae raised her hand tentatively to her face: cheeks wet, nostrils wet. Pulling her hand back, the Kleenex was half dissolved in a mush of mascara, powder, and a streak of tawny red lipstick.

"Mae." He cupped the side of her face in his palm, his generous warm palm. "What, what do you need?"

She shrank away from his hand, even though that made her skull feel impossible to hold up, so she let it drop against the back of the chair. *When had she sat down?* He withdrew his hand apologetically.

"Don't, Mae, I'm just trying to help. You're sitting here like a zombie, alone, in tears, and I just hate to see you..."

She wiped across her cheeks with the backs of her hands. "I got it," she countered. "I just, lost track. More Kleenex?"

"Here." He stooped down to dab at her eyes.

She snatched it away. "Don't touch me."

Eyes downcast, he nodded. "Um, want to go in the ladies' room? Your mascara is..." He made a smeary motion in the air, careful not to touch her cheek.

"Oh. Keep, just keep Kristy away while I go clean up." She glanced about, but no Kristy, no Sophie, no grave strangers nearby.

Tommy offered one hand. "Let me help you to the powder room. Kristy won't see."

"No!" Mae rose unsteadily. "By myself. Back in a few minutes." She eased one foot in front of the next, focusing intensely on the doorframe that would take her out of the room. Her heels dragged on the carpet, as if she were wading through mud. Faintly heard Michael's voice back near Tommy, asking, "Is she okay?" Mae held up one hand to warn him off, couldn't turn her head or she'd fall, kept scraping toward the hallway. Almost there, and in the background, Michael and Tommy's voices blurred together, something about Tommy telling Michael he'd wait for her, he'd watch, wouldn't leave. Well, that was something, not much, but at least he wouldn't leave.

Chapter Sixteen

Not Alone

November 1979

Mae didn't even let the brownie defrost, just chomped down on a corner, never mind the edges of her teeth buzzing in protest. She rolled it around in her mouth, warm spit getting it soft and even a little slimy, no matter, chocolate and hashish, the best combination in the world. Her tongue was happy, and soon the buzz would settle in. *This was such good stuff, scored really good stuff this time. Gotta remember that kid next time I'm in Rogers Park.*

Mae nibbled on the next corner, closed her eyes, focused on the chocolate film coating her tongue. *Should've thought of this long ago! Tommy's so nuts if hair smells like smoke, if I burn incense. Expects me to be Samantha Stevens, just stick to all the surface housewife stuff, but hell, no, here are my magic powers, and they are mine, and they are sitting in the back of the freezer for whenever I want them, asshole. So there.* Took a bigger bite and grinned, sank into the edge of the kitchen counter, loved the quiet, loved the chocolate, loved the trace of bitter aftertaste. *Yes, c'mon, baby, work your magic for me. Let me feel you, c'mon, got wife and mommy duty all too soon.*

She glanced at the clock. *Shit! Already?* Kristy home in the next five minutes, and a swim lesson day too. *Shit.* Mae checked: brownie gone, just some chocolate smear on her fingers. Licked them clean. *Counter?* No crumbs. Tugged open the freezer door, made sure they were tucked back, behind the fish sticks and the mound of ground beef, a small box of kuchen perched above them. *Mrs. Beihl, thanks! That was a good day.*

I'll come again this month. Won't forget about you, promise. Mae pressed the freezer door closed and considered brushing her teeth. *Nah, might spit out some good stuff. Let it dissolve a little longer. Kristy won't think a thing of me smelling like chocolate.*

Mae rinsed off her fingertips and checked the wall calendar as she dried her hands. It was her turn to drive—well, no big deal, barely ten minutes each way. Nice that Kristy and Sarah were getting along, making friends. Mae checked the clock again: where was Kristy anyway? Mae started to set up a juice glass, a small plate, a fresh paper napkin folded in a triangle, tucked under the edge of the plate. *There. Wait to see what she wants, gotta get something in her before swimming.*

"Mom?" The mudroom door banged for emphasis. "Home!" Mae could hear the shoes getting kicked off, bouncing off the floorboards.

"Hi, baby! How was your day?" The backpack hit the linoleum with a resounding thud.

"Fine." Kristy emerged, her cheeks weirdly pink, one with a bigger blotch than the other. The top ridges of her ears looked like they were burning.

Mae frowned. "Is it that cold out?" She reached out to feel Kristy's face but barely grazed it as Kristy slipped past her into the kitchen chair.

"Not so much, it's just we ran home, got swimming, remember?"

"I know, my turn to drive. But you have a little time now, so let's get you warmed up—want hot chocolate?"

"Mom, I'm not really cold. How 'bout peanut butter and apple?"

Mae rested her hands lightly over Kristy's ears, but Kristy shrugged away. "Mom! Not cold!"

Mae held up her hands in surrender. "Fine. So sue me for caring." She turned toward the frig. "Was that a yes to hot chocolate?"

"No," Kristy sounded petulant. "I said peanut butter and apple."

"Please?" *Watch your tone, missy.*

"Please."

Most insincere please I ever heard. Mae washed the apple and set the peanut-butter jar and a knife on the table in stony silence.

"Thank you," Kristy followed up more meekly, her brow tensed up. *Good. Point taken.*

Mae pulled out a chair and sat down beside Kristy. Kristy offered an apple wedge; Mae shook her head with a wink of approval for improved manners. "No, you eat that: you're the one who'll be in the pool soon. So what did you learn today?"

"Dunno, not much." Kristy crunched down the apple. "Math's a lot harder here."

"You're good at math!"

"Kinda, but they are farther than at my old school. I'm behind."

"Want me to go in and talk to your teacher?"

"No, Mrs. J's being nice about it, but she said I gotta do extra worksheets on the weekends. Maybe Daddy can help."

"Hey, I think I can do second-grade math."

"I know, just thought Dad might want to." Kristy chewed noisily, smacking from the peanut butter. Drooling, too, wiping with the back of her hand.

"You have a napkin. And try to chew nicely."

Kristy rolled her eyes but picked up her napkin, sealing her lips shut while she chewed.

Crap, killed the conversation. Mae stood up. "Either Daddy or I can help with math." Kristy nodded. "So finish up and get ready for swimming." Kristy nodded again. Mae tried to catch her eye. Kristy was licking her fingers. Mae opened her mouth to correct her and then decided better of it.

♦ ♦ ♦

"Mrs. Panos, did you know that we are coming into the shortest days of the year?" Sarah had good company manners, trying to be conversational from the back seat.

Mae liked that. "You know, I'd forgotten that, Sarah, but now that you mention it, I have been noticing how early the sunset is."

"Actually, the shortest weeks are almost a month away," Kristy countered, "right before Christmas."

Mae winced at her daughter's one-upmanship. "Honey, you're both right. It'll be getting darker faster for several weeks. Then the days will start to get longer again. I think that's what Sarah meant."

"Yeah," Sarah agreed, sounding unperturbed. Probably didn't care, just trying to be a good guest. Mae tapped the steering wheel with her thumbs: long light. *Should've left a few minutes earlier.* They were going to be late if they caught every red light.

"Less than five minutes," Mae announced. The light changed, and she turned left.

"Mom, c'mon, tip us on the turns!" Kristy begged from the back seat. "Dad does!"

"Well, he shouldn't!"

"It's fun. C'mon, we have seat belts on. Please?"

"Honey, driving is not some carnival ride. Traffic's heavy. We can't be horsing around in traffic."

"Aw," Kristy complained. "Dad would." Mae heard her mutter to Sarah, "My dad's more fun." The sunlight streamed in broad sheets across the windshield, forcing Mae to squint even behind her sunglasses. *Damn, better get the car washed soon.* Well, a turn was coming up, and then the sun would be out of her eyes.

She took the right turn smoothly, relaxing a bit in the shade of the elms lining the side street, but then, glancing at her wristwatch, muttered a quiet, "Shit." They were late and still a few blocks away. She edged up the speed, only a little with all the kids on the sidewalks. "You guys jump out and run inside as soon as I pull in, okay? No dawdling in the locker room: we're a little late."

"Okay," they responded in unison.

There was the YMCA. Mae took the last left into the parking lot a little fast—*so late*—and heard Kristy gasp happily at the centrifugal tug. The setting sun's rays slipped across the windshield like an instant, golden shade: Mae could see nothing but a penetrating yellow film. Still, she knew the door was just a few yards up on the left, so she let the car roll forward, barely braking.

Stop.

Her foot slammed down on the brake, and they all lurched forward violently. Her hands were riveted to the steering wheel. Her brain scrambled: *what*? Kristy and Sarah were shrieking with delight at being thrown, but had there been another cry? A flicker of movement, a slip of, some flash of pink, a blur...? And the voice, a man's voice: inside and outside her head at the same time, the voice that simply, quietly commanded, "Stop," and she instantly did. Her foot had flown to the brake before she even knew it, and now it was welded, practically pressing through the floor, disconnected from her brain, immobile. *What? Oh God, whatever it was, it was bad.* The girls were still giggling and reaching for their towels, unbuckling their seat belts.

"Good one, Mom!" Kristy planted a kiss on her cheek from behind the seat. "Should we get out now?"

"No!" Mae whispered. She sensed Kristy's confusion. "I mean, yes, but careful."

"Unlock the doors?" Kristy prompted.

"Right." Mae had to stare at her left hand to uncurl the fingers. She willed the hand to the controls on the door, watching it tremble, not understanding, not connected. With the loud clack of the lock release, the girls tumbled out. Mae willed the hand onto the control for the window, rolling down the window with a deep sense of dread.

A woman was staring at her, eyes popping in disbelief and terror, accusatory eyes. Twisted around her legs, the arms of a little girl, maybe five, maybe six, a little girl in a bright pink fall jacket, sobbing, "Sorry, Mommy!"

The mommy grabbing at her daughter's arms and shaking her daughter as she crouched down, eyeball to eyeball, yelling in the little face just inches from her own, "Didn't I tell you to be careful? Didn't I? Didn't I tell you not to run around cars?" Scanning up and down her daughter's body anxiously, frantically, she grabbed her close, crying with her. She stared at Mae, shaking, with accusatory eyes.

Inhaling with a shudder, Mae croaked out a shaky "Is she okay?" The mom nodded, crying too hard to answer. Mae nodded back at her. *Get out, get out and walk up to them. Go check, go say sorry, go be with them.* But she still could not pry her foot off the brake, didn't know how to find her body. She nodded back, sober, ashamed, nodded so very, very sorry and turned to creep forward through the glare, so this mom could see she was so very, very sorry and was creeping, so very afraid she would hurt a daughter in her little pink jacket. And as she turned behind the building and the sun instantly swept off the windshield, Mae crept to a stop and turned off the car, turned it off wrong when it made some gear-grinding cry of complaint, no matter, just sat there trembling, crying for the little girl and her scared mom, crying her apologies and her thanks to that voice, the voice that scared and saved her.

♦ ♦ ♦

Even in her own driveway, it was daunting, how to get out of the car, to uncoil her fingers from the steering wheel, to command her feet to swing out onto the pavement. Every part of her body wanted to stay pressed against the metal brake, the taut leather of the steering wheel, the stiff upright seat back. But she had to get inside, be home, be away from the damned windshield, the accusatory eyes that were still somehow reflecting, trapped in the window and flashing out at her with each shifting slant of the setting sun.

Sucking in a huge breath, as if she had to dive very deep, Mae threw open the car door and slipped past it. She shoved it closed and ran her hand along the front of the car, partly for support, partly double-checking: *no dent, no blood, guess she's really okay.* Mae was still holding her breath tightly until she could stumble inside of the mudroom door. Only then did she exhale, an unfamiliar, creaky groan threading through the stale air. Mae covered her ears with her palms, fingers splayed, and scrunched her eyes closed, willing all of her attention to the rumble in her ears and the vacuum behind her palms. Ow, the vacuum hurt, no matter, no matter... in fact good, she could focus on just that, on that sucking pain, that rumble of her own pulse. Nothing else.

Mae, settle down! Mae could feel her ribs shudder when she inhaled. *Okay, you're home. Calm down. Calm down. A brownie—need some magic. Magic disappearing act.* Mae let her eyelids ease open, just enough to look toward the freezer. *No, I'll throw up, for sure I'll throw up. Okay, upstairs, got two joints upstairs. Go upstairs, go.* Mae pushed off, lurched through the kitchen, tried to take the stairs two at a time but ended up climbing on all fours, had to get to the bathroom, to the medicine cabinet, to that ugly little seafoam-green plastic tampon holder, that double-barreled plastic case, to two joints shaking out into her palm. She stared at them, through them, through the saran wrap cocoon resting so daintily on her lifeline, or was that the heart line? Her eyelids drop closed. *I'm all right now, and she, she's okay... her mom said she was okay...*Ugh, suddenly her eyes were uncomfortably full, tears surging up to press against the inside of her eyelids, but just then, too, the last glinting rays of the sunset bounced off the outside of her lids, and she had to acquiesce to the sting, opening her eyes just enough to let fat tears roll down her cheeks, and through the slit of watery film, she saw the golden letters floating on the bathroom mirror:

pray

Mae could not even gasp. Only her eyes moved, opened so big that the tears were spilling down her face, tucking under the curve of her jaw and trickling down her neck. The last setting rays were bouncing all over the bathroom fixtures, off the silver faucet, the white porcelain toilet seat, but all Mae could take in were the glowing letters floating on the mirror: *pray*. The letters wavered, fading slightly, then glowing even brighter: *pray*! Mae cast down her eyes, saw she had dropped the joints, dropped the plastic case, but had never heard them bounce against the tile floor. She pulled her eyes back up to the mirror, afraid it would not be there, afraid it would, and it must have known, because it was just a trace but then glowed sharply to repeat: *pray.* Again it waned a little, as if about to sink away. Then Mae saw the can of VO5 hairspray on the counter, its reflection arcing from the near-horizontal last rays of the afternoon, and the last letters of its golden scripted label being thrown up onto the mirror. Mae rotated the can ever so slightly: now "spra" floated on the mirror. Mae shook her head, a shuddering no, and wiped the tears off her chin, her throat, sensed the light dropping—finally, sunset—and, checking back to the mirror, saw it was gone, had dissolved away. *Thank God.*

She glared at the naked window: the big maple in the yard was stripped of most of its leaves. No privacy. *Curtains by tomorrow. Kristy's room would have to wait.* Mae double-checked the mirror, now its usual smooth silver, like gray water with no ripples, water that had swallowed something whole, unperturbed, as if nothing struggled underneath. *Holy... call Cynthia... see if she'll pick up the girls, say the car sounds funny, beg off, switch days.* Mae got on her knees to retrieve the joints, the cracked plastic case. *Just call Cynthia, then you can have one, no, just half a joint, on the patio, then gotta find a new hiding place. But first get Cynthia to get the girls, and then you're okay. You're okay. She's okay.*

Chapter Seventeen

Not Thanksgiving

Ow, dammit! Mae inspected the tip of her index finger. A sole bright drop of blood was welling up. *The needle must've gone deep. Man, really stings.* She watched the blob of blood swell, hold its shape, some shiny, invisible surface tension creating a perfect ball until Mae brushed her thumb firmly across it, smearing it thin and even down the length of her finger. *Gonna get on the fabric.* She licked the side of her finger and stared down the tiny new bead that seemed afraid to emerge. With a gentle nudge from her thumb knuckle, she pushed it back.

Mae arched her back and shook her head back and forth in slow motion. *Been sewing too long. Get up and move.* Pushing off the sewing table, Mae stretched, contemplating the large ruffle still clamped firmly under the feeder foot of the old Kenmore.

Kristy's bedspread: take two. Kristy had not been thrilled, had not offered the beaming face Mae was expecting after two weeks of measuring, threading, weaving rose-colored ribbons through the eyelet ruffles. Kristy was supposed to clap her hands in excitement, her voice squeaking with glee as she took in a bedroom transformed with starchy white eyelet, delicate rosy ribbons, pillow shams in not one but two pinks, one powdery, one more peppermint. But no, she stood there, uncertain, taking in the shirred bed skirt and the scalloped edges of the curtains and looked... bummed. "It's pretty, Mom, but, it's just..." Knew not to say it.

Fine. Mae studied the reworked flounces, now stripped of their ribbons, and glanced down at the wastebasket, over half full with snips of pink satin ribbon. *Must be twelve, fifteen dollars' worth tangled up in there. What a waste.* Mae reconsidered her decision to pitch it all, but she didn't want to see it again, not even packed away for a Halloween costume three or four years off. No, rejected.

"What?" she'd heard the falter in her own voice, knowing full well this was her vision, not Kristy's. But it was so sweet, so girly, those crisp whites, soft pinks, all ruffles, ribbons, eyelet. She'd wanted Kristy to glow, to gasp in appreciation, but no, just a halting thank-you, not even a step into the room. "What?" Mae had echoed, now more reproachfully.

"It's nice, just, remember, I said hot pink, not..." Kristy's eyes stopped darting about, just settled on the carpet. Her mouth was pressed into a tight line.

"Yes, but sweetie, bright pink would be too much. I knew you'd get tired of it, but this, this is classic, and there's still lots of pink, see?"

Kristy nodded, compliant but not even a polite smile.

With a surge of certainty, Mae grabbed the corner of the bedspread with both hands. She heaved it off with one flourish, sending pillows bouncing and rolling across the floor.

"Mom?" Kristy protested. "Wait, what are you doing?"

"Obviously, I got this wrong."

"No, Mom, wait!"

Mae held up one hand for silence. With no eye contact but with great authority in her voice, she continued: "Go downstairs while I fold this up. I'll put the old blanket back on your bed for now, rework this in the next few days. When your dad gets home, you tell him he needs to get some hot-pink Rit dye at work tomorrow, at least four of those little boxes." Mae leveled her gaze on Kristy. "That's your job."

Kristy turned away with a shamed nod, and Mae stood tall at the foot of the bed, clutching the folds and ruffles tightly against her breast.

The phone rang. *Now what?* Mae scurried into the master bedroom. "Hello?"

"Mae?"

"Hi, Cynthia."

"I hate to call you on Thanksgiving: you up to your elbows in turkey?"

"Actually, no, we're heading to my aunt's soon, and all I'm bringing is cranberry sauce and pie. It's all packed in the frig."

"Oy, am I jealous! I've still got a table to set and a turkey that went in a half hour late. But that's not why I called. Two things: first, you want to have Kristy come stay overnight tomorrow night while we're at the Candy Cane kickoff at Deb's? I already have a sitter—Ellie's daughter—and she can watch two as easily as one."

"I was going to use a lack of a sitter as my excuse not to go," Mae teased.

"Oh no, you don't: if I have to go, so do you! I'll even wear my red sweater. But you're the new kid on the block, so you have to go."

"I guess. What time?"

"Send Kristy over early: they can eat together. We're supposed to be there at six, right?"

"Think so. So I have to get dressed up?"

"No, just something with red or green, or one of those little Christmas vests if you've got one. If it's like last year, it's just cocktails and heavy hors d'oeuvres. After a few rounds, people bundle up, wander up and down the streets to check out the decorations. That's when we duck out, but most find their way back to the punch bowl from what I hear."

"Can't wait."

"Aw, I'm corrupting you before your first Candy Cane Lane party. Sorry."

"Well, then don't expect me to chip in on the sitter."

"Hey, if you want to stroll around in the snow, don't let me stop you!"

"Snow! It's snowing?"

"For about an hour now. Haven't you looked outside recently?"

"No, I was working on Kristy's bedspread."

"Thought you finished it."

"Long story." Mae pulled back her draperies to peek out. "Shit. And it's getting dark. I'd better start to clean up to go to Sophie's."

"Tom's not working today, is he?"

"No, they're closed today, but he's gotta work tomorrow. He and Kristy must be watching TV downstairs. I should go. Oh, wait: what was the second thing?"

"What?"

"You said you called for two reasons."

"Oh. Well, listen, neither of us has time right now. I just...never mind, we'll talk tomorrow."

"No, what?"

"I was wondering if you were, well, getting hints about the whole decorating thing. I noticed you don't have anything on your lawn, just lights around your windows and all."

Mae bristled. "I have lights on the roofline, the windows, and a huge wreath up."

"No! I'm *glad* you don't have plastic reindeer, believe me—that way our house doesn't look as naked. I've gotten a few not-so-subtle nudges the last few days, you know, to add more. Wondered if you were getting hassled too."

"No, but then I've been holed up most of the week, even forgot to get the mail yesterday. Are people really going to call me up?"

"Well, they do get a little freaky as opening night approaches. Just be prepared for persona-non-gratis treatment at Deb's unless Tommy brings home some light-up elves."

Mae twisted the phone cord tightly around one finger. "Gee, can't wait for the party. Sounds like a real blast."

"Forewarned is forearmed, kiddo. Listen, one holiday at a time, but I'd better get back to my turkey. So, yes for Kristy tomorrow night?"

"Yeah, thanks. See ya." Mae hung up the receiver and uncoiled the cord. She checked the clock: *shit, after four thirty. Good thing the food was ready.* "Guys?" she called down the stairwell. "Time to clean up! Half hour!"

Mae heard the TV click off as Kristy's complained, "Aww."

"Scoot," Tommy insisted. "Go see what Mom wants you to wear to Aunt Sophie's."

Then, calling up to Mae, "Here comes Kristy. I'll be up in five."

"Fine," she called back. *Good, can change before he comes up.*

♦ ♦ ♦

What's? Wake up, Mae, wake up! "No!" Mae swung blindly, hit something solid as she opened her eyes.

"Whoa, easy there, Bruce Lee! Just kissing you good-bye—gotta leave for work."

"Shit, Tommy, scare me a little, why don't you!"

"Nightmare again?"

"No, never mind. Bye." She blew a dismissive kiss in his general direction and rolled over, burying her head under the pillow.

"I'll stop by around lunchtime with the spotlight and the Rit dye." *C'mon, Mae, he's trying.*

Mae pulled the pillow aside and peeked with one eye. "Noon? I'll have lunch waiting."

"Sure, noon."

Mae lay still on her back, eyes closed, listening to his steps creaking down the staircase, and then the faint click of the mudroom door. Stillness. Kristy must not be up yet. *Crud, no going back to sleep now.* Mae tried curling up on her side. Nope, wide awake, bothered by Tommy's expression as he left. *Did he have to look so wounded? Are we that messed up?* Her left foot started jiggling as she pondered their exchange, felt guilt welling up into her chest. *Get up, quietly, grab a toke. No, Kristy could be up any time. Oh! Vodka, yeah, vodka and OJ. Just a little bit to settle down.* Mae kicked back the covers and arched her back to feel the little cracks release down her spine.

♦ ♦ ♦

"So there's not really a *hot*-pink dye, but I got a couple of boxes of red you can mix in with the pink. Carly said that'd brighten it up. I probably got too much, but I can return the extras once you figure it out."

"Who's Carly?" Mae asked absently, cutting his sandwich on the diagonal and transferring it to a plate. "Cheetos? Want Cheetos? With the tomato soup?"

"Carly: the one who works in housewares. With the perm. The one you don't like."

Mae flapped her free hand, gesturing acquiescence. "Right, ditzy blond chick." She shook out a small mountain of Cheetos, drowning his sandwich. Mae grinned as she licked the orange dust off her fingers. Then, composing her expression, she turned to serve his lunch. "Here ya go."

Tommy stared at the mounded plate, then looked up at her, puzzled. "Really? All this for me?"

Mae giggled as she plopped down next to him. "I'll help you. Oh, where's my drink?" She jumped up but had to grab the edge of the table to steady herself; he didn't notice. Mae snatched her orange juice and lowered herself carefully.

"God, Mae, you gotta be kidding."

"What?" she murmured, taking a sip. *Be cool.*

"Orange juice and Cheetos? That's disgusting."

Whew. Mae shrugged lightly. "Guess I'm in the mood for orange food." She snatched a Cheeto from his plate, grinning as she bit into it.

Tommy shook his head. "Guess so. Hey, if OJ and Cheetos put you in such a good mood, have at it. Want orange soup too?" He offered the cup of tomato soup, but she shook her head vigorously, stuffing two Cheetos in her mouth. With a lopsided smile, he set the soup spoon down and fed two more to her. *Those dimples!* Mae chomped with an appreciative nod.

Tommy scooped up a dozen or so more and lay them in front of her. "Just for you," he offered gallantly, settling into his sandwich. "So anyway," he continued between bites, "Carly said for that much fabric to dissolve two packets of pink and one of red, maybe only half the red and then throw a white rag in to check if you want more red or pink. She thought two and a half, three boxes max."

"Oh well, if Carly says so!" Mae rolled her eyes.

"She's just trying to help. Do it your way; I don't care." *Looking at her too closely.* Mae took a big slug of her drink. Tommy frowned. "I can't believe you're drinking that."

Did he know? "Juice. Vitamins. Energy."

"Just do me a favor and wait to throw up after I get back to work, okay?"

"I'm not gonna throw up, wise guy."

"Where's Kristy anyway?" He fished the other half sandwich out from under the Cheetos.

"At Sarah's already."

"Hmm, so what're you doin' this afternoon?"

"Just dye the curtains and bedspread hot pink for Her Majesty and then clean up for the Candy Cane extravaganza."

"Oh right, I meant to tell you: by the time I close today, I probably should just head straight over to the party. Mind meeting me there?"

"Nope, that's fine. I'll walk over."

"You getting dressed up?"

"Dunno."

"Well, I was just going to grab a fresh shirt and my red sweater vest now and change right as I lock up. Sound okay?"

Mae smacked her lips. "Sure." She grabbed another Cheeto.

Tommy pushed the plate toward her. "Here. They're yours. Gotta run." He pushed in his chair and kissed Mae on the top of the head. "Just gonna grab my vest. See you there about six? Six fifteen?"

"Somethin' like that." Mae didn't look up from her Cheetos. "See ya."

"Okay, bye." As he bounded up the stairs, Mae refilled her glass half full of orange juice, waiting, listening for the steps down, the creak of the front door.

"Bye!" he called. Click of the door latch.

"Bye!" she echoed, reaching for the vodka bottle behind the olive oil, eyeing it carefully: almost empty. Still, what was left glinted prettily. "What the hell!" She poured out the last of it—only two, maybe three shots—and carefully filled the bottle with tap water, not quite half full. *Yeah, looks about right.* Mae screwed the cap on, positioning the bottle behind the bourbon.

♦ ♦ ♦

The agitator swished left, right, left, right. *Ick.* Made her a little woozy. Left, right, left, right, the two reds and two pinks flowed together, splashing bloody-looking drops across the top of the washer. Mae shuddered and closed the top of the machine. *Gross. No more booze till the party. Just finish this, then a long shower.*

Mae stumbled into the kitchen to check the oven timer. Almost twenty minutes before the rinse cycle. She tapped her hands absently on the counter. *Now what?* She shuddered again. *Yuck, too much orange. Hated when he was right. Felt all floaty, vision was floaty… no, wait, snow?* Mae squinted out the window: snow, a real flurry. *Shit, haven't gotten the mail in two days. Shit. Then again, a little cold air might help.* Dragging one hand along the wall for balance, Mae grabbed her jacket, got an arm shoved into one sleeve. Flipping her hair over the bulky collar, she got her other arm in as she tugged open the front door. *Great, a fuckin' blizzard.* Hunching her shoulders to keep the snow off her neck, she stepped right into a burst of wind. *Shit!* Clutching the collar tighter, Mae wobbled down the driveway, feeling the vodka sloshing each time the wind shoved her backward or sideways. *Shit—ow!* She found herself on her ass near the curb. *Shit, fuck! Shit, fuck!* On hands and knees, she pulled herself up on the post of the mailbox, clinging tightly while she dug out the letters and bills crammed inside. Clutching them to her chest, Mae leaned against the box and tried to suck in a few deep breaths of the bracing air.

It was hard to see, even squinting against the stinging snowflakes. Their gray swirl muddled her sense of up and down. *Focus, Mae, focus.* She fixed her eyes on the mailbox next door: not moving, could help her be steady. Just then a particularly sharp gust of wind popped the box open and a red, no pink, no red paper whipped out, a blur of red scuttling frantically along the curb, catching on her toe as if it needed to catch its breath. Mae leaned over to snatch at it and fell heavily on top, still clutching her mail to her breast. *Damn!* Feeling the crumple paper under her hip, Mae dug it out carefully and peered through the frenetic snowflakes:

> **Last chance! Candy Cane lights go on promptly at 5:45 p.m. on Friday! We're going for the "three-peat," and the CCL Committee thanks you for your beautifully decorated yards! Still, we have a few neighbors not as fully in the spirit as you (see list below) so PLEASE find a way to suggest they do more (but tactfully: shh)!**
> **Your CCL Committee,**
> **Deb, Debbie, & Debz**

Mae's eyes dropped down the list: Fisher, Goldman, Panos...*well, fuck them, fucking Candy Cane Committee!* She lurched up onto her feet, supported by the mailbox, contemplating Cynthia's twinkling white lights, a generous dose of them blanketing the shrubs under their bay window. Then, turning slowly to assess her own home, Mae took in the large wreath on the front door, the red spotlight positioned below it, and the neat line of bulbs clipped to the gutters, all the way around the house, and outlining the first-floor windows...*well, fuck them!* Tears stung her eyes as she stumbled toward the front door. Kicking over the spotlight, she slammed the door behind her, sending the wreath bouncing against the other side.

♦ ♦ ♦

Mae stopped the drier to check again, but it was still damp. *Dammit, come on!* Had to keep the temperature low, though, or it would shrink. She reset the drier for another fifteen minutes, checked that there was no more chocolate on her fingertips before she sat back down at the sewing machine. Mae licked her fingers to make sure, savoring the aftertaste of hash hanging on the surface of her tongue. *Man, such good shit.*

She hunched over the seams, pinching them into a rough overlap and racing to feed them up under the needle. The motor surged as the needle zigzagged frantically, locking the strips together. *Those fuckers.* She glanced at the clock: nearly five fifteen. "Lights on promptly at five forty-five," she intoned aloud. *Almost ready.* She fed the material as fast as she could, debating between twine and clothespins, wondering if she had a laundry marker. *Ow!* Mae blinked, confused: the machine had jammed. *Damn, not now! What happened?* Mae inspected more closely, muttering, "Shit cakes." Her left index finger was wedged under the feeder foot, the needle buried right through the center of the nail. Mae tried to turn the manual wheel. Jammed. "Son of a bitch!" she yelled, giving the wheel an extra twist and wincing as the needle abruptly dragged back up to the surface of the nail.

Mae flipped up the presser bar and slid the finger out. Blood welled up where the needle had punched all the way through her finger. Mae examined the nail, now whitish except for a purple center and a fat, shiny ball of blood sitting on top. Sucking on that, Mae was suddenly calm: all her upset feelings were now concentrated in that boring ache under her nail. She felt strangely composed. She reached into the garbage for a scrap of fabric and bound up the finger tightly with one hand and her teeth. *Pain's not so bad. Pain is good. Back to seams.*

Chapter Eighteen

Not Christmas

Mae rang the doorbell, fighting back a Cheshire-cat grin. Hearing footsteps, she licked her lips. The door swung open, and there was Deb in a sheer green blouse and a snug Christmas vest, tiny knitted trees all around the waist. Black slacks, leather boots with tall stack heels. *Wow.*

"Mae, there you are!" Deb exclaimed, pulling Mae into the foyer. "I've had to keep your husband company for nearly a half hour. Why so late?"

Mae let her grin break wide but slowly, sweetly. "You know, just a last-minute urge to do some extra decorating," Mae purred. "I knew the judges could drive by any time after six, so it was now or never!"

Deb wrinkled her nose appreciatively, oozing, "Well, that's the best possible excuse for being late! Let me take your coat and get you a drink, so you can catch up!"

"If you insist!" Mae demurred, unbuttoning her coat and slipping out of the sleeves. She bit back a triumphant grin in response to Deb's confused expression. Mae smoothed the skirt of her silk suit and smiled brightly. "Overdressed?" she ventured.

"Oh no, not at all," Deb responded quickly if unconvincingly. "You look great. C'mon, let's get you that drink."

"I like the sound of that!" Mae laced her arm through Deb's. The suit was snug—the silk had shrunk a little—and was now hot pink. The skirt was just long enough to allow a side slit, and the men were noticing.

Deb extricated her arm as Tommy emerged from the crowd, looking both perplexed and amused. "Here's your girl!" Deb announced. "I'll go get her some eggnog." With a sidelong glance, Deb click-clacked away as Tommy moved very close, blocking everyone's view of Mae. "Is that your wedding dress?" he whispered.

"Yes!" she responded brightly and too loudly, taking a step back so he could admire her handiwork. "Decided to dye it. Silk takes color so well."

Tommy stepped close again, and in a low voice, he countered, "Mae, it's hot pink, not exactly Christmas colors, and it's...really, really showing everything."

"I know!" Mae beamed, sidestepping him to show herself. "I still have hot legs. I think I look good. And they seem to!" She nodded toward a cluster of the husbands, blowing a kiss hello.

"Yes, I'm sure they do." He studied her face. "You all right? You look flushed."

"I'm just totally in the Christmas spirit, totally up for a party!" Mae beamed at Deb and a proffered glass of eggnog. "Aren't you sweet! Hostess with the mostess!" Mae took a delicate sip. "I taste rum!" Mae drained the cup. "Delish!"

"Careful, Mae!" Deb laughed. "It's sweet, but it's strong."

"Think I can handle it. Oh, and look at your earrings! Aren't they just too darling!" Mae flicked at the little dangling red ornaments with her finger. "Too cute!" she insisted even as Deb pulled back awkwardly. "Anyway," Mae continued, "just point me toward the punch bowl. As you said, I have some catching up to do."

"Follow me," Deb responded, weaving her way into the thick of her guests.

"Wait." Tommy gripped Mae's arm. "I don't think you need to catch up," he murmured. "I think you got a head start on us, didn't you?"

Through a gritted smile, Mae asserted, "Joseph Thomasini, take your hand off me right now, or I'll make a scene."

"I think that ship has sailed. Keep your voice down."

"Only if you let go!" Mae twisted loose, smoothed her skirt, and sashayed in the direction of the husbands, calling brightly to them, "Buy a girl a drink?"

Debbie's Greg stepped forward. "More eggnog or a martini?"

"Yes!" Mae cooed, waving her empty glass. "I'm playing catch-up, so surprise me!" She patted his shoulder. "Love your vest—ooh, cashmere?" She let her hand glide down his back and then rubbed her cheek against his chest, resting her head there to hear his heart quicken. "I just love cashmere, don't you?" she whispered, nuzzling her nose into him. "Hmm..." And then with tug, she was jerked back.

"Tommy," she warned, shaking off his grip and then hesitating: Tommy was standing a few feet away, staring at her. *Wait, but who...?* Mae looked down at her arm and saw Greg's hand letting go. Checked his face: flushed, but no gleam in his eyes, no spark, nothing playful, more like—*oh God*—like he was assessing a grease stain on his tie. Mae felt a flush mottling up her neck, burning her cheeks, as if the pink suit were bleeding upward. She took in a few more faces, an unexpected blend of disapproval and unkind bemusement. Mae stumbled closer to Tommy, saw him reach toward her—*thank God, yes, take my arm*—but only to pluck her glass out of her hand. Mae reached toward him; he shrunk back in stony silence. *C'mon, Tom, help.*

Tommy took one step close, his fist closing on the back of her collar, tugging her up onto her tiptoes. *Tommy, don't! I'm not steady.* He spoke right past her: "Greg, sorry, clearly someone started before the party." Shook her by the scruff of the neck like a puppy, pulled her up even higher so she tottered and had to grab at him, tried to catch his eye, but he resolutely looked past her as he directed a subdued, "Excuse us," to everyone and to no one, and dragged her toward the foyer, letting her skitter on her tippy-toes.

Look at me! I'm here. Don't act like I'm invisible. Mae shuddered, really deeply from her gut. *Oh God, gonna throw up.* Mae dug her nails into his arm, gestured for the door. "Hold my hair?" she begged as he pulled the front door ajar, threading her past the threshold and letting her legs collapse under her on the frozen front step. She crumpled over, holding the vomit in her mouth, scrambling on her knees toward the shrubs, vomiting on the glowing candy cane. Heard the door close behind her.

♦ ♦ ♦

Bleh. Gross. Oh God, help...my mouth tastes so...jeez, somebody help, take care of me...? Oh God, can't do this alone, gonna throw up again. No, Mae, breathe, just breathe through it. Calm down, breathe...

Click. Stepping out, Tommy closed the door behind him. Mae peered up: his head seemed so far away, and her head was barely above his knees. She felt a giggle bubble up her throat at their mismatch, but she clamped her hand over her mouth and waited expectantly. He was holding something. *Is it my coat? You didn't want me to be cold?*

Tommy wrinkled his nose. "Oh no, you gonna hurl again?" He reached for the doorknob, but Mae grabbed at his pant leg.

"No!" she pleaded with a tug. "No, stay! I'm okay, just cold..." She checked his arms: no coat, just a grocery bag and a roll of paper towels. "Oh," she murmured. "Am I...will you...?" She shuddered. The blowing snow was muddling the little bit of thought she could muster.

Tommy dropped the paper-towel roll. It bounced once and rested against her leg. "Me? No way. Clean up this mess, and if I were you, I'd do it quickly, 'cause people are coming out in a minute or two to walk along the street. Here's a bag to put it all in. Hurry up."

"Help me?"

Tommy pulled his leg away. "I helped you by suggesting they go out through the mudroom door. More for their benefit than yours. Better hurry."

"Tom, at least keep me company, you know, block their view of...me? Please?"

His gaze bored down on her from way up there, piercing through the bursts of snowflakes. "I thought the whole point was to *be* seen." Sounded nasty.

"Oh c'mon, not like this, not like..." she gestured vaguely. "I need help," she whimpered, not fighting the tears brimming up. *I'm crying, for God's sake. Help.*

Tommy rested his hand on the doorknob. "Cynthia wanted to come help you, but I told her no. Clean this up, Mae. Your mess. I'll be back with your coat in five minutes to take you home. You're gonna sleep this off, and tomorrow we get to some kind of understanding before Kristy gets home. Got it?"

She nodded, vainly blinking back hot tears and sharp snowflakes blowing into her eyes. "But I'm so cold," she faltered. Everything felt numb, except for the melting flakes on her lashes. Snow was resting on her legs, on her frozen stockings. *Too numb, can't feel the edges of my body, can't tell where I end.*

"Then hurry." Tommy disappeared behind the door with a resolute click of the latch.

Taking a halting breath, Mae turned back to face her mess. Hoped to see a delicate blanket of snow covering everything for her, but no, the heat of the vomit was melting the snow, adding an oily patina to the garish spatter of red and orange. Sealing her lips tightly, Mae tore off a paper towel and started to wipe down the lighted candy cane, tried to look past it. *Don't think about it, don't look down.* She kept her eyes above the streaks, focused on the clean part, and let the stained paper towel drift down and rest over the puddle on the ground. *Don't look down, Mae, just drop sheets over it.* Her hands frantically tore off more paper towel, scattering the sheets all over the ground next to the stoop. Her shaking hands made the paper towels flutter nervously, but she could see out of the corner of her eye that a layer was accumulating, with a dusting of snow like powdered sugar. *More paper towels, make it a thicker layer.*

Voices threaded around the corner of the garage. *No, not yet, don't come out yet!* Mae sucked in as much frosty air as she could hold, and squinting so that she could just barely see, she turned toward the puddle, loosely scooping up the mound of paper and tossing the squishy warm pile into the grocery bag. Then she scooped up snow accumulating at the edge of the stoop and threw it over the stained grass, scooping more as she heard their chatter grow closer. *Now what?* Mae shrunk back against the brick wall, still and tiny, closed her eyes, wouldn't look as the crowd grew quiet walking down the driveway and then started to whisper and chuckle as they moved further down the sidewalk, closer to the corner, louder even though they were further away, louder even through the whispery gusts of wind and the screen of the snowfall. Mae pressed one cheek against the brick, could only tell it was rough, couldn't tell whether it was hot or cold, couldn't tell up or down either. Didn't look up, didn't want to see one arched eyebrow, not even a sympathetic sideward glance, no, wouldn't open her eyes for anything, not until they were gone, totally gone.

Mae startled at the clack of the front door but stayed frozen, still. *See what he says first.*

"Stand up," Tommy commanded.

Mae shook her head. "Can't." Pressed her face into the wall, the steady frozen brick.

"You have to. We'll walk home. I'll get the car tomorrow." She felt his hand grasp her elbow.

"I can't," she protested. His other hand clamped on the waistband of her skirt.

"Up," he insisted, pulling. Mae clutched blindly at his arm and scuffled to get her feet under her. "Okay, here's one sleeve." He threaded one arm and then the other into the coat, pulling the collar up against her neck. *Thanks, Tom.* She pressed her face into his shoulder—*better than the brick*. Heard the crumple of paper as he picked up the bag. "Walk," he directed. She stumbled; he sighed. "I'll go get the car."

Mae could see nothing but a penetrating, yellow film whisk across the windshield like an instant, golden shade. Still, she knew the door was just a few yards up on the left so she let the car roll forward, barely braking. ***Stop.***

"No!" Mae grabbed frantically. "No car! I'll walk, I can walk. I'm, I'm afraid of the car."

"What? God, you're messed up. Fine, we'll walk."

Mae nodded meekly. "No car."

"No, no car. C'mon, home. Step."

Step, step, focus, no car, gotta walk. No car, walk. Okay, she was finding her legs again. Tommy was holding her close, not too fast; she was starting to feel upright again, could feel her body again. *Step, step.*

"Tom?" she offered. "I'm getting better."

"That's debatable. Just walk."

As they turned the corner, Mae could make out the neighbors further down the sidewalk. They weren't moving. *Oh.* She shivered with simultaneous horror and glee. *Our house!* She felt Tommy slow, hesitating.

"What's...? Mae, why's everyone at our place?" He pushed her faster, but Mae started resisting, stumbling, postponing. *He wasn't going to get it.* But he pressed right up to the crowd, then froze. "No," he whispered.

Mae took in a couple of the faces, the expressions. She clapped her hand over her mouth, but couldn't contain the croaking laughter. "If you could just see your faces," she protested, deflecting Debbie's dagger glare with a floppy wave of her hand. "It's priceless!" Mae moaned happily, clutching at Tommy's collar. "Oh my God, Tom, look at their faces!" she sputtered, giggling. Mae turned to proudly view her handiwork. She'd secured the banner well: FUCK XMAS! flapped with each gust of wind, each flap like a new chant. The hot-pink fabric glowed red with the spotlight on it.

Whoa! Mae collapsed onto the sidewalk as Tommy sprinted toward the front door, tugging at the banner. "Sweetie!" she called after him, "I got it up there pretty good! You might need scissors..." With a huge jerk, he snapped down one end. "Or maybe not." Mae chuckled, turning toward the crowd. "Oh come on, you guys, it's a joke!" Mae cackled. "A joke for Chrissake! Lighten up!"

Snap! Tommy had the banner down. Wadding it up, he threw it in the shrubs and then, hesitating, ran his hands through his hair. "I'm so... sorry," he called out.

"It's a joke, Tommy!" Mae shrieked. "Don't you apologize!" She started to crawl toward him through the snowy lawn. Stopping halfway, she turned back and gestured toward the crowd. "Look at their faces! It's hil*ar*ious!" Mae grinned at the sea of stunned, scowling neighbors, deflating a little. "Well, maybe not as much at this point, but at first, come on, it was pretty damn funny!"

Tommy strode up to her and yanked her to her feet. "Mae is sorry. I am sorry," he announced.

"Oh no, I'm not!" Mae wriggled loose. "Don't you apologize for me. It's not my fault if you guys don't get it. I bet Cynthia gets it!" Mae scanned the crowd and locked onto Cynthia's incredulous face. "You get it, right, Cynth?"

"No, Mae," Cynthia faltered. "Why would I get it?"

"'Cause you feel the same way, right?"

"No, why would I?"

"'Cause you're Jewish!"

"You just had to ruin it for everyone else, didn't you?" Debbie cut in, seething.

"Everyone else, everyone else! Well, what about me? This is my take on Christmas decorating, and if you don't like it, screw you!"

"Yeah, well, screw you, too," Debbie shot back. "Loser! You pathetic, drunk loser!"

Tommy squeezed her arm, muttering, "Inside, Mae." *Like when he pinned her wrists. That horrible time. When he pinned her to the bedroom wall.*

His disengaged expression. They'd stared at each other, totally confused. Then his fingers had tightened at the roots of her hair. He was pressing so hard into her that she couldn't inhale. His other hand had tugged at her belt and ripped her zipper open. No. Oh my God, no!

Mae twisted away ferociously. "Don't you manhandle me! Don't you fucking touch me!" Mae threw up her hands. "What's wrong with all you people? It's Christmas! You know, be jolly! Laugh at a goddamn joke!"

"Mae, you're drunk, go inside," Tommy warned, hands up in surrender, but Mae was wary, stepping away from him.

"Christmas, people! Cookies and candy canes and Baby Jesus and the three kings and—oh, wait!" Mae clapped her hands excitedly. "Even better! Four princesses! Get it? The three Debs, and a JAP!" Mae pointed proudly at Cynthia. "Cynthia! Take a bow!" Mae beamed, clapping her hands again.

But Cynthia didn't bow, didn't move. "JAP?" she echoed, incredulous.

"Jewish American Princess! No shame in that! Be proud of who you are: sure beats these wasp-y types," Mae explained, poking her finger toward the Debbies. Mae gestured between Cynthia and herself. "We're our own people, right, Cynthia?"

Cynthia, silent, turned away. Gary slipped his arm around her shoulder. "C'mon, honey, let's get inside."

As they eased through the crowd, Mae called after them, "Cynthia! I'm just jokin' around! Look, you can call me a CAP, okay? Okay?"

Suddenly Tommy's face was right in front of hers. "Mae, go inside this minute." She backed away from him. "I won't touch you," he whispered, "if you go inside right now. Go."

Mae took one more step back. "Obviously nobody gets my sense of humor," she announced indignantly. "You're all so, so parochial!" Mae wrinkled her nose at the bunch of them and marched through her front door. Her heart skipped, hearing Tommy just a step behind her. Mustering her bravest voice, she tried to take charge: "Don't touch me, that's the deal."

Tommy snorted. "Like I'd want to touch you? Just tell me where it all is, the bottles, the stash."

"What?"

"The stuff." Tommy dragged open the doors of the entertainment system. "Here? Is it in here?" He roughly pushed the albums back and forth. "Behind here?" He pulled the lid off a ceramic pot, peered inside, and threw the whole thing on the floor.

"Hey, stop! Are you crazy?" Mae protested, chasing after the spinning ceramic lid. "Stop! Stop it!" she cried as he ripped through the shelves. "It's not there! There's nothing there!"

Tommy paused, turning to face her. "Okay, then where?"

"Bottles...in the kitchen. I, I finished the vodka. But nothing else..."

"Oh, bullshit!" Tommy raged, yanking out an end-table drawer and dumping it out. He kicked through the contents with his foot, muttered "Dammit!" and threw the drawer against the wall.

"Stop!" Mae shrieked. "You're scaring me!"

Tommy froze and peered at her closely, as if she were a bug he didn't recognize. Then he chuckled nervously. "I'm scaring you? You kidding me? I'm scaring you?"

Mae nodded, trying to look more angry than scared. Tommy took a menacing step toward her, while Mae held her ground. She pushed her chin out toward him.

In an almost-whisper, Tommy spelled it out. "Mae, you have one chance—one—to tell me where the pot or the hash oil or the whatever-the-fuck-it-is, is, before I rip the house apart. Now, right now. Tell me now, and don't tell me there isn't any."

Mae narrowed her eyes and, in her darkest, most controlled tone, replied, "There was some, but it doesn't matter where, 'cause it's gone, I finished it today." She held her breath.

"Some what?" he countered, matching her tone, her stiletto eyes.

Mae hesitated. With a softer, reasoning tone, she responded, "Some hash oil, but it's gone, so there's no point ripping the house apart." His expression wasn't yielding, so she tipped her chin up again, bracing.

"I don't believe you. You're a liar, and you're messed up."

"Well, you're a bully, and you're fucked up."

Tommy slapped Mae so hard that she bounced on the carpet. "Bully!" she screamed, holding her cheek. Mae watched him bite his fist, swaying back and forth indecisively. She rubbed her cheek lightly, making sure he knew it hurt. At the same time, though, she felt relieved now that all her pain was concentrated on her throbbing cheekbone. *Better.* Her mind was clear. Her gut was calm. Her heart didn't hurt. *Better.*

"I'm—oh God, are you all right?' Tommy's voice sounded boyish. He awkwardly reached one hand toward her, but she shrank back, so then he did too.

Mae nodded. *Better. Good, it felt good.* Mae clambered to her feet and stepped up to him.

"Oh God, Mae, we can't keep doing this," Tommy implored.

"Hit me again," Mae interrupted. "Do it. Hit me!"

"What?" Again he sounded like a little boy.

"Hit me," Mae insisted. "It helps."

"What? No!"

"Do it!" Mae shoved him. "I want you to!" She shoved him again. "Hit me!" She took a swing at him, but he grabbed her wrist.

"Stop it, Mae!"

Mae started slapping at him with her other hand. "C'mon, fight back!"

Tommy grabbed her other wrist and forced her down on her knees. "Cut it out!" he cried.

"Hit me!" she begged. "Just one more time, hit me hard!"

Tommy released her and stumbled back, collapsing on the sofa. "What's wrong with you? This is more than being drunk or stoned. Jesus, Mae, stop."

Mae crawled toward him. "Tommy?"

"No! Get away from me!"

"But, Tommy, listen, we can—"

"'We'? Mae, there is no we. We are sick. We are over. We are...over." He tipped his head back and covered his face with his hands, groaning.

Over? No. Mae pressed her palm against her pulsing cheekbone, but the pain was radiating out, pulsing down her neck and seeping back into her heart. Shaking her head, scattering tears, Mae scrambled up the stairs on her hands and knees, scuttling into the shadows of the empty master bedroom. Reaching up from the carpet, she flipped on the light, cringing at the brightness, falling back against the wall of the bathroom, hands up against the wall in surrender. *That wall.*

She had crawled along that wall, slipped back through the door of the bathroom, and closed and locked the door, pressing her back into the door, sliding down to the floor. Hate him, I hate him.

Mae punched at the air, at the light. His staccato sobs downstairs made her feel like her cheekbone was going to explode, too much, too much pain inside the bone, the heaviness of the bone. It pulled her down until she curled on her side on the floor, gasping for air, gasping at the shredding inside her heart. *Ouch, ouch, ouch.* Mae crawled over to the bathroom tile, grabbed his razor and tugged out the blade, pressed the edge into one palm, watched the blood bead up, felt the pressure dripping away. *Thank God, bleed, let it out, let it drain, bleed.* Mae hitched up her skirt and cut carefully, right through her stocking into her thigh, tearing the stocking away so it would not mess the perfect line of blood. *Longer, a longer line, let the blood out, yes, look at it, more, another line, parallel. Yes, look at the parallel lines of red. One more, for the Trinity.* She cut one more, long and deep and straight, and now her mind was clear, her heart was calm, because all of the pain was dripping away, rolling down her thigh, turning the bathroom grout pink, and now she could breathe and just be.

And the sparkles of the tiny gold lights...her eyes were nearly closed now: each mascara-choked lash tugged down, down, until just a sliver of light remained, just a fog of white, a trickle of red, and pale points of gold, barely gold, multiplying and washing everything else away. Just the shade of closing lashes, the dusting of gold everywhere, and the stone-cold heaviness pressing on her eyes, draining down her cheeks until she was almost paralyzed, but her lips could form one word, the only word she'd needed but hadn't made her own until just now. "Stop," Mae whispered, her lips curling up into a faint smile.

Chapter Nineteen

Not Sure

November or December 1979

The water's too deep, can't see the bottom. Dark air, dark water. Lake Michigan? What if something touches, seaweed or a corpse? How big do the fish get? Waves breaking over my head, cool but oily, up my nose, clogging my ear. Still can hear voices in the distance. The beach? So tired, gotta find the beach. Waves pushing one way, the next, some colder current below pulling my feet. Ew, slimy! Seaweed? A drowned swimmer? Splashing too much, too tired.

Nicky and Alex, yelling, laughing but so far away, echoes. Where are they? Where's the beach? They don't know I'm out here, but when I try to call out, another wave pushes into my throat, pushes fishy, slippery water over my tongue, makes me gag, choke. Can't yell, can only gasp for air...

Ow, ow, ow. Where...? Wait, what's this room? But look! God, look, there he is, sitting in the chair in the corner, patient, a little blurry, as if there were a cloudy current of water washing between us. He's leaning forward, elbows on knees, fingers laced together, thumbs braced against each other. Waiting, content. Smiling? Not quite, just a hint, but oh, his eyes welling up with love: "Right here, kiddo."

"Papa!" Mae croaked, wincing. Her voice caught in her throat, tangled on barbed wire, slashing to get past. *Try again.* "Papa," she mouthed, hoping he could see her try. He blinked. Didn't respond but didn't look away, either. Mae tried to reach for him, but she couldn't find her arms, that icky floaty feeling. *Try again, Mae, reach!* Grimacing, she rolled one shoulder, but the arm didn't follow, didn't reach, tugged back.

"No, Mae, don't," a woman's voice coaxed. Mae cautiously rolled her head to the left. "Don't try to move, Mae. You really can't."

Mrs. O'Toole? What—in the infirmary? Am I in the infirmary? Why's Nora's mother here? Why is her hair red? Where's Mama? Oh, but Papa! Mae craned her neck to reach back through the blur: yes, he was still there. He nodded, winked. Mae let her head sink back onto the pillow.

"That's right. Don't strain, Mae. Just rest, okay?" She smoothed Mae's bangs back. "Just rest. I'm here. I'm here with you. Rest."

Sighing, Mae closed her eyes. No sense, this made no sense. A ripple of nausea made her shudder. *Ick. Flu? In the infirmary with flu? Papa, not Mama? Just rest.* Mae moaned, sinking deeper into the mattress.

"That's right. Sleep."

Mae opened her right eye just enough to check: he was still there, not going anywhere. She let the lid droop closed again. The dark was good. The dark was safe after all.

♦ ♦ ♦

Ew, can see it growing. Gotta stop sweating, it's growing out of the sweat, there, right there on my belly. A pink mushroom welling up from my belly button, icky pressure, but don't touch it. Don't touch. Leave it alone. But it's brittle, it's crystal, like crystal, could snap it off, send it skittering across floor. They said don't touch, but I can snap it off, make it gone. Snap! Now it's rolling on the floor, off, thank God! No, no, what's that itchy feeling? Arghh, I'm itchy all over, can't scratch, can't. Wait, it's going away, now it's only itchy at my waist, at, at my belly button… oh no, no, no, can feel another one starting to grow. There are more. No!

Throbbing, left temple throbbing. Ow, ow, ow. Damn, just want to sleep. Mae reached up to rub her face, but her arm snapped still, frozen, just inches off the mattress. *What the—?* Jarred awake, Mae tugged harder, felt the bed shudder, felt the squeezing on her wrist. *What the fuck!* She squinted, trying to make sense of it: an ace bandage, wrapped two, three times around her wrist and knotted to the side railing of the bed. *What the fuck!* Mae tried a sharper jerk. The bed bounced a little. Rolling her head, she saw the other wrist tied down. *Son of a bitch.* Mae wriggled both arms, twisting and undulating her fists like a baton twirler, ignoring the pinching, and then, rolling and kicking, she shrieked in frustration, not even recognizing the throaty croak filling the room. *Damn, my throat hurts!* But she kept the ragged yells coming—someone had to help her.

"Mrs. Thomasini, Mrs. Thomasini!" a nurse bustled in. "Shh! No, don't struggle: you'll hurt yourself." She firmly held one wrist down against the mattress. "Stop. You're okay, but stop."

Mae complied, more out of sheer confusion than cooperation. *Who was this girl? Plump, pale, couldn't be more than seventeen, eighteen, playing nurse in her snug white uniform...?* Mae's eyes darted erratically around the room: hospital bed, window—dark outside, night?—the chair in the corner, vinyl dulled by Lysol. Mae looked back at the child-nurse. "How?" Mae croaked. *Ouch.*

"Shh," the girl insisted, one hand on Mae's wrist, the other almost touching Mae's lips. "Don't, that's going to hurt. You had a tube down your throat, and it's out now, but you'll still be sore for a couple of days. Lie still, don't try to talk. My name's Rose. Did you hear me? I'm Rose. I'll take care of you. But you need to lie still."

Look, dozens and dozens of roses, yellow and white and red. Not pink. Dozens, hundreds, but can't smell them, and they don't have thorns, how can they not have thorns? Nurse, nurse, the roses need their thorns! Don't let them open, or petals will fall off! Tell Nora, tell Emma: they need their thorns. Ow. My throat hurts.

"Shh." Her eyes were patient, as if they'd seen too much for her age, but this girl was so young, this child-nurse giving directions. Mae glanced all around, taking in the switches on the headboard, the chart clipped to the foot of her bed, the chair—*shouldn't be empty, where was...couldn't quite remember who...?*

"Mrs. Thomasini, look at me," she ordered. "Good, now listen: you're in Resurrection Hospital. Understand?"

Not really, but Mae nodded feebly.

"Good, okay. Mrs. Thomasini, you're in the hospital, and it's almost midnight. I know it's confusing, but try to understand. It's Tuesday night. You've been here several days. You've been sick."

Mae shuddered and strained to rest her hand on her stomach. *No! Another little lump, another mushroom growing.* She tried to push it back down.

"No, don't pull on the restraints. That won't help. Your hands are tied down to protect you. You were scratching and swinging at the ER docs. Gave one a black eye. Tore out some of your own hair, too, so you're in restraints till we know you won't hurt yourself. Please trust us: we know what's best."

Mae stared dully: *couldn't be more than eighteen, but you know what's best. For me.* Barely shaking her head, Mae groaned, "Off." *Damn, her throat was raw.*

"Off? No, I'm sorry, I can't. That takes doctor's orders."

A tear trickled down the outside of Mae's cheekbone, resting on her earlobe. The girl-nurse wiped it away.

"Aw, Mrs. Thomasini, just a few hours till rounds, and I'll put a note in your chart that you requested no restraints. Maybe, could you sleep a little, until morning? You do need rest."

Mae rolled her face away, focusing on the empty chair. She sank limply into the mattress.

"That's right, relax." She sweetly dabbed at Mae's tears. "It's confusing, I know, but we're taking good care of you, so don't you worry. Just get some sleep. And here." The girl-nurse pressed the call button into Mae's left hand. "See, this reaches. So you be sure to buzz me if you want anything." Mae nodded, gripping the buzzer firmly.

"Good." The little nurse patted Mae's arm for emphasis. "I'll be here all night. My name is Rose, and I'm just a buzz away. But the best thing you can do is sleep. Feel like you can do that?"

Mae nodded and let her eyelids drop. She felt little Rose smooth her blanket, listened to the light footsteps on the tile floor. Mae slowly opened her eyes, focused on the weirdly yellow light streaming in between the slats of the shade. *Parking lot?* Her gaze drifted to the empty chair in the corner: the Lysol streaks glowed a little, too dull to have color but bouncing light into the air. The cushion was depressed. Too many bodies sitting there too many hours, hollowing the cheap foam and vinyl. A record of past visitors. Empty. Mae's tears receded. Maybe empty was better. The heaviness in her forehead started to recede as well. At least hollow didn't hurt.

♦ ♦ ♦

"Mae?" His voice was tentative, sweet, made her fight to open her eyes, but the lids fluttered drunkenly, sinking and wriggling and sinking again, but she wanted to see if he was back: *Papa wouldn't leave again.*

"Mae? That's it, open your eyes!" he begged, but not Papa's voice. Mae frowned and managed to force her right eye open: no, the chair was empty. A whimper bubbled up her throat, and discouraged, she let her eyelid fall closed.

"No, Mae, come back, please? Look at me, Mae!" Mae rolled onto her left cheek and forced both eyelids up, enough to see Tommy through the veil of her eyelashes. His face was so close she could smell the shampoo on his curls. "Mae?"

Let him know: he sounds scared. Mae nodded feebly, managing a *t* sound as she exhaled.

"Yes, it's me. Yes, oh God, yes, it's me, Tom. I've been here a lot."

Mae frowned, shook her head.

"No, Mae, really, I have! I know, they told me you woke up during the night, and I'm sorry you were scared, but you've hardly been alone at all.

I've been here, or your mom, or Michael, Nora, but you've mostly been out of it, Mae. We've all been here."

"Kristy?" she whispered. *Ow, damned throat.*

"No, not Kristy. She wants to see you but not yet, not when you're..."—he searched for words with his hands in the air—"like this." He gently touched her left wrist, and she remembered, yanked, but the restraint snapped back.

"Off!" she mouthed as forcefully as she could, her eyes brightening with a surge of angry humiliation. She snapped both wrists to make sure he understood.

"No, don't, easy!" Tommy tried to pat her arm, but she shrank away from him as far as the ties allowed. He sat back and bowed his head. Mae distrustfully studied the blond ripples and waves, couldn't see his face except for the tip of his straight, Roman nose. She braced as he raised his face to her, but she wasn't prepared for the sorrow and surrender clouding his expression. Now *his* eyelids looked impossibly heavy.

Tommy cleared his throat and laid his hands very deliberately in his lap, lacing his fingers together so tightly that the knuckles turned ghostly white. Mae's eyes darted hesitantly between his knuckles and his taut mouth. Couldn't stand to look him in the eye.

"No, Mae, I won't touch you. Don't be, be scared of me," he implored, pale, defeated. "It—look, we've made a mess of it. I mean, I really let you down. I never wanted to be someone you had to be afraid of, or that you had to try to escape somehow..." His voice trailed off as he ran his fingers through his hair, started to reach for her, and caught himself, pressing his fists into his thighs. "I'm sorry," he choked out, guttural and garbled. "I meant to take better care of you, I really did." A huge tear rolled down his nose and splashed onto his leg. He dropped his head, curled down almost into his lap, slumped shoulders all but disappearing. Except for a jagged breath every few seconds, he seemed frozen.

The weight of his defeat crept over Mae, immobilizing her as well. She waited for him to look up, wanted to somehow let him know that she, too, felt the heavy muck layered over them. She waited, but he didn't move, wouldn't raise his face to her, and she felt her own face growing dull, was afraid she was fading away.

"Roses," she wheezed.

"What?" he searched her face. "Say again, what?"

"Roses," she whispered with all the breath she could find.

"I'm sorry, I can't understand what you're saying. Roll? Roll over?"

"No!" she croaked, tearing up.

"I'll get the nurse. I'll get someone to help."

"No!" she mouthed, shaking her head back and forth. *No, no, no. Don't leave. I'm too little to be left alone. Where's Papa?* "T—" she exhaled.

"Yeah?" he sniffed. Wiped his eyes with his sleeve. "What? What can I do?"

Mae wiggled her wrist. "Please?"

"Um, no, at this morning's rounds, he said no, not till you can talk with a psychiatrist. But I can tell the doctor you want them off—is that what you want?"

Mae nodded faintly. She motioned with her fingers to come closer. The darkness in her head was growing. She was sinking into it. "Safe," she whispered.

"Yes, you're safe."

"No!" she groaned, tugging on the bandages. "Safe!"

"Oh, it's safe for them to be off?

"Uh-huh," she exhaled, eyelids fluttering like butterflies.

"Safe, okay, I'll tell the doctor you said that, and that you want doctor to see you, so they can come off. I'm not sure, is that what you need, Mae?"

Her eyelids wouldn't stay open, but she could hear the trace of his voice. "Good," she mouthed.

"Mae, can you hear me? I promise we'll get Kristy in soon, once the restraints are off. Would that be good? Mae?"

The black space between them was dense and unbending. She couldn't make a sound, couldn't find her face, not sure if she was sending a trace of a smile to him. *Trying.*

"Yes, Mae, rest now. I'll be right here, promise. And I'll take care of, of it all..." His voice was washing away.

Sinking under the waves. Toes in the muck. Sinking into the slime.

♦ ♦ ♦

Nick, looming like a skyscraper, giant concrete Nick, glassy eyed, peering down at Mae, grim, disapproving. Stony, nasty silence. Mae scurries up North Michigan Avenue, darting between shoppers, glancing back to check if she's eluded his gaze, but no, need to hide! He could reach down and snatch her, gotta keep head low, duck in some shadow, the shadow of the old Water Tower that survived the Chicago fire, pretend to pass it, then dive into its shadow, hug the yellowish stones, crumple up tight like the McDonald's wrappers, be small, be small, cling to the rock, find little nooks to press into, hang on. His gaze sweeps like a search light, the Gestapo determined to take back an escaping prisoner. Don't breathe, grip tighter. The stone below her middle finger gives way, crumbling like a vanilla cookie, and a trickle of water spills down a crooked path like tears curling over a cheekbone. No! Press, stop the flow, but more water washing away bits of stone, pebbles popping and water bubbling with excitement, escaping in noisy gurgles. Shh! Please, quiet, don't! Mae presses both palms against the flow, but the water's staining the ground. His gaze locks on the puddle. No, no! Mae shrinks back, tiny as she can be, tucks into the shadow. I'm a shadow, just a shadow, don't illuminate me. I'll be gone, gone, just leave me to be a shadow. She closes her eyes tightly, but water gurgles, eases into a big puddle, a big shiny disk that bounces his light onto her scrunched-closed eyes, light tapping on her eyelids, warming her cheek: I see you.

♦ ♦ ♦

"Mary, can you hear me? Mary?"

What? No, keep your eyes closed, maybe he'll go away.

"Mary, wake up."

Sees me. Mae batted her eyes open a few times, focused: oh, the doctor, and three child-doctors at his elbow. *The restraints!* Mae arranged a timid smile for them and wiggled up on her pillow. "Morning," she offered, low and raspy.

"Good morning, Mary." The doctor was glancing down her chart, then paused to lock into eye contact. "How are you feeling?" It sounded like a challenge.

"Good," Mae whispered, carefully submissive. She glanced at the interns to acknowledge them, then readdressed the doctor. "Better."

He did not respond and her assertion floated in the space between them. He clicked his pen. "Better? In what way?"

Gonna make me beg? Fine. "S-sleeping, eating a little, and...not so sore now." Eased a second soft smile to them, suggesting nothing hurt.

"Then your throat is feeling better?"

Mae nodded. *Talk!* "Yes," she responded clearly.

"Good." The doctor turned to the interns. "ER admission for...?"

"Polydrug ingestion," answered the tall girl with a pixie haircut.

"Diagnosis?"

"Alcohol and cannabis intoxication, self-inflicted lacerations," she volleyed back confidently.

"And...?"

With a sidelong glance at Mae, the girl addressed the doctor: "Possible suicidal ideation."

"No!" Mae protested vigorously. They all turned to look at her. "No," she insisted. "Not suicidal, never suicidal."

Again, her assertion hovered, a tiny, erratic hummingbird they might easily brush aside. "Really," Mae added, seeing their skepticism. "I'm Catholic." The interns turned to the doctor, who looked as unconvinced as they looked uncomfortable.

"Let's see how the wounds are healing." The doctor folded back Mae's blanket and flipped up the hem of her gown so they could inspect her thighs. Mae tried not to blush as they gathered closely to scrutinize her cuts, peeling up the sticky gauze pads.

"Nice stitches, healing well. Replace this." The doctor lifted the corner of a pad stiff with clotted blood and handed it to a student. He turned his attention back to Mae. "So I understand you'd like to be out of restraints." He walked to the side of her bed, a more conversational distance between them. Mae tried to tune out the intern fumbling with the bandage.

"Please?"

"What's your understanding of why you've had them on?"

"Was, uh, drunk—kinda fought being brought in."

"Mm-hmm?" *He was looking for more. Shit.*

"I'm...I can lie still without restraints. I would. Really."

The doctor was quiet, seemed aware that everyone awaited his judgment. "You say you're not suicidal?"

"No."

"Never were?"

"No, never."

Silence. "Those cuts are deep," he noted. "You lost enough blood to be in the hospital for almost a week now."

All eyes were on Mae. "Yes, uh..." she faltered. "Stupid, that was stupid, stupid of me to ever get that fucked—excuse me, messed up. But no, not trying to kill myself. You know, I have a little girl, a daughter."

Silence. Then from an intern, gently, "Then why?"

Mae's eyes settled gravely on the young man. He looked nice enough, sincere, wanted to understand. *But how can you understand? Early twenties and in med school, done everything right, think you can plan your life? Think you can make everything turn out right, don't you? You're so wrong, but how can I explain it won't work, that you can't...*

"Mary?" the doctor's impatience cut in.

Mae looked down at her restraints and then up at the doctor. "Hard to explain. The pain, the cutting helped me feel less...I dunno, less confused, less lost, like a fog. And I needed a focus, you know?" She glanced to check the young man's face. *Was that enough? I don't want to tell you the rest.* His face was slightly perplexed but sympathetic. "But won't need that anymore. No drugs. No drinking even. So no more fog, no confusion." Her resolute tone seemed to bounce off the doctor's white jacket and his impassive expression.

"You plan to stay sober."

"Yes," Mae insisted. Her throat felt shredded, but she kept her voice strong.

"That's harder than you think. You were in withdrawal for three days. I suspect you can't remember much of it, can you?"

"No," Mae murmured, "but that means I'm clean now, right?" A hopeful smile.

"Getting sober and staying sober are two different issues. Tell you what, Mary. I'll order restraints off on the condition you see Dr. Gregorich, from psychiatry. You'll need to plan for psychiatric support at discharge. You willing to do that?"

Mae sighed. "How many times?"

"That's up to her. Could be once, could be more."

Mae nodded. "Then these come off? She tugged lightly and turned toward the interns, but they watched the doctor expectantly. She held her palms toward the doctor. "Please?"

"The nurse will take care of that shortly." He jotted something in her chart as he turned toward the door, interns in tow.

Mae sank into the pillow, biting the inside of her cheek to counter the flashes of pain in her throat. She opened and closed her fists a few times. *Shortly. In just a little bit.*

♦ ♦ ♦

"So where's Rose been? Haven't seen her lately." Mae tried to be chatty, while the nurse made small, deliberate cuts through the ace bandage.

"Rose?" She frowned, eyes fixed on her methodical snips. "There's no Rose on our unit."

Now Mae frowned. "I talked to her a couple of nights ago, when I woke up at night. She was the first one I talked to." *Come on, hurry up, get these off.*

"Don't pull," the nurse corrected. "These are extremely sharp, and you don't need one more cut."

Mae tried to relax her arm and brush off the chastisement. "Better?"

"Hm." The nurse nodded, positioning for the next cut.

"But Rose?"

"Not on my staff. Maybe there's someone new on nights, but not that I'm aware of."

Mae sifted through the shards of memories she'd held onto across the last few days: *the yellowish light at the window, Rose pressing the buzzer into her hand, the streaks of light in her hair. Was she young, or was she old with streaks of gray? Wait, what did she look like again?*

"There!" the nurse announced, whisking away the last layer of gauze and turning over Mae's hand to examine the wrist. "Skin looks good." She looked up at Mae with a crinkly smile. "That has to feel good, eh?" She lightly rubbed both sides of the wrist, moving moved it closer for Mae to inspect. "Feel okay?"

"Feels great!" Mae sighed. The skin looked a little whitish, kind of ghostly, but some pink was inching into it from her palm. Mae rotated her wrist left, then right, then left again as the nurse positioned herself on the other side of the bed.

"Be still now," she warned. "Just rest it on your tummy while I get this one."

Mae obediently laid her hand on her stomach, the fleshy part of her thumb cradled in her belly button.

"Good," the nurse noted somewhat automatically, intent on the other bandage. Mae watched without comment, smiling a little at each click of the scissor tips connecting through the gauze. Her eyes flit over the nurse's uniform, lighting on the golden plastic name tag—KATHY—and then up to her face, to her broad cheekbones, her slightly heavy but very even brow, her lips pursed in concentration. Pleasant if no-nonsense, nursey. Another staccato snap.

"Kathy?"

"One second please!" A louder snip and the bandage relaxed into loose spirals. Again Kathy brushed her hands over the skin, patted it, and only then looked up at Mae. "Yes?"

"Oh!" Mae sighed, flapping her newly freed hand gently. "Thanks."

"Sure." Kathy laid the scissors on the shiny rectangular tray near the door. "Better?"

"Heaven," Mae gushed. "Can I take a shower now?"

Kathy chuckled. "No, slow down. You're still confined to bed till the doctor clears you."

"But I feel so..." Mae tugged on an oily lock of hair. "Ick."

"I know, but you've been in bed quite a while, so it'll be harder than you think to move around."

"Just the bathroom?"

Kathy shook her head. "Got to keep those cuts clean." But her brow, still very straight, somehow softened a smidgen, and she patted Mae's arm. "Tell you what. Let's raise the head of your bed a bit and let you get used to being more upright. I'll arrange a sponge bath and shampoo for starters. Baby steps. Gonna be harder than you think." Kathy pressed a small button on the side of the bed, and a motor whirred determinedly as Mae's back and head were pressed up. The vibration jarred Mae's vision and set off a whirling sensation in her head and stomach. Mae groaned; Kathy snapped off the motor.

"Okay?" She obviously thought not. "Lookin' a little green around the gills."

"A little," Mae admitted, closing her eyes.

"No, open your eyes, focus! Closing your eyes will make it worse."

Mae dutifully batted her eyes open, focusing first on the empty chair and then the foot of her bed. She wiggled her toes, and once her eyes felt comfortable with the shifting blanket, she then let her eyes settle on Kathy's cryptic expression. Mae took a deep breath and blew it out forcibly.

"Better now?"

"Yeah," Mae exhaled.

"It'll get easier, but see why we need baby steps?"

"Yeah," Mae repeated, resisting the impulse to nod, needing to keep her head still.

"Would you rather lie flat?"

"No, gotta get used to this."

"Okay, but lie quietly. Remember, you still have a catheter and an IV. Want an emesis pan just in case?"

"I guess."

"Here, tucked by your side, but if you just rest, I think you'll be fine." Kathy gathered up the scraps of bandage. "You know how to call if you need help?" She reached for the call button.

"Yeah," Mae whispered, yielding to the fatigue overtaking her. "Rose showed me."

Kathy frowned as she set the button near Mae's hand. "Right. Well, I'll check back in ten, fifteen minutes, unless you call me first. Lie still."

"Okay." Mae dutifully rolled her head onto her right cheek as she arranged her hands on her belly. She stared absently through the slats of the blinds, losing herself in the diffuse midday sun.

Chapter Twenty

The Question

I can wait. Mae shifted back in her chair.

Dr. Gregorich continued to sit quietly, expectantly. Her expression was obtuse, with barely a crease around her broad, full lips, barely a shimmer of movement around her deep, focused eyes. Not a stand of her salt-and-pepper hair moved. Yet she was alert: unnervingly alert.

I can outlast you. Mae kept eye contact and a faint smile but no more. A wall: a bland, pleasant wall. A wall with no windows.

Dr. Gregorich tilted her head slightly. "How do you feel?"

"Fine." Mae brightened her smile for emphasis.

"Hm." Dr. Gregorich nodded. "You're much quieter than in the first session."

Mae shrugged. "We pretty much covered it all then. Not much else to talk about."

"No?"

"Nope." More quiet. Mae's sigh filled the tiny office. She instantly regretted it.

"What?"

"Nothing, it's just—look, is there...I mean, I understand why I need to see you, to be able to go back home, but really, if, if I've told you everything, covered all that ground, then can't you just sign off on me? I just want to go back to my daughter and my home and do the regular stuff, only, you know, sober. I'll stay sober and be fine."

The doctor nodded. "You'd like to be discharged, get home." *Was she agreeing?* Mae waited for the doctor to say something more. Dr.

Gregorich looked faintly sympathetic, but no, no response. *Honest to God.* Mae's jaw tightened. *Careful.*

"Look," Mae ventured in her best let's-be-reasonable tone, "medically, I'm much better. Stitches healing. Lots of rest." *Lots of nightmares.* "Eating," she continued. "All that stuff. Withdrawal's over, not going to use any more. My family wants me home. I want to be home." *Was she persuaded?* "Can still come in for appointments, call, whatever you want. Believe me, I'm good at that: I've spent my whole life doing what other people say I have to do." *Shit.* Mae flinched internally. *Fucking shut up, Mae!*

The doctor frowned, pursed her lips.

Don't say it, don't! Mae scrambled to add something more benign. "So my point, see, is that I'm clean, I'm basically a cooperative person, so just set me up to see you outpatient—whatever schedule you say—and you and I'll talk, but I also can get things back to normal for Kristy."

Silence. *What? Shit!*

"And for Tommy, too. That goes without saying." *Shit. Made it worse.*

"What?"

Mae shook her head. "Nothing important."

The Raised Eyebrow. *Hated that.* "What's not important?"

Mae slumped back in her chair. *Careful.* "Look," Mae eased the word out, blanking any irritation in her own voice. "Don't, please don't start reading into what's, you know, a normal wish to go home, to get out of the hospital and go home. That's normal, right?"

"Which part?"

"Which part what?" Mae countered abruptly. "I want out of the hospital." *Duh.*

"And you want to go home?"

"Of course I do!" Mae shook her head. "Who doesn't want to be at home?"

Silence. Now Dr. Gregorich was the blank wall.

Come on! "Me? You're suggesting I don't wanna be in my own home? See, that's exactly what I meant, about reading into something that's completely normal. Why imply something like that?"

Silence. Then, "How are you feeling right now?"

Mae sighed and shook her head. "Exasperated, thanks to your insinuations! What is this anyway? What do you want me to say?"

"What do you want to say?"

"No, no, no!" Mae continued to shake her head. "You know, I know, that's not how it works. There's some magic something you're waiting for me to say, so you can write in my chart that it's safe to send me home, that I'll be a good little wife and mommy, so how 'bout we cut the crap and you tell me what you need to hear, and I'll say it, you sign off on it, then everyone's happy?"

"Then everyone would be happy?"

"Are you going to twist everything I say?" Mae demanded, gripping the arms of the chair. "Is this, like, part of therapy, to provoke me?"

"You feel provoked?"

"Honest to God!" Mae clasped her hands on the top of her head. "This is why people hate psychiatrists: they won't give you a straight answer!" Mae fell back in her chair. "I'm sorry, but really..."

Dr. Gregorich leaned forward. "What are you sorry for?'

"What?"

"You said, 'I'm sorry.' Sorry for what?"

Mae turned her head and looked at the doctor out of the corner of her eyes. "I don't...don't get what you mean."

"What are you sorry for?"

"It's just an expression," Mae retorted woodenly. "I just—I didn't mean to be rude or anything."

"What would've been rude?"

"I dunno." Mae sighed. "You know, I'm getting tired. Is our time almost up?"

"Almost, but stay with me. Why did you feel a need to apologize? For what?"

Mae shook her head. "I really don't know. It just came out. Didn't mean a thing."

Dr. Gregorich leaned back in her chair. The Raised Eyebrow.

Nope. It's almost over. I can wait. I can outlast you.

♦ ♦ ♦

Just want to drop off. Why can't I sleep? Mae flopped onto her other side. *Ouch!* One of the stitches pinched. *Want to sleep in my own bed.* Mae squirmed, punched down the pillow. *If I could just get a little bit stoned, just one toke, maybe two. That's all it would take.* She rubbed her cheekbone against the starchy pillowcase. *Forget it, Mae, it's not happening.*

Mae wriggled her shoulder, nestling into the mattress. *Keep your eyes closed. Stop thinking. Just breathe slowly, one...two...*She rolled her hip back. *Ouch! Dammit, they could at least give me a pain pill.* She pulled one pillow out from under her head and clutched it. *Pretend it's Kristy, pretend we're snuggled up on the couch.* She tried to relax into the pillow, gently patting and stroking it. *Relax, think of Kristy. Relax.* Sighing softly, she patted the pillow. *They don't understand. I could be a little bit stoned, don't have to be completely clean. Could handle it if I set my mind to it, just use a little. Oh, would be so much easier to sleep. Just wanna sleep.* Mae lay very still, trying to trust the sleep would come, embracing the pillow. No sleep, still no sleep, and she peeked out her left eye. The room glowed slightly from the parking lot lights, diffused up by the ceiling, but defined strips of light right by the window blinds. Her eye rested on the stripes of glow-white on the empty vinyl chair by the window. Something so forlorn about that old chair. *Close your eyes, Mae, keep them closed.*

♦ ♦ ♦

The lights in the room are flickering. Almost sparking, so bright that Mae can see them through her eyelids. Call button, call button, something's wrong here, a loose connection or something. Rose pads into the room: "What do you need? Not comfy?" Mae points out the sparks, but Rose just chuckles, says, "This room is haunted. You know ghosts communicate with lights." Then she chuckles again. "Just kidding."

And when Mae yells, "That's not funny! You're scaring me!" the sparks shoot further, burning her arm, flecking the sheets with brown dots and tiny holes, and finally Rose moves close to shield Mae. Mae can see white streaks in Rose's hair—she is old!—and Rose bends close to whisper, "Don't be afraid of ghosts. They're yours, Mae. People make their own ghosts." And then the streaks in her hair glow silvery white, and the rest of her glows a bilious green, and with a tiny whirl, Rose shrinks into a spider plant in a pot in the corner. And the ghosts lift Mae up off the mattress and let her dangle, suspended, and Mae wishes she had the restraints or the weight of Tommy to hold her down, doesn't want to drift like this. What if she drifts away?

♦ ♦ ♦

"Hey, baby!" Mae circled her arms around Kristy, sunk her face into Kristy's sandy, unbrushed hair. Mae's left arm was pressed into the cold aluminum railing of the hospital bed, but no matter: she could smell Kristy, the wonderful smells of Breck and Dial soap and little-girl skin. Mae rubbed her nose against Kristy's scalp, surrendering to the squeeze of those little arms. If only the clock would stop: she could stay suspended in this moment forever. Mae kept inhaling Kristy, intoxicated, until an unexpected wriggle pushed Mae's funny bone into the bedrail. "Ah!" she grimaced as Tommy swooped in.

"Easy, Kristy!" he gently corrected, cupping Mae's elbow. "Mom's really glad to see you, but, remember, hospital?"

Mae felt Kristy release her and pull back, but Mae kept one hand on her daughter's back to extend the embrace. *What? What had she been told?* Mae looked up at Tommy, glanced over at Mama, then Sophie: *cryptic smiles.* Eyes back on Tommy, she reassured him, "I'm fine, really. You all here, this is the best." He nodded. *Choked up?* Mae reflexively reached up to stroke his arm. Kristy in the crook of her right arm, her left hand resting on Tommy's sleeve—*no, this was the moment she wanted to last. For this moment, they were good.*

♦ ♦ ♦

Swimming, trying to move forward, but the waves slap, push that clammy, dead-fish smell up her nose, and she has to stop, tread water, try to find shore, but the haze, a heavy pink haze, like malevolent cotton candy, reaches right down to the water, can't see so Mae listens for those faint voices, listens for the backsplash of waves on the rocks, tries to edge closer. At least the water's not too cold...the current tugs but not too bad, just need to find shore.

Mae stretches, longer strokes, cupping her hands to pull into the waves, pull closer to those faint voices on some hidden beach. Shore, get to shore. Pushing sideways into the waves, letting the left side of her face absorb the slap of each wave, careful not to inhale as the water breaks against her cheekbone, waiting for the ebb to grab a quick gasp. Getting closer, just keep pushing closer. Keeping strokes even and strong, really strong for a girl, and peeking out with her right eye—horrors—a monstrous turtle swimming alongside her. Mae sputters, treads water, but the turtle also slows, with a watchful eye. It's okay, just start swimming again, it will move away. She strikes back into a rhythmic stroke, but the turtle keeps pace. Ignore it, swim toward the voices. Keep one squinting eye on the creature and put everything else into strokes, slowly edge away. The distance starts to increase, and thinking, "Thank God," but suddenly the turtle's neck shoots out, long as a snake, and its beak sinks into her cheek, then pulls back, and blood spills everywhere, over her face, over the surface of the water as the creature silently drop below the red puddle, red diffusing to pink streaks, blurring the water, the fog, her face. Blurring.

♦ ♦ ♦

"You're very quiet," Dr. Gregorich observed.

"I guess." Mae stared at the border of the rug, the band weaving over and under, Celtic knots. Liked the symmetry: over, under, twist right and over, under, twist left then over, under. Mae started to sigh but caught it, stifled it, stared at the rug.

"Tell me how you feel?"

Mae met her gaze: concerned but reserved, more distant than the few feet between them, on opposite sides of the massive maple desk. Mae shrugged. "Not feeling much."

"No?"

Shit, give her something. "No," Mae reiterated. "Guess I'm tired."

"Tired?"

Mae nodded.

"Trouble sleeping?"

Every night. "A little. Miss my own bed, you know?" Mae stirred in her chair. "Yet another reason to go home." She tried a genial smile. "You prefer your own bed, too, right?"

Dr. Gregorich simply looked at Mae.

Mae's jaw muscle twitched. Hated when something she said just hung there. *Ignore it.* "So a bit tired, just need your okay to go home. Then I can get some decent sleep."

"What's happening now?"

"What? At night? Just don't sleep so—I dunno, so deeply. Lots of dreams."

Dr. Gregorich nodded. "Dreams?"

"You know, room's not dark enough, not quiet enough. I actually miss Tommy's snoring," she quipped.

"But the dreams?"

"No," Mae countered. "Nothing memorable." *The turtle beak sinking into the flesh of her cheek, the skin practically falling away without protest.* "It's really hard for me to remember dreams." *Pink, hot wet red and pink spilling everywhere.* "But, uh, you just know you had them when you wake up and then you're tired from them."

Dr. Gregorich was quiet.

"So tired. You know, like pregnant-tired," Mae tried a girl-talk tone.

The Raised Eyebrow. "Pregnant-tired?"

"You know what I mean." Mae nodded toward the silver-framed picture of two little boys on the doctor's shelf. "Remember how tired you were then?" *C'mon, talk to me like a mom.*

Dr. Gregorich glanced toward the photo and then locked in on Mae. "You feel pregnant-tired?"

"Not literally! Just saying I'm really tired, that I'd sleep better at home. That's all." She slumped back in the chair, scowling.

"You're angry?"

"No, tired," Mae corrected, "and maybe a little grumpy 'cause I'm tired. Let me spell it out for you. One: I'm tired. Two: I want to go home, and then I'd sleep better."

Dr. Gregorich was quiet.

"And three: I am not pregnant. I'm not afraid I'm pregnant; I'm not wishing I were pregnant. I'm just describing how tired I am. Metaphor. Forget the pregnant."

The Raised Eyebrow.

"Look, even if I were pregnant, which I'm not, it's not like I could do anything about it."

"What would you want to do about it?"

Jesus! "No, that's not the point! Why are we even talking about this? I'm not pregnant, and I'm sorry I ever...even said it, you know, descriptively. Bad example anyway, because the tired I do feel can be fixed—by going home—but that kind of, of tired, there's no fixing."

"No?"

Mae's eyebrows shot up. "No! Unless you mean tear the little thing into a dozen tiny pieces. Yeah, that'll teach a baby to dare to be inconvenient!"

Dr. Gregorich flushed slightly, remaining very still as the mottled pink in her cheeks slowly faded.

Mae felt a gratifying surge of power and settled into the slippery leather chair and the silence. *Now what?* The two women quietly assessed each other.

Finally, flatly, Dr. Gregorich noted, "Interesting you brought up pregnancy."

"Interesting you brought up abortion." Mae's observation hung heavily in the space between them.

"Did I?"

"Oh, I think so. You know, it may be legal now, but so what? Legal doesn't equal moral. I'm Catholic. You know I'm Catholic, right?"

Dr. Gregorich nodded.

"So it's weird you'd say that."

Dr. Gregorich frowned.

"Okay, intimate that. That's not part of my world, not part of my reality. It's not like, like a Catholic woman can be a feminist. I mean, at least not what you'd consider a feminist."

"What would I consider a feminist?"

"You know, myself first, my body, my life, my decisions. It's not that simple, it's never that simple." Mae's voice crept up in pitch. "Maybe, maybe you get to be part of the decision, but you don't get to make big decisions, even if you want to, you can't, because..."

"Because...?"

Mae threw her hands out beseechingly. "How can you? It's not just your life—it—you affect other people, other people's lives are changed too, so you, so you try to get the life you want, but it's not that easy. It's not that easy at all. So all you can do is try, but what you get is..." Mae stopped for air. "I don't know..."

Dr. Gregorich leaned closer, hands braced on the desk. "What did you get, Mae?"

Mae shook her head gravely, blinking back tears. She couldn't find her voice: it had ebbed away. The doctor's concerned eyes penetrated through the glossy film of tears, made the tears trickle down Mae's cheeks. Mae shook her head. No voice.

"Mae?" she prodded, kindly.

A sob welled up Mae's throat and spilled out, a shuddering, wordless complaint. "Don't know," Mae gasped. "Not what I expected."

"No?"

Mae shook her head violently. "No," she wheezed.

Pause. "And that hurts."

Mae nodded fiercely, and tears shot out like rain—no, hotter than rain could be. Her head felt impossibly heavy: she braced it in both hands, then braced her elbows on the chair. She was sinking, caving in. Her heart, a stone slab crushing, pushing her under. Sobs shivered up, wrenching weird sobs in a voice she didn't recognize. And after a few minutes, silence, and then one sigh, welling up from the soles of her feet, one sigh of resignation, and she could lift her head again. Mae met the doctor's eyes forlornly, glad to not be alone.

The doctor sighed for Mae. Her eyes were shadowy with the sadness that filled the room.

"What do I do now?" Mae asked, her voice husky with old tears.

The doctor studied her gravely. "That's a really important question. The Question."

Chapter Twenty-One

The Homecoming

"Okay, so Ma's setting up a buffet, and Sophie and Kristy'll be here soon with balloons or some such, and Tom's getting you unpacked upstairs. I got dessert duty, so how's this look?" Michael stepped to the side to show off his platter of cookies. "Fancy enough for your homecoming?"

Mae barely glanced at the imbalanced pattern of cookies. "Yeah, nice, thanks." She drummed her fingers on the edge of the kitchen table.

"What?"

"Nothing, just—dunno, edgy, need something to do."

Michael shrugged. "Guest of honor isn't allowed. First day home, kid: enjoy! You'll be up to your elbows in dishes 'n' laundry soon enough."

"I guess." Mae's chair scraped heavily as she pushed away from the table.

"And a floor to polish tomorrow," he observed drily. "You *are* jumpy. Wanna take a walk around the block or something? It's not all that cold."

"Oh God, and run into the neighbors? No, not ready for that."

"You ready to be here?"

"What? Oh sure, listen, it's a relief. Couldn't stand one more day in that hospital. This is great. I just need...to get my bearings, get used to the changes."

"Like no booze bottles?" He grinned wickedly.

"Shut up!" Mae poked him. "No, I mean, yeah, that's weird, but no, just little stuff, like, like Tommy rearranged the furniture and the shelves, and I had them a certain way...now it just doesn't feel quite right, like, like my house."

Michael looked unimpressed. "So your biggest problem is you got free cleaning services. Man, I could use that! Look, even your frig and freezer are all cleaned up...must be love!" He tugged the doors open to display the tidy shelves.

"Yeah, but see, rearranged..." Mae's eyes drifted up from the frig to the nearly empty freezer space. "Shit," she murmured.

"What?"

"Where's...?" she hesitated. "Where's, what happened to the food I had in the freezer?" She stepped closer to peer at the containers. "I mean, I had, had a number of, uh, of prepared dinners." She shifted the few containers left, right, left again, double-checking.

"Probably ate things up while you were in the hospital. Why?"

"Nothing," she responded feebly, avoiding his eyes, still checking containers.

"Mae?" Michael darted in front of her to catch her eye.

She flinched. "Nothing!" she insisted, closing the freezer door firmly and turning to head out of the kitchen. Then her eyes rested on the dessert tray, and she froze.

"So," she added nonchalantly, "Mom did all this baking?"

"Pretty much, but you're being sexist, Maisie. I made the peanut-butter cookies."

"From scratch?"

"From a tube, if you must know." He popped one in his mouth. "Not half bad."

"And...the brownies?" she ventured.

"Those, don't know, probably Ma. No, wait, that's right. Tom gave 'em to me to mix in with Ma's cookies. Said he didn't want Kristy eating all of them."

"Kristy's been eating them?" she cried out.

Michael startled. "Jeez, Mae, settle down! Just a couple this morning, while they thawed. Christ, a little sugar won't kill her."

Mae grabbed his arm. "Where is she now? With Sophie, right? Where? How soon till they get back?"

Michael's eyes narrowed. "Mae, what's your problem?" When she looked away nervously, he grabbed her chin. "Mary Therese Panos, what?"

Mae's throat tightened at the darkness of his eyes.

"Nothing," she faltered. "Just, they...have freezer burn. They could give someone a stomachache." She twisted away and started to pick the brownies off the tray. "Um, help me with this. Let's take them off." Her fingers darted rapidly, haltingly, picking them off the platter.

Michael snatched one and pushed it right under her nose. "Freezer burn my ass. Are these loaded?"

Mae didn't answer.

"Mae, dammit, what's in them?"

Mae couldn't even blink.

"Pot?"

She nodded.

"Shit! Much?" His eyes drilled into her.

"I, I don't remember. Maybe hash oil too," she whispered.

"Shit, what were you—?" He clapped his hands on his temples.

"I know!" she pleaded. "What, what do we do?"

"Shit," Michael muttered, turning away from her. Even his stooped back seemed to rebuke her.

"Sorry," Mae whimpered.

The back of his head shook slowly. "Yeah, that helps."

"Michael, Mae?" Mama peeked in from the doorway. "How's it going in here?" Mae jumped and Michael froze, his back to both of them.

"Oh, just about finished," Mae chirped.

"You're supposed to be resting," Mama chided.

Michael turned slowly, and Mae anxiously scanned his face: stony. He addressed Mama without looking at Mae. He offered a halfhearted smile: "Not my fault! I told her to sit, but Miss Fusspot had to rearrange everything. Definitely have our Mae back."

Mama chuckled. "Well, bring it in when you're ready. I think Sophie's back. I heard car doors." She disappeared again.

Michael and Mae looked at each other wordlessly and then moved in unison toward the doorway. "Thanks," she whispered. "Explain later?"

Michael turned to face her. "Bet your ass we'll talk later. I'm gonna check out Kristy, but this is not over. Not by a long shot."

♦ ♦ ♦

"Mommy!" Kristy shrieked. Mae caught the wide-stretched arms, gasping at the hurtling hug that almost knocked them over.

"Whoa!" Tommy protested. "Easy, don't break Mom her first day home."

"Kristy, sweetie," Ellie added, rubbing Kristy's arm to get her attention, "how about we let your mother sit down, and you sit right next to her?"

Kristy fiercely shook her head, drilling her nose hard into the fleshy space between Mae's lower ribs. Mae stroked the half-buried head, fingers catching in a roil of waves and ringlets, some still streaked blond from July and August sunshine. Mae looked up and murmured to her mother, "I'm fine, really, Mom." But Michael's dark gaze cut through her misty contentment, and Mae fumbled to extricate herself from Kristy's bear hug. She squatted down to examine the little face: *flushed beneath the freckles, eyes bright, maybe a little glassy. Were her lips pale?*

Kristy whooshed out of sight as Michael swung her up over his shoulder. She squealed in mock protest, and Mae reached after her. But Michael spun Kristy twice and then plopped her down on the couch, landing next to her with a big flop. Bouncing the cushion to elicit one more giggle, he advised her in a broad stage whisper, "I'm much funner than your mom—just stick with me, kid."

"'Funner'!" Ellie tsked, but Michael ignored her. He tickled Kristy until she was a gasping puddle next to him, all the while looking her over. When she swatted at him to stop, too breathless to talk, he kept her down with one hand on her belly and looked up at Mae, deadpanning. "How'd you ever get such a good kid? Must take after her dad." Kristy squirmed to sit up, but Michael pushed to keep her down. "You rest! Doctor's orders!"

"You're not a doctor," Kristy teased, wriggling to get free.

"Hey, missy, I'm a medic, close enough!" He softened his voice. "Really, do Uncle Michael a favor and just rest there a second, 'cause otherwise everyone's going to yell at me when you barf up lunch." He caught Sophie's eye. "Here, Aunt Sophie'll sit down with us"—he patted the empty cushion—"and make sure we behave. Won't you, Aunt Sophie?"

"Well, I'll try," Sophie bantered, slipping next to Kristy, "but it's awfully hard to make Uncle Michael behave."

Michael kept one hand on Kristy's tummy and shot Mae a hostile glance. Mae flushed and turned away as he added, "We can't all be grown-ups, can we, Mae?"

Mae found Tommy trying to read their faces, so she mustered a light voice and a perky expression: "So, Mom, shall we finish setting up lunch?"

"No," Ellie responded firmly. "I want you to sit down for a moment, too." Ellie felt Mae's cheeks. "Do you feel warm?" The cool brush of her mother's fingers made Mae close her eyes and give over to the tingle racing across her scalp. She gulped, trembling all over. *I almost hurt her, could've killed her,* Mae wanted to confess. But instead she felt Tom grasping her elbow and Ellie's tightening hold on her face. "Mae?" Ellie demanded even as she and Tom steered Mae toward a chair.

Mae tried to shake her head against Ellie's palms while they guided her down. "No," she protested. "No, I'm fine." Her eyes opened to find both Ellie and Tommy looking unconvinced. "Medic!" Tom called back to Michael in a half-joking tone. *No, not Michael.* But already Michael was peering into her eyes, steely, all business, and then looked down at his watch as he positioned his fingers on her wrist.

"Michael," she complained.

"Shut up," he ordered, taking her pulse.

The room was still for a few seconds as he looked Mae again in the eye, this time a more sober, even tired expression. "Feeling a little bad?" he inquired softly. Mae nodded, staring at her toes. He sighed and turned to address the others. "She's just a little off, not surprising given the circumstances. I'd suggest that both she and Miss Kristy snuggle up and rest on the couch a few minutes, then light lunch and naps all around. Anything more than that and we may be facing..."—he paused, finishing with a dramatic whisper—"vomit!" Kristy shrieked, and he pointed straight at her. "And I am *not* cleaning up after you! So scoot over and make room for your mom."

Tom escorted Mae over to Kristy, who obligingly nestled her head into her mother's lap. Relief muddled with self-reproach as Mae stroked Kristy's head. Arranging a hint of a smile on her face, Mae wordlessly watched her family arrange her welcome back with plates of sandwiches, cookies, and sugared fruit slices from Marshall Field's. Scents of burning pine from the fireplace plus cinnamon tea steeping in a chubby china pot made her want to cry. *No, look up, smile.* Couldn't look down at her lap, at the little girl she could've hurt. *Pink blur, jolting brake even as she heard that voice, "Stop!"* Mae's hand froze on Kristy's shoulder. *Two, two little girls almost killed—how did she manage not to? Was it luck? Was it random? Could never be that lucky a third time, if that's luck. Luck?* Mae inhaled deeply, watched, pretended to be part of the family.

♦ ♦ ♦

Mae's eyes opened to an almost pitch-black living room, so still she could practically hear the slow burn of the lights on the Christmas tree in the corner. The tree had a faint halo, quietly illuminated against the weighty shadows surrounding it, surrounding her. Her eyes wove slowly across the kaleidoscope of lights and ornaments. Her fatigue dragged her gaze down to the shiny boxes and ribbons at the base: silvery packages in a pretty tumble, hiding most of the scalloped skirt she'd made, a cherry red skirt to cover the tree stand. *Huh. Hadn't missed Christmas.* The corners of her mouth curled up a little, and she wriggled contentedly under the crocheted afghan.

"Mae?" Tommy whispered.

Where...? Tried to force her eyes to focus: there, in the winged-back chair, he must've been dozing there. "Yes," she whispered.

"You feel okay?" He made no move to join her.

"Yeah. Guess I nodded off." *Blurry shards of recollection: a ham-salad sandwich, could still taste the pickle...good-byes...nap...murmuring, a woman's voice...Cynthia*? "What time is it anyway?" Mae asked, her voice a bit husky.

"Don't know, lemme see..." Tommy stepped closer to the tree to squint at his watch, green and gold and red lights bouncing off its crystal. "Um, just about nine. Seems later, doesn't it?" He retreated to his chair but sat forward, resting on his elbows.

"Kristy?"

"Oh, put her to bed a while ago, worn out. Oh! I'm supposed to tell you she blew you a kiss good-night. Told her not to wake you up."

"Oh." Mae smiled ruefully. "Thanks, but that would've been all right."

"No," Tommy insisted. "You looked so tired, pale, like you were wiped out. You feel okay?" *Didn't seem to remember that he'd already asked.*

"Yeah, I'm, I'll be fine." There was a long pause, and her assertion just seemed to drift, unanchored, and then fade into the void. *Say something, Mae.* "So I guess I didn't miss Christmas..." She nodded toward the tree and gifts. "Must've felt longer in the hospital than it really was."

Tommy didn't move. She couldn't make out his face, even though he was facing her, as the light of the tree barely touched the back of his head, brightening only the lines of one ear.

"Mae, what date is it?" His voice had a weird edge.

Mae hesitated. *Okay, must be after Christmas, of course, it's after Christmas.* "I mean," she faltered, "I know it's a bit after..."

"You don't know?"

"No!" she snapped in embarrassment. "What? Twenty-eighth? Thirtieth?"

Stillness, then gravely: "January third, Mae. The third."

Mae swallowed hard, hoping her face was as obscured as his. Casting around for a response, she finally uttered, "Oh." Wanted to hide in the dark, didn't really want to see his expression. "But the gifts?" she ventured.

"We were waiting for you." His voice was thick, a little choked.

"You didn't have to do that," she protested weakly. "I mean, Kristy..."

"Her idea," he added. "I had her open one thing on Christmas Eve, just like every year, but she wanted to wait for you for the rest...maybe tomorrow, maybe we can do that. I could go into work a little late. Breakfast and presents?" *Hated the effort in his voice.*

"Sure," Mae tried for a lilt of enthusiasm. "Or, if that's a problem with work, when you get home, that'd be good too."

"Nah, morning's fine. Kristy went to bed early, so she'll be up. Shall we—let's see how you feel in the morning."

"Okay," she agreed cautiously, eyeing him as he stood up and lumbered closer. He stopped just short of the coffee table, but his back was to the tree, his face still blank in the shadows. *Don't, don't say it.*

"So..."

Don't say it.

"So if you're comfortable there, why don't you just stay on the couch? If you feel like you can fall back asleep."

Oh. Mae frowned but then, realizing he could probably make out her face, smoothed her brow. "Yeah, good idea...I'll sleep here."

"You sure?"

She nodded, surprised by the tightness behind her eyes. She cleared her throat and blinked hard. "Yeah," she repeated. "I can nod off again. I'll just let you and Kristy wake me up...okay?"

His head, faintly silhouetted by the tree lights, nodded in affirmation. "Okay. Good night then." He turned toward the stairs. In the shadows his body loomed massive, and yet...the same shadows made her feel puny, adrift, and her skin yearned to be tucked under the crook of his arm, close in bed.

"Tom?" she called after him, not sure what to ask.

"Hmm?" He stopped.

"I—" she sputtered. "I'm glad to be home, that's all." *Invite me, please, or—or come stay with me.* She held her breath, needed to hear his voice clearly, the tone more than the words.

"Yeah?" Then a perfunctory: "Me too. Good night." He continued up the stairs. She listened to the floorboards squeak, first down the hallway, then in their bedroom.

Mae clutched the edge of her afghan and pulled it up to her chin. *Just...just being thoughtful, probably realized the first night would be weird.* Noticed she'd started to shiver. *Just saving me the stairs since I'm tired.* Mae focused on quieting the shivering, knew it wasn't that cold in the room. *Don't think about it. You're tired, muddled. Everything seems worse when you're tired, Mae. Sleep.* She rolled her face away from the tree so the lights wouldn't wash around inside her eyelids. *Sleep.* But she was on guard against the dreams that might come, the dreams that often came: *the one with the blur and the "Stop!" and only the pink jacket that kept her alive, the flash of pink or else she'd have killed her, someone's little girl. If the jacket were white or yellow or—stop! Stop, Mae, you didn't, she's okay, just...stop...*Mae sunk deeper into the sofa, wishing she could hold his hand, could fall asleep. She rolled onto the other cheek, studied the tree, wanted to dream about the tree. Staring at the half-hidden bulbs, blue and green and red and gold, her stomach sunk with the certainty that he did not want her upstairs—that "Yeah?" and that polite afterthought of a "Me too." *God. He wasn't waiting anymore. He's tired of treading water, tired of waiting.* The lights burned into her retina, but she couldn't find her eyelids to make them blink. She was getting used to the dark, but she still couldn't see.

Chapter Twenty-Two

Not How She Remembered

January 1980

Kristy was tearing into one of the last boxes, wrestling with a knotted ribbon. Mae listened to Tommy teasing their daughter, actually sounding relaxed, having fun. *Fun.* Blessedly, Kristy's enthusiasm for ripping into the gifts kept her oblivious. Mae and Tommy forced polite smiles when Kristy looked up.

The doorbell rang. Tommy's eyebrows shot up as he asked Mae, "Expecting someone?"

She shrugged, shook her head as he strode to the door.

"Well, hi!" he exclaimed, sounding confused as he let Michael in.

"Uncle Michael, look! A Barbie Dream House!"

"Hey, peanut! Wow, what loot!" Michael turned to Tommy. "Say, I was hoping to borrow Mae for a couple of hours, but looks like you're going to work, huh?"

"Yeah," Tommy allowed, "but Kristy's headed across the street to play after breakfast, so that could work out, if Mae feels up to it." They both turned to look at Mae, who shrank back under their scrutiny.

She ran her hand through her hair. "Gee, I dunno, I'm such a mess..." She gestured to her rumpled clothes from the day before.

Michael folded his arms. "There's a new cure for that: it's called a shower and a change of clothes." His tone was shades lighter than his expression.

"What's up?" Tommy asked.

"Oh, wanna borrow her expertise on decorating. Got a new listing that could use fresh paint. But not sure what colors, and we all know Maisie's always got opinions about that!"

"Thought you realtors were hooked on eggshell."

"Yeah, well, thought I'd dare to be different." Michael turned back toward Mae. "So? Consultation? Won't keep you long, promise."

Mae started apologetically, "But..." gesturing toward Kristy.

"Tell you what," Tommy suggested. "How 'bout you let Michael supervise cereal with Kristy while you get cleaned up? I'll call Cynthia, ask if Kristy can head over a little early. I'm sure it'll be okay."

"Okay," Mae conceded. "Just need twenty minutes to shower."

Michael clapped his hands authoritatively. "All right then! Captain Crunch!"

Mae stood up stiffly. "Make sure she has juice too!" She could feel their gazes on her back as she slowly climbed the stairs.

♦ ♦ ♦

The cold tile felt soothing against her heels, the back of her calf muscles, along the back of her thighs and radiating up. Toes all in a row, knees aligned, her legs were still graceful, slender, smooth, until halfway up her inner thighs, where the puckered lines of thick scar tissue made the skin as rippled and lumpy as water barely skimming a sandbar. And the parallel lines—like a chevron, if she pressed her thighs together—*like some quilt pattern. Poor skin.* She traced the lines with a fingertip. *Sorry, I'm sorry. I'll do better, I promise.* Mae noticed the grout was still tinged a little pink from that night. Clearly it'd been scrubbed, probably bleached. She cringed at the image of Tommy or her mother bent low, an old toothbrush in hand, trying to get out the stain, Mae's stain, trying to get it looking normal, clean, to answer the complaint of the puddled blood.

Poor skin. Poor Mama. Got to do better. She kissed a fingertip and touched it to the tile. *Sorry.* A knot inside her loosened a bit. She kissed the fingertip, touched a scar. *Sorry.* Again, she kissed the finger, transferred it to the next scar. *Sorry.* And again, a kiss, a touch, a sorry, down one thigh and up the other. Even as she wondered if she was being weird, inventing some crazy ritual, she surrendered to the contentment welling up low from her gut, filling her ribs, her heart. *Peace*, she blessed each scar. *Peace, poor body, peace.* Mae tipped her head back and closed her eyes, felt the strength of the sunlight soaking in, too gentle to cauterize but still penetrating, top-down against the last cool tingle emanating up from the tile. Mae felt her heartbeat, pictured warm, wet, red blood suffusing her fingers and toes, rosy like Kristy's lips. This was it, how she needed to feel in her damaged skin...but now she needed to move, to take a shower, be a sister, a mom, a wife. If she could get back.

♦ ♦ ♦

"Where are we going?" Mae felt uneasy with Michael's reticence as they drove further and further east on Touhy Avenue. "You have a listing in Rogers Park?"

Michael shook his head. "Nah, just heading toward the lake." He signaled to go north on Sheridan Road.

"What?" Mae knew they were just a few blocks from where Sheridan swung around Calvary Cemetery, and then they'd be in Evanston. "I don't—are we looking at colors someplace or not?"

"Not. Cool your jets, almost there."

"Almost where?"

"Just this tiny park I like, okay?" He shook his head, frowning. Mae folded her arms in protest but decided to be still. With arched eyebrows she eyed creamy marble mausoleums and rose granite obelisks guarding the front rows of the cemetery, behind them hundreds of modest headstones flecking the manicured lawn stretching back at least a quarter mile. *Lake views for the rich, even after they're dead.* On the right, Lake Michigan had sealed the massive, angular concrete blocks buttressing the shoreline with a thick glaze of ice. They sparkled like chrome, slightly tinted with frozen seaweed, a deeper green than the spray of the surf or the gunmetal blue of the choppy, irregular waves washing around and over chunky ice floes.

The road swung back inland as they proceeded a few more blocks, past sturdy red-brick apartments standing shoulder to shoulder, almost identical with trim courtyards, separated by the slimmest of walkways or the occasional shaded alley. The repetition of the brick box, shadow, brick box, shadow lulled her, tugged at her eyelids, but then unexpectedly Michael took a sharp right and wound along a narrow lane and a patch of frozen grass, just shy of a new batch of concrete blocks and icy spray. He turned off the engine and slumped back, resting his gloved fingertips on the bottom curve of the steering wheel. Mae watched him watch the waves, waited for him to lay into her, braced for a lecture if not a scolding.

Silence. Mae slumped back, parallel, and fixed her eyes on the waves. "Just say it," she sighed, resigned to a drenching reproach.

He gripped the wheel tightly and turned to face her. "Mae." He was insisting on eye contact. "Want to go to an AA meeting with me?"

The breath she'd been holding burst forth in a nervous laugh. "What? You kidding?" His absurdity was a relief. She poked at him, trying to solicit a grin, a confirmation that he was teasing her, some goofy icebreaker before the inevitable lecture.

But he didn't smile back. She narrowed her eyes, offered a baiting grin. His expression was stony, so she tried to be brighter. "Seriously?" she asked skeptically.

"What's going to change, Mae?"

"Look, Michael, I get that the whole brownie thing could've been bad, and I'll quit, or, or at least cut back. Come on, I'm not clueless here..."

He turned back to the horizon. "How?"

"Look, the liquor's cleaned out of the house, the pot's gone. I just won't buy any more. And I'll have a rule, just two, no, just one drink at a party. Just have to set my mind to it."

He turned away, staring through the windshield, far out past the surf.

Exasperated, Mae slapped at his arm. "Hey, over here!" she protested, but she was unprepared for the weird blend of distrust and love in his eyes. He shook his head.

"Mae, you're gonna fuck it up."

"No," Mae insisted, "I'm clean. I'll stay clean. Lighten up."

He frowned. "You think that'll fix everything? And that's assuming you do stay clean, which you seem to think you can do all by yourself, even though almost nobody can."

Mae struggled with which insult to answer first. "Look," she reiterated, "no dope is a given, and if I decide no drinking, I'll stop drinking. And yes, that'll fix everything."

"So you and Tom are okay."

"I, I think so."

"You love him?"

Pause. "Not sure."

"Hm." His tone was more sympathetic as he added, "Think he still loves you?"

"Of course," she mumbled. "Well…I…not sure we're staying together."

"No?" The concern in his voice cut through her. "Sorry," he offered as she wiped a tear away with the back of her mitten. "So what about you, Mae?"

"What?"

"What do you want?"

"Like it matters? C'mon, Michael, you get what you get, not what you want…" One more tear welled over and rolled down her cheek, cooling by the time it reached her lips.

He admonished, "Join the club."

"What!" she protested.

Michael shook his head. "Jeez, Mae. You get what you get, just like everyone else." Her jaw dropped. He shrugged. "You think it's just you? Ever occur to you how much Tom's compromised? Engineer, remember? He wanted to be an engineer. But no, he manages an Ace Hardware and has given up on the engineering thing, I guess. Never hear him talk about it, but also never hear him complain. He thinks Kristy's worth it, you too. For what it's worth, I think he still loves you, don't ask me why."

"Nice, really nice, why would he love me?" She swatted him.

Michael shoved her hand away. "You know, Maisie, I love you, but you are something of a brat."

"Please!" Mae insisted, "I've done my part!"

"Yes and no. Been a good mom to Kristy, that's important, but mostly you've done the surface stuff—you know, the laundry, hot dinners, flowerpots by the front door. But face it, Mae: you can't be any prize to live with, what with the pot and the attitude."

"I don't have any attitude!"

"No? How 'bout the poor-me-I'm-stuck shit?"

"Well, I am stuck! This is hardly the life I would've chosen!"

"Jeez, Mae, once again, join the club! And by the way, you did choose this!"

"No!"

"Yes! Okay, so you didn't choose to get shipped off. That was hard. You know it, I know it. Ma knows it. But she did the best she could with what she got dealt, Mae. And she felt bad, still does. Do you even realize she's still trying to make it up to you?"

Mae pulled back, braced against the cold plastic of the car door. "But..."

"But you chose to be a stoner, and you chose to keep Kristy. You chose to create a family with Tommy. Look, I'm sorry if you guys aren't happy. Maybe it's time to end it. I know I'm on the outside looking in, but, as your big brother, I'm gonna tell you this much..." He looked out over the water. "Before you break up with Tom, be sure. Figure out what you're really angry about, 'cause I'm not sure he deserves what you dish out."

"Meaning?"

"All the little shit: the hundred little ways you let him know he wasn't your first choice."

Mae hung her head, blushing. *Enough.*

Michael's voice grew softer. "Look, Maisie, I don't know if there's other bad stuff between you guys, but why keep punishing him for laying a pretty girl at a party?"

Mae frowned at her lap. "There is other bad stuff, and it's not all my fault." She watched out of the corner of her eye as his gloved hand covered hers.

"It's not about fault, Maisie. Do you want to talk about, about the other stuff?"

Mae shook her head.

"All right." As low as his voice was, as it trailed away, the stillness was palpable.

The crash of a wave splattering the rocks, slapping spray against the windshield made them both startle. "I just think, if you're in, be really in. Not halfway."

Mae watched the droplets freezing on the windshield.

"Mae?" he prodded.

"I know, I know what you mean. Just thinking."

"Thinking is good. Think. Talk. Talk with your shrink?"

"Yeah, seeing her next week. Gotta check in every other week for a while."

"Good. You gotta keep talking it out till you're sure. It's hard stuff to be managing all by yourself. At least I can't—that's why I go to meetings."

Mae checked his expression. "AA meetings?"

"Yep." No joking tone, no grin.

"You go to AA meetings," Mae clarified.

"I go to AA meetings at least once a week," Michael announced slowly and evenly, as if she were a little dim.

She twisted sideways to face him. "You?" came out sounding a little stupid.

He grinned. "Jeez, Mae, can't you see past the tip of your own nose? When's the last time you saw me drink?"

She wrinkled her nose, trying to order the fragmented memories of the last few months. *Too jumbled.* "I dunno."

"Meetings, they help."

"But you're not an alcoholic."

"I used to drink a whole lot. Got drunk most every night before bed, trying to sleep real deep, pass out, not dream, nightmares from 'Nam." His face sagged. "But it hardly ever worked. And then it was during the day, between appointments...drove drunk. Could've killed someone."

Glare sheeting the windshield, a blur, jarring brakes. "But you didn't," Mae countered.

"By the grace of God, Maisie, grace of God."

Stop! His voice, inside her, outside her, surrounding her.

Mae frowned. "Well, I don't think you're an alcoholic."

Michael floated a wan smile. "I know you're trying to be nice, so thanks, but I think I am, so that pretty much means I am."

"I just can't think of you that way. Is *she* making you do it?"

"Ma?"

"No, your girlfriend."

"Her name is Caroline, which you should know after this many months. And no, no one is making me do anything. I think she likes me better sober. I know I like myself better sober. That's what counts."

"I just can't think of you as an alcoholic..."

"Tell you what, think of it as I was headed that way, so I'm facing it down now, before I end up like Pop."

Mae gasped with a faltering, "What?"

Michael was adamant. "A drunk like Pop." Mae shook her head, and Michael insisted. "Pop was a drunk. Drove drunk all the time. Were you too little to get that? Remember the fights? Ma not wanting us to drive with him?"

Mae's headshaking turned into a violent shudder.

"Wow." Michael turned apologetic. "Sorry, I figured you'd put two 'n' two together by now. Yeah, Pop was a drunk, a really charming drunk. And he died drunk 'n' was damn lucky he didn't take anyone else with him in that crash." Michael's whole expression darkened. "But you know, in a sense he did. Think how everything changed for us. Everything."

Mae clasped her head in her hands, as if she were holding it together. "No," she insisted. "Stop talking about him that way." But she felt dread washing up, and she hated the pain in her brother's eyes, hated his certainty.

"Maisie, you all right? You look sick."

She shook her head.

"What? Not sick or not all right?"

"No, you're wrong!" *Take it back, take it back. You're just saying this to scare me, to throw me.* "How can you speak of Papa that way?" she rebuked him.

"Shit. Look, Mae, I've been living with this awhile, figuring out how to forgive him 'n' all, and I thought, well, obviously this is new to you, and okay, it'll take time for you to get a handle on it."

"No! I don't believe you."

Michael grimaced. "You don't believe me?"

"No!" Mae was resolute. "Mom would've said something in all these years. I don't know where you got this, or why you want to say that about Papa, but you are wrong, dead wrong." They stared at each other mistrustfully. The moment felt frozen. *Take it back, Michael. At least say you're not sure. Come on!*

"Okay then," Michael announced abruptly, turning on the engine. He shifted into drive with a lurch and took a tight left turn to head south on Sheridan Road.

"What, that's it? You got nothing else to say?" Mae argued.

He didn't take his eyes off the road.

"Michael!"

"Yeah, I got more to say," he responded flatly, "but not here."

"Where are we going?" Mae tried to sound annoyed, not anxious.

"To Ma's." He wouldn't look at her.

"No, Michael, take me home. I've had enough."

He did not respond.

"Michael, take me home."

Without a glance, he responded firmly, "Just shut up."

♦ ♦ ♦

“This is too stupid. We’re not going in there,” Mae insisted, even as he hit the curb parallel parking.

“Yes, we are,” Michael responded flatly, easing forward to straighten the car.

“I’m not. I’m not hurting Mama with this kind of talk. Can hardly believe you’d be that cruel.”

Michael shoved the gear into park and pulled the key out of the ignition. “Know what would be cruel, Mae? For Ma to have to go through this again. ’Cause of me or you. So grow up, Mae, face facts, ’n’ look at what’s right in front of you. ’Cause you gotta stop.”

Stop! That voice. A pink blur. Mae shuddered. “She’s not going to like this, not one bit.”

Michael’s hand rested on the door handle. “Probably not, but she’ll do it for you anyway. She’s stronger than you think.” He popped his door open and slid out, slamming it behind him. As he climbed gingerly on the front bumper to squeeze over to the curb, Mae threw her car door open and slid out, slamming it even louder.

“Be as indignant as you want, but don’t be a brat once we get inside.”

“Shut up!” Mae muttered, brushing past him to climb the porch steps first. Still, when they got to the front door, she couldn’t raise her hand to press the buzzer. Hated that Michael noticed.

“Let me.” He gave the security button a long push. They both waited in silence, staring at the buzzer.

Don’t be home, don’t be home.

Then, a crackling electronic voice: “Hello?”

“Hey, Ma, it’s me ’n’ Mae. We stopped by.”

“Michael! What, well, of course, come up!”

The buzzer droned loudly as Michael tugged open the door for Mae. “After you.” He gestured with a sweeping arm.

“Fuck you,” she retorted, edging up the narrow flight of stairs, arranging a smile on her face as she heard the bolt thrown on the apartment door. “Hi, Mom!” she called sweetly as she approached the landing.

"What a nice surprise!" They brushed kisses on each other's cheeks, and Mae slipped past, tugging off her mittens and fumbling with the jacket zipper, while Michael kissed Mama. She shoved her trembling hands into her pockets, making no move to take off her jacket. Her mom noticed.

"Oh, you're cold, sweetie? Let me turn up the heat a little." Ellie moved toward the thermostat.

"No," Mae protested, "I'll just keep my jacket on. We're not staying that long."

"Don't be silly." Ellie adjusted the setting. "Hot tea?" she offered.

"Sure!" Michael agreed. "Sounds good." He slipped off his jacket, holding out his hand to collect Mae's. She complied with the most malevolent look she could muster.

"Sit down, sit down!" Ellie called from the kitchen, over the familiar clatter of the aluminum teakettle, the rush of tap water, the poof of the gas flame. "Such a nice surprise! I'm so glad I was home—just back from errands."

"Lucky, huh, Maisie?" Michael baited.

"Fuck you," Mae mouthed back at him.

"The water will just take a minute," Ellie noted, settling down on the couch next to Mae and reaching for her hands. "Oh, sweetie, your hands are like ice! What are you two doing running around on such a bitter day?" She sandwiched Mae's hands in hers, rubbing them lightly.

"Ah, it's not so bad out," Michael countered. "But, yeah, I'm glad we caught you in, 'cause Mae and I were talking, and I really think we need, well, your perspective."

"Oh?"

"Yeah." Michael glanced at Mae and then focused on his mother. "Well, you know, Ma, how I go to AA."

"Yes?" Ellie encouraged him, even as Mae pulled her hands away and interrupted.

"Wait! You knew that? You knew and didn't tell me?"

"Mae," Michael began.

"No, really!" Mae complained to her mother. "How could you not tell me that?"

"Well," Ellie hesitated, looking back and forth between them, "sweetheart, that was for Michael to tell you. It felt...private, so I knew he'd tell you when he felt it was the right time. Which I take was today?" she turned to Michael.

"In fact," Michael clarified, "I asked Mae to come to a meeting with me."

"Oh!" Ellie blinked in surprise, turning to check Mae's expression.

Tell him, tell him that's ridiculous! Go on, Mama! Be indignant!

"And, Mae, are you, that is, are you going to go with him?"

"What? No way!" Mae protested.

"Oh."

"I can't believe you didn't tell me, either of you!" Mae exclaimed, slumping in her seat.

"You're getting off the point," Michael observed.

"No, I'm not!" Mae countered. "This is my point! You guys should've told me. A long time ago, apparently!" She folded her arms tightly.

Ellie shrugged. "I'm sorry you're upset, Mae, but it was for Michael to tell you, not me."

"Ma," Michael added gently, "I really think this is about Pop. I think that's what Mae really is upset about, and she needs to hear it from you."

The teakettle whistle trilled. Ellie popped up from the couch. "Just a minute!" she called as she scurried to take it off the flame.

"Knock it off!' Mae muttered.

He shook his head.

"The tea can wait." Mama settled back down with them. She took a deep breath and composed her expression. "So you were saying?" she asked Michael.

Mae shot him a beseeching look. *Don't!*

"Ma, you need to tell Mae about Pop, about his drinking, 'cause she doesn't believe me. She doesn't want to believe me."

Mae strained to see her mother's face as Mama dropped her head for a minute. But when Mama turned to look at Mae, her eyes were a steely blue, every bit as resolute as Michael's tone.

"I'm sorry," Mama offered. "I hoped never to have to say it in so many words, Mae, but, well, the drinking problems did not begin with your brother, or with you."

"How can you talk that way about Papa? How can you?"

"I don't mean to sound unkind, Mae. Your dad, he was a wonderful man in so many ways! But he drank, well, too much, and he lost jobs, and he took risks, you know, driving, and it was a, a problem between us, and between John and Nick." She flushed. Her eyes grew shadowed despite her even tone.

"But no one has ever said this before, in all these years!" Mae pushed, skeptical.

"Oh, sweetheart, you adored your dad, we all did. There wasn't a mean bone in his body, and goodness knows he never ever meant to hurt anyone. So when he died so abruptly, you lost so much, so young. How could I take away the vision you had of him? We had hard years, losing him, then each other..." She stared down at her knees, looking far, far past them.

No! You don't get to float off someplace else! "You let it happen," Mae charged grimly. "How could you let that happen?" The challenge in her tone brought her mother back, but Mae recoiled a little at Ellie's wounded expression. Still, the gauntlet was thrown down. "How could you let Nick separate us?"

Michael sighed loudly. "God, Mae!"

"What?" Mae shot back. "You're just fine with how it all played out? With what they did to us?"

"What *who* did to us?" Michael yelled. "No, I don't like what Nick did, but it was Pop who separated us, Mae. Pop first, and then Nick made it worse."

"Papa was in an accident." Mae could hear the venom in her own voice. "What Nick did, what Mama allowed Nick to do, was different. That didn't have to happen, so shut the fuck up."

"Mary Therese! Enough of that!" Mama scolded. "If you're angry, I'm sorry. If you're mixed up, I'm sorry, but you will not talk to your brother that way!" Ellie's face was taut and white with anger. "Apologize!"

The tense silence was cut by Michael. "Ma, I don't care, but she's mad at all the wrong people, that's all."

Mae's eyes stung as she studied her brother's face, tried to line up something coherent to demand, to counter, but her brain felt locked up, traces of arguments drowning in tide pools of misery.

"Mae"—her mother rested one hand on top of Mae's—"you feel let down. You didn't understand at the time, and maybe not even now, but there were dark times. Your dad, he'd lose another job, and I'd try to make a little extra money waitressing, but while I was at work, he'd take you and Michael to the bar with him. I never knew what I would come home to."

"Mama, so he drank some."

"Some? Mae, he drank all of the time, and he was careless, careless with your safety, careless with money, ours, Nick's...Nick's business almost went under at one point because of John." She peered fiercely into Mae's eyes. "Not some, Mae, all the time."

Mae's eyes welled up.

"Oh Maisie, sweetheart..." she continued, her voice softening. "John was sweet, charming, a 'hale fellow well met' whom everyone liked, and he loved you, he loved us all. But he did not take good care of us. No. So, I did the best I could by you. Maybe I should've found a different way, found a way to keep you at home, but this was what Nick offered, to educate you and Michael. You need to know, Mae," Mama added. "You need to know, I didn't fight to keep you. When it became too much, I asked Nick to send you away."

"What!" Mae gasped, pulling her hands back.

"I, I...had troubles, on and off for years after your father died. I was overwhelmed, couldn't stop crying and shaking for days at a stretch. Don't you remember dinners, where you and Michael were eating, and I just sat crying?"

"No, I don't," Mae insisted, but she saw Michael nod.

"I'm glad you don't remember, but I lost my job, couldn't leave home. Sophie tried to help, but I think it was too hard for Nick to see you two at their house so much. After losing his own boys, he had become so...closed. And he was hurt by your father's drinking, his irresponsibility. In time, I just couldn't manage, and he wouldn't take you into their home. So when he offered boarding school, I said yes, because you needed to be away from me, and he gave us that. I always felt so terrible, when you or Michael got resentful: you blamed Nick, when he was only doing what I asked. But he said it was better that you be upset with him, that he had big shoulders, and he did not want you angry with me. I do believe he would have sent each of you on to college, but then Michael was drafted, and you, well, your life took a different turn...God had different plans for the two of you."

Mae snorted, and Ellie jumped up. "Mary Therese!" she warned.

"Plan? I'm sorry, Mama, but you really think my mess of a life is some kind of plan?"

Ellie lowered herself very deliberately, sitting right next to Mae, her face so uncomfortably close that Mae felt her mother inhale. "I most certainly do," she responded gravely. "Look at what you have: a husband who loves you, a precious daughter who adores you, the chance to raise her yourself." Ellie's voice broke, and they both flushed deeply, cheeks and necks mottling red.

Mae's heart tugged down her whole chest, so collapsed it was hard to breathe. She forced herself to meet her mother's eyes. "Sorry," Mae whispered.

Ellie barely shook her head. "Don't be sorry, Maisie. Be thankful for them."

"I am, Mama," Mae asserted weakly.

Ellie appraised her soberly. "It looks like you don't want what you have."

"I do, I do. It's not like I'm going to throw it all away."

"Your father didn't mean to, but he did."

"You think I'm an alcoholic then?"

"That's neither here nor there, what I think. It's what you think, what you stand to lose."

"I can say it if Ma can't," Michael chimed in, half joking. But when they both turned to look at him, he added, completely seriously, "But Ma is right, Maisie: at the end of the day, it's your call."

The space between them all was painfully full. Mae put her hands to her temples, pressing hard to find some words, some order in her head.

"You know," Ellie's tone shifted, "I never made the tea. Shall I make it now?" Her voice was so kind that Mae wanted to hide her face.

"You know, Mom, if it's all the same, I think I just want to head home. I don't, I don't feel like tea just now. Would that be okay?"

"Of course," Ellie agreed, leaning in to kiss Mae gently on her widow's peak. "Next time, then."1

Mae sat with downcast eyes, listening to the rustle as Michael picked up their coats. He silently helped her into her jacket, let her tug on her own mittens while he gave his mom a peck on the cheek and pulled out his keys. "Ready?" he asked.

Mae nodded, heading toward the door. She brushed a kiss on Ellie's cheek and clutched her, pressing her nose into her mother's neck. With a long breath, she inhaled a little of her mother and stood stock-still while her mother rubbed her back. When they pulled back from each other, Mama cradled Mae's face in her hands. "Mae, it took me years to find my strength again. Maybe you can sooner...I hope so, sweetheart."

Mae waited for her mother's hands to drop away before she followed Michael out the door.

Chapter Twenty-Three

Going Home

Four, maybe five miles streamed past without a word. The January sunlight sheeted almost like frost on the windshield, glinting so bright that Mae looked out through a veil of eyelashes. Mae shook her head with an exasperated sigh.

"What?" Michael frowned. *Or was he squinting too?*

"How could you keep this all from me?" She punched him in the arm.

"It wasn't all that well hidden," Michael observed dryly. "You saw what you wanted to see. You wanted to blame Nick, see Mom as weak. Mom was actually the strong one."

"Strong? She sent us away!"

"To protect us, until she could find her way. Must've hurt her like hell to ask Nick, to have you believe she wouldn't fight for us. She was fighting for us, Mae. She tried to trust in a bigger plan."

"How very Catholic," Mae sneered.

"Didn't pick up on that until now?"

"Of course, just that whole plan thing, I mean, c'mon! Maybe, maybe that's her generation, but seriously, a plan?"

Michael didn't respond.

"What?" she demanded.

"Doesn't matter what I think. You have to figure out what you think."

"You, too? You really think this is anything more than random?"

Michael wouldn't look at her. "Mae, nobody knows."

"But what do you think?"

Silence.

"Tell me please?" she asked more gently. "Michael? What?"

He cleared his throat but kept his eyes forward. "Well...yeah, I do think there's, I dunno, something bigger out there, yeah, or else I would've thrown in the towel a long time ago." The glare of the windshield washed over his face, making his expression hard to read.

"Really," Mae noted acerbically.

His quick sidelong glance was surprisingly dark. "You mocking me? Then don't ask. Just knock it off. Stop."

Stop!

Mae shuddered, raising a hand in appeasement. "No, sorry, didn't mean to sound snotty."

"You did," he grumbled.

"Sorry, really," Mae insisted. *Please convince me.*

Michael assessed her out of the corner of his eye. "You're asking something pretty damned personal."

"Please?"

Michael was still, but she could feel him weighing his words. "Don't think it's random. That's all."

"But you can't know."

"No," he concurred, "but it's not something you know. But if you slow down, pay attention at the right moment, it's something you feel, something you mostly normally don't feel when you're too busy rushing around, all disconnected, like your head's not with your body." He frowned, looking unhappy with his explanation.

The glare, a shadow as something moved, a pink shadow. Mae tried to shake off the memory, to follow what her brother was trying to say.

"So," she ventured, "you feel that? You can feel that?" She felt a heaviness in her chest, a dread that she would never feel that herself.

Michael wiggled his fingers lightly on the steering wheel. "Sometimes."

"How do you know?" Mae asked as respectfully as she could. "I mean, when?"

Michael's face drooped a little, got distant even as his eyes stayed locked on Touhy Avenue. "It's hard to describe, and it's kinda, well, fleeting—wish I felt it more. But the first time, the first time I really felt it, deep, like right through my bones, through the soles of my feet down to the center of the earth, was in Saigon, in the hospital, one night when there was this guy I had to prep for surgery. Hopkins?" He frowned. "No, Hoskins, Jake Hoskins...yeah, anyway, he didn't look too bad. Vitals were pretty decent, but anyway, I'm cleaning him up, and out of the corner of my eye, I see something move..."

A blur, a pink shadow. Mae pinched her thumb, let the sting help her focus on Michael. "And?" she nudged.

"Not even moved, more like a shiver or, or a ripple maybe?" He slapped at the steering wheel. "But I knew I saw something. So I check his leg, the one with the deep gash, and the skin was doing this, this weird rippling thing, and at that exact moment, a maggot started to poke out of the edge of the wound—"

"Eeuuww!" Mae protested.

"I know!" Michael agreed, talking faster. "And I had to duck back, throw up in the emesis basin next to his bed. He was sedated, so he didn't realize."

"Jeez, Michael, how gross."

"No, that's not my point, not 'cause it was gross: it was because of this moment, realizing that this mindless little thing, this nasty little critter, already knew, knew what I didn't—not until just then—it already knew he was a goner, it was already breaking him down. And sure enough, despite being stable, not half as bad as most the guys I saw, he died on the table."

Mae waited. There had to be more, couldn't come down to a maggot. *Please.*

"So then, just maybe two, three hours later, it got real slow on the ward, but I had this guy on the unit, Billy Czarnecki, bad off, his breathing, his color, but surprisingly lucid...and get this: he was from Chicago! And he was a Cubs fan, even though he was from the south side!" Michael grinned, slapped the steering wheel for emphasis. "Ever hear of that?" he marveled. "South sider, Cubs fan! But, but I was unsettled from earlier, with Hoskins, you know, and now it's quiet like it hasn't been in weeks.

Here I am on that shift, so I end up being able to just sit with him, sit there moaning about the Cubs with him, and it really lit him up...if it hadn't been so quiet, if I hadn't been on that shift, well, he'd probably have just been alone, alone with his thoughts when he died. But I was there, and I could just feel it, could feel that I was where I was supposed to be, in fuckin' Saigon, at fuckin' two in the morning, two pathetic Cubs fans rehashing the season. That moment, it felt so clear I was part of something, well, vast, some wonderful web, there was no way that was a coincidence. I could feel the, the order of it all, that I was supposed to be there with him, his last hour and all..."

Mae waited for him, could see he was back there briefly, weirdly content with those memories. But she felt left behind, wanted to feel connected to something vast and coherent and wonderful, but he was slipping into it without her.

"Michael? You, you really felt that, that you were part of something bigger?"

Michael nodded.

"But, but then what we try for, the decisions we make, they don't really matter, if we end up where we're, what, directed?" She could hear the disappointment in her voice, the despair at the prospect of the very thing that had him so animated. But she wanted to understand it, to feel the bigness of...*what?*

Braking for a red light, Michael turned toward her apologetically. "Maisie, I'm not smart enough to know. But sometimes I feel, well, yeah, you gotta try: try to have the life you think you want, and help those you love, try to help them have the lives they want, and maybe you end up with the life you were meant to have." His cheeks flushed. "At least, that's how it seems to me. Sometimes that feels right to me."

"Huh." Mae ached, void of feeling the rightness of anything. "Light changed." She pointed, directing him back to the road, then turning to stare out her side window, tipping her face away. At the next red light, she felt his eyes resting on her. "Wish I were as sure as you."

"Believe me, I'm not that sure. Not all the time. But that feeling—well, it helps."

Don't have that feeling, don't have it. "Next left," she observed somberly.

"Right." He turned onto Brophy, then into her driveway, popping the locks. "I feel funny leaving you like, you know—maybe you don't want to be alone now. We could just go get coffee someplace. Like an AA meeting?" He floated his best Michael grin.

Mae's smile was faint, wry. "Wow, tempting as that offer is, no. I'm home. Alone is fine. I'll think and maybe, maybe bake." Michael appraised her and then, apparently reassured, shifted the car into park but kept the engine running.

"Baking, huh? As in dessert, for company?"

"You wanna come for dinner? Just say so."

"So."

She shook her head. "Pathetic. Yes, of course, you can come for dinner. Six?"

"For cocktails?"

Mae shook her head. "For Cokes."

"Cokes at six. I'll bring the peanuts."

Mae patted his cheek and climbed out of the car. "Wanna bring Caroline?"

"Really?"

"Yeah, about time I get to know her. Bring her along if you want."

"Yes, ma'am. Six, with Caroline, and with nuts for the family nut." He winked.

"Jerk."

"Lightweight."

Mae shoved the door closed and waved. Michael backed away. Mae let herself in through the garage and laundry room, into a perfectly still house. She eased onto a kitchen chair, pulling off her mittens, arranging them on the kitchen table. And then she sat. Thinking.

Chapter Twenty-Four

Almost the Epiphany

Mae handed the kitchen towel to Caroline. "Here you go. We made short work of that!" She watched Caroline dry her hands and fold the towel neatly, placing it to the right of the sink.

"Here okay?" Caroline checked.

"Sure, anywhere. Just appreciate the help."

"Well, Michael could've helped with the dishes too. All he did was carry them in."

"That's all right. That was enough."

"Sometimes a little bit of Michael is enough," Caroline noted, her tone dry but her eyes glinting with affection.

Mae nodded knowingly. "Welcome to my world. Run while you still can."

Caroline laughed out loud. "Nah, thanks for the warning, but I don't think I want to run."

"Glad to hear it."

Michael popped his head in and hesitated, his eyes darting between the two faces. "Something tells me I shouldn't have left the two of you alone." When both women rolled their eyes, he insisted, "Okay, that's it. We're outta here before Mae corrupts you any further." He strode up, slipping his arm around Caroline's waist. "Remember," he whispered loudly, "you can't believe anything Mae says about me: she's psycho."

Mae punched him in the arm. "Shut up!"

"Violent too." He grinned, giving Mae a quick peck on the cheek before he started to steer Caroline out. He stopped to rub his arm. "Jeez, Mae, you don't know your own strength."

"Oh, poor baby, did your little sister hurt you?" Caroline cooed, patting his shoulder.

"It does hurt!" he protested, resting his head on her shoulder as they strolled into the living room.

Mae leaned against the counter a moment, contemplating the doorway, listening to the clang of hangars and the muddled good-byes. *Go join them.* She pushed off the counter and ambled into the living room, fatigue slowing her stride, but she knew they wouldn't leave without more good-byes and thank-you kisses. Then, standing in the doorway and waving, Mae half watched them pull away, half lost in some misty connection to other times—mundane but comfortably familiar—anchoring her every bit as much as the fresh air. She pressed the front door closed and leaned against it heavily: definitely tired. Tom and Kristy's heads were almost touching as they sorted through some boxes under the tree. Wordlessly, Mae returned to the kitchen to check, but no, nothing needed doing in there. She sunk onto a kitchen chair and let her eyes sweep across the wiped counter, the empty sink, the dishes dripping in the rack. Something needed doing, she sensed, even though it looked fine.

"Mae?" Tommy stood in the doorway. "Tired?"

"Yeah," she admitted, "more than I expected. But it went well, didn't it?"

"Oh yeah," Tommy agreed, pulling out the chair across from her. "A really good dinner. Everyone enjoyed it."

"Good."

"Anything you want me to do?" He glanced about the kitchen. "Looks pretty good already. Garbage? Anything?"

Mae surveyed the room. "No, not really." She focused on his face: he looked tired too, his eyes dull despite the bright kitchen light. Muted. "You know what you could do for me?" The words sprang out of her mouth: she wasn't even sure what was coming next.

"What?"

"Would you consider..." she hesitated, struggling against the clarity of the impulse. "I mean—only if you want—would you, well, go to therapy with me? You know, see Dr. Gregorich together?" Her mouth hung open a little with her own surprise at what had just spilled out, and yet she knew, down in her bones, it was exactly right.

"Really?" He looked equally surprised. "What, like, marriage counseling?"

"I guess." She raised her eyebrows hopefully.

He leaned closer across the table. "Sure. Absolutely."

Mae smiled faintly, saw light welling up in his eyes, the blue-gray-green flecks, saw the deep frown line she hadn't noticed before, his attentive expression. She leaned in a shade closer too, tilting her head. "Okay then, I'll call on Monday, ask her how that'd work." They nodded in unison, shy but pleased.

"Dad!" Kristy called from the other room. "Come help!"

"What, baby?" he called back, his eyes still locked on Mae's.

"The Wise Men, I can't figure out where to put them."

"Just a sec!" Then, to Mae: "We're rearranging the crèche. She wants to add the kings. You know, almost the Epiphany."

Mae smiled. "Right, it's coming up."

"Dad!"

"Coming," he called.

Mae stood up. "I could help," she offered.

He stopped to wait for her. Taking her hand, he announced, "Kristy, kiddo, make room for Mom. She wants in. She can help us figure this out."

◆ ◆ ◆

"You want to drive, or me?" Tommy leaned on the hood of the car, dangling the keys.

"What? Um, I don't care. You, you drive, okay?" Mae waved and ran to the foot of the driveway, grabbing Cynthia in a fierce bear hug. "I'm gonna miss you!"

Cynthia chuckled as she squeezed back. "You're moving less than a mile! Plus having us for dinner Sunday—which is crazy when you're still unpacking—but you asked, we're coming, so you're still stuck with me!"

Mae pulled back but hung onto Cynthia's hands. "Well, I can whip the first floor into shape by then, but if you try to go upstairs, I'll tackle you." She pulled their hands up close to her heart. "But we'll celebrate, and you'll finally meet Nora and her family—know you guys will hit it off—then, well, I'm just so glad you're coming. Promise?"

"Promise: six sharp, with dessert."

"Yes!" Mae let go and then, uncertain, shoved her hands deep into her pockets. "Well, I guess..."

"C'mon." Cynthia propelled her toward the car. "A little scary, a lot exciting."

Michael tugged open the car door for her. "Scram! The buyers will be here soon, 'n' I don't want you scaring them off. After they walk through and take a few measurements, I'll lock up."

"Kristy!" Tommy called in the direction of the house.

"Back here!" she chirped from the back seat, peeking over the box covering her lap. "Been here forever, and yes, my seat belt's on."

Mae contemplated the house through the windshield. "Forever, huh? Jeez, we really weren't here very long at all."

Tommy stared at the house. "Could've been good. Nice house. If we'd, well..."

"I screwed it up. Sorry."

Tommy caught her eye. "No, we messed up, so now we'll figure it out, not all at once, just a little at a time, right?" He pinched a couple of inches of air between his thumb and finger.

"Don't!" Mae pushed his hand away.

"What? I just meant—"

"No, I know. I just..." Mae faltered. She clasped her hands in her lap, then ran her hands down her thighs, smoothing her jeans. She winced.

"That one still hurts, huh?"

Mae nodded. "It's healing."

"Good. Time's on your side."

"Yeah." Mae bit her lip, looking up at him. "Time's on our side, right?"

"Sure hope so, Maisie. I think so."

"Hey!" Michael rapped the hood of the car. "The only neighbor who's gonna miss you is waiting for you guys to go, and me too! Get going!"

Tommy nodded and turned the ignition key. Mae peered up at her brother through the window. "Be sure to lock up."

"Jeez, Mae, I know what I'm doin'!" Then, with half a grin: "More than you can say!"

"Yeah, yeah." She tipped her head back on the headrest, let her eyes close lightly. "But that's okay. It'll come to me." Smiling, she said it once more, to no one in particular, to everyone: "It'll come to me."

About The Author

Margaret D. Kasimatis brings three decades of experience as a psychology professor to her debut novel, *Not Pink*. She uses her expertise as a clinical psychologist to tell the story of Mae, a quirky but deeply unhappy woman.

In addition to her novel, Kasimatis has published several poems and a short story. Her children are grown and live all over the globe. Kasimatis currently lives in Wisconsin with her husband and their dogs.

Made in the USA
Lexington, KY
15 August 2018